I0772426

CREATOR'S END

THE SKYWARD SAGA
BOOK 4

A.R. KNIGHT

Earth. Home. The pale blue sphere looms in front of us, dominating the view and, at the same time tearing at my heart.

This should have been a moment of triumph. Happiness. Instead all I can see are the long lines, the blots against the white clouds and sapphire oceans that show the presence of the Sevora. That show who's come to take my home away from me.

"We go in." I issue the command because somebody must.

Three of us on this ship and, of them, I'm the only one labeled an Empress. The only one given a direct, divine responsibility for a people I'd left behind.

Not anymore.

"You know that's a whole lot of enemies between us and where you're wanting to go," T'Oli replies.

The Ooblot has its white, liquid-like self spread between a number of terminals and controls at the front of the ship. By rapidly thawing and freezing parts of itself, T'Oli flies the craft in a lazy arc towards the Earth, trying to get away from the Sevora ships, to find a path through the atmosphere that doesn't involve a suicidal gauntlet.

"We've already survived a planet full of them," I come forward, stand next to T'Oli. "You can get us through."

I have no idea if that's true, but I say it anyway. Because I hope, and sometimes that's all I've got.

"Then you're going to want to sit down," T'Oli says. "Because once they realize we're not friendly, things are going to get real exciting."

As we get closer it's clear that in front of us isn't just a motley collection of spaceships—not that I know what I'm looking at when it comes to these things—but a formation. The Sevora arrayed their craft in a grid that moves along with the Earth itself.

"Orbit," T'Oli says when I mention it. "They've matched the speed of your little planet there, so they can stay above the same spot while doing whatever it is they're doing."

I put aside my momentary blown mind—Earth has a speed? Why does it spin?—in favor of more important issues like, "What *are* they doing?"

"Turning us all into slaves, probably," Viera says.

The Lunare is slumped back in her netting, arms folded and wearing a look that would reduce most people to gibbering apologies if she directed it at them. I know why she's looking that way, but I'm trying not to think of it. Mostly because if I remember Malo now, if I remember how I left him lying there in a crumbling cavern infested by the enemy, I'll fall apart. Which is something I can't do right now.

Later, though. Later I'll give Malo the grief he deserves.

There's a crackle, then a strange voice, flubbery like a Whelk's, comes bubbling out of the speakers, "Approaching shuttle, identify yourself."

"And that's not what you want to hear," T'Oli says. "They're already guessing we're foreign. Must not be transmitting the right codes for this."

I have no idea what T'Oli's talking about, but I wave for the Ooblot to let me speak anyway, and at a dual-blink from T'Oli's twin eyestalks, which rise up from its gray puddle of a body like reeds from a muddy riverbank, I start.

"Sevora, this is Kaishi, Empress of the Charre people. I demand you stop your incursion into my territory. I demand you leave my home, and never return." I'm more confident than I thought I'd be, and my voice sounds strong.

I earn silence.

Then bright points begin to appear across the grid of Sevora ships, each one appearing as a lumpy sliver across Earth's backdrop.

"What is that?" Viera asks as the same question forms in my mouth.

"Your response," T'Oli says. "They're targeting us now, and they're going to follow up with energy weapons in a moment. Think miners, but bigger. If that fails, they'll send up smaller fighters to roast us up close. We're dead, basically."

I point behind me, down towards the shuttle's lower deck. Where we came in and, if I'm right, where we'll be going out.

"There's another way off this ship right? For emergencies?" I remember the Oratus shuttle having one, and the space station *Cobalt* had things called vac mods.

"It's a defenseless ball, but yes, technically," T'Oli replies. "Good if you don't have any other options."

"Do we have any other options?"

"Seeing as we'll be in range of their cannons in about five minutes, after which we'll be reduced to something close to molecular bits by a frenzy of laserfire, and you've already said no to running—"

"We get it," Viera interrupts, shakes herself out of the nets. "But even if we jump ship in the escape mod, what's preventing them from just shooting that out of the sky too?"

"A decoy," I say. "Something big and bright to distract them. T'Oli?"

"The shuttle's only going to explode if they hit the right parts," T'Oli, I think, does the Ooblot equivalent of a shrug. "They miss, it'll just pop holes in everything and our ship'll disintegrate when it hits Earth's atmosphere."

"Earth's what?" Viera asks.

"Can you make it explode?" I trump Viera's question.

T'Oli swivels one eyestalk to Viera and one to me. "I suppose I could push all the energy we have into the engines. It'll make this shuttle go way too fast, but if the batteries overheat, it could ignite the oxygen we've got—"

"Do it," I order. "Then meet us at the mod."

"Okay," T'Oli says.

Viera blinks, then follows me down to the shuttle's lower deck. A second later, T'Oli's fix goes in and we lurch forward as if we'd suddenly fallen off a cliff. Then we start to float, our feet raising off the ground, my hair poofing out around me.

"Forgot to say that this takes power away from everything else," T'Oli announces as it flows to meet us, its hardened body looking like milk. "Better get inside before the panels go dark too."

"Does anything ever phase you?" Viera says as the Ooblot wanders over to a panel in front of a small arched door.

"No." T'Oli sends part of itself up the wall, over the control panel, and then hardens it.

A light above the panel blinks green, and the door opens to a cramped space with two long gray-metal benches. Benches set far too low for human height, but that, if we bend over and crouch, we can use. T'Oli, for its part, flows in behind us as the shuttle's lights flicker out.

The mod doesn't make a sound as it disengages from the shuttle. A set of lights around the hatch blink from green to red, and the viewport out the back swivels as the mod points itself to Earth—something T'Oli says the thing does automatically.

"So there's something else," T'Oli says as we settle in, which involves Viera and I bending around each other and T'Oli puddling up beneath the viewport.

"Something else?" Viera says. "Other than the exploding shuttle and the fact that we're now plummeting towards Earth in a tiny pod?"

"We're heading to the other side of your planet," T'Oli says.

"The other side? Why?" I've never been to the Earth's other side. Don't know what's there, but I do know my people won't be.

"Because if we kept going with the shuttle, we'd run right into the Sevora ships," T'Oli replies. "You sounded like you wanted to live, so I changed the trajectory. At our angle, it's going to be hard for them to see us with the explosion, even harder to shoot us."

I stare at the Ooblot. Confusion is melting away to anger. "Earth isn't like Vimelia, T'Oli. There's no tubes to fly people around. No way to get from one side to the other quickly."

"Oh," T'Oli says. "Well, it'll be a long walk then."

We glide around the Earth for what seems like a long time. T'Oli spends the journey educating Viera on the finer points of astronavigation and I tune them both out. Take the cramped, dull interior of the escape mod and vanish inside my own mind.

We'd all been there, on Vimelia, at the edge of our escape. Ignos had shown up, with a new host—why does that bother me?—and even though Viera had blitzed them down with a showy display of miner accuracy, the Sevora had decided to crash their own ship into our route to stop us from getting away.

Why, I keep wondering, are we worth so much to them? Why commit so many forces to stopping us?

Why kill Malo, when we didn't have the weapons, the numbers to threaten them?

Plenty of my tribe had vanished during my childhood—hunters departing on raids never to return. Others dying of disease or animal wounds. It's a part of jungle life—appreciate the time you have because it might run out at any moment.

Malo, I realize, is the first human to die off of Earth. He'd probably laugh at the thought, before remarking that falling in service to one's kind or something makes the sacrifice worth it.

Not to me.

There's only one way I can think of to fill the void where Malo's presence used to be, and that's by taking what we have, rallying my people, Viera's people, all of them to stand up against the creatures that took Malo away. That will take us all away if we let them.

We won't.

Coming into Vimelia, I stood in the cockpit with a calm Sevora voice in my head telling me everything as it happened. Explaining what was going on, what was worth worrying about and what, crucially, was not.

As the vac mod begins its rough-and-tumble turn towards Earth, as our viewport becomes a blinding glow of orange-red fire, my only options for solace are a white-faced, fists-clenched Viera and T'Oli, an alien whose primary mode of being is obtuse bemusement.

"Hitting the air pressure now," T'Oli announces as the fire grows hotter. "You've got a thick atmosphere on this one. Congratulations."

My eyes feel so wide that they're going to burst out of my skull. The novas blowing around the capsule are incredible, though I'm less excited by the heat seeping through the walls of the escape mod. My back is warm: even my feet, covered by ill-fitting Flaum boots, feel like they're stepping in desert sand. I remember to breath only when spots start flitting in front of my eyes.

"You'll want to use the handles," T'Oli says. "Going to get bouncy for a while."

The mod rumbles hard, shaking and rattling us around. I manage to grab onto the edge of the seat while Viera holds the handle on the hatch door, turning her face away from the viewport. She's closed her eyes now, but I force mine to stay open. Because the fire's starting to die away now and what I see morphs my mind.

From space, I'd recognized my corner of the planet. The browns and greens, even interrupted by Sevora ships, that marked my home-land. Even if I didn't know exactly where Damantum sat, the colors and arrangement fit. What I see here though is a spidering swath of blacks and blues. A mass of tendrils against the huge oceans, and most of that land is the color of ash, with patches of browns, greens, and one large orange oval towards the center.

"This isn't Earth," I say.

The mod's settled itself enough that my fear of death isn't quite enough to conquer my curiosity, my wonder at what's happened to the other side of my planet.

"Definitely is," T'Oli replies. "Though I'll admit the differences between the halves of your planet are striking. Not what I expected."

We continue our hurtle down, and things transition wildly in temperature, from hot to cold to warm again as the black expanse draws closer and closer to us. I'm noticing too, now, that T'Oli is still fiddling with controls by the front of the mod, making subtle changes in the direction of our descent.

"Where are you aiming us?" I ask.

"Towards one of those green patches," T'Oli replies. "Statistically, that's the most likely place to have things we need. Food, water, lack of deadly remnants."

"Deadly remnants?" Viera asks.

"What we're looking at," T'Oli says, "I'd guess, is a ruin. Something's gone wrong here. We want to stay as far away from it as we can."

"But we're landing in the middle of it." Viera's reply has a tint of resignation—of course we're going to wind up right in the thick of a new problem.

"No," I say. "Looks like, if we go to the west, the land continues around the horizon. Maybe we can get home that way?"

"Maybe," T'Oli says. "Going to need a lot of luck either way."

Viera shoots the Ooblot her dagger eyes. "You keep talking like this, I'm going to kill you before long."

"If you don't position yourselves for impact," T'Oli replies, "you won't get the chance."

I can't see the oceans anymore, or the orange lake. The viewport only has gray and black rock, and it's rushing up at us fast, too fast. I start to scream when the mod jerks, judders as flames appear around the edges of the viewport and our crashing speed slows.

And we settle on the unknown world I call home.

Criminal. Rebel. Fighter.

Traitor.

Useless words. Unable to capture the depth of feeling swarming through Sax as he stands, with Bas, on the bridge of the *Mobius*. Plake is at the controls, her skin only visible on her head, with everything else covered by rainbow feathers. She's orienting the *Mobius* now, pointing it towards a mustard-yellow planet whose surface swirls with passing storms.

"This is your idea of a place to hide?" Bas asks as the planet comes into view. "Rathfall?"

"When was the last time you heard of the Vincere coming here?" Plake replies, that burble of hers tickling Sax's ears.

Vyphen always sound like they're underwater.

"Rathfall won't have what we need." Sax flexes his claws. They're still not moving perfectly, and he's worried the heavy stunning might have done some permanent damage. "Evva won't be here, and we won't be able to find passage to the Chorus this far on the outer edges."

"The Chorus?" Plake laughs, then turns to the red slug-like creature at the back of the bridge, the eternally armed Agra-Red. "You hear them? They're traitors and they want to go to the Chorus!"

"I think it's true—Oratus without the Vincere just want to die," the Whelk says.

"That's—" Sax can't finish the words before a buzzing alarm cuts him off.

The sound's the same no matter the ship. A signal to find your crash netting and get situated, because you're about to hit atmosphere and going from zero air to lots of it makes for a bumpy ride. None of them have to move far; panels in the ceiling above them pop open and the black, padded stripes fall down to connect with magnetic loops in the floor. Making himself safe is as easy as falling backwards and getting caught.

Sax doesn't bother restarting the conversation, because it's too late. The view outside is entirely swirling yellows now, and the *Mobius_*is already rattling in its descent. Plake wouldn't change course this deep. After they land, Sax and Bas will have to find another way off-world, back to where they need to be.

Entering Rathfall's atmosphere is a visual treat, once Sax decides the *Mobius* is well-built enough to handle the turbulence. The planet is the product of hyper-pollinating plants and the giant, mindless insects that swarm from each flower to the next, scattering so much of the pollen that the planet's covered in the stuff. Ordinarily, the shading of starlight would have resulted in a super-cooled atmosphere, but the plants dealt with their own problem, burrowing deep into Rathfall's soil and rock to release heat from the planet's core.

The plant's practice was quickly co-opted and refined by those who found Rathfall's natural cover a perfect opportunity for businesses the Amigga didn't want in the open. With guidance, the plants now keep Rathfall's temperature equalized, and with that balance, trade flourishes.

Outside, the pollen scatters and bursts as the *Mobius* plows through pockets. Some sticks to the windshield for a second, exploding out against the pressure in grainy-yellow patterns. Flames appear as the ship hits the harder parts of the atmosphere, flicking in whites and blues along the edges of the glass. Sax thinks he can make out larger shadows flitting in the distance—the bugs about their work.

When they get beneath the upper pollen cloud, into the pocket of pressure that splits Rathfall's canopy with its floor, it's as if the *Mobius* is suspended for a moment in between worlds. Sax can see clear to the left and the right, with the windy tendrils of pollen above and the roiling, thicker mass of it below.

Plake pulls the *Mobius* out of its dive and settles into a streak across the surface, heading towards, Sax has no doubt, one of the Spires.

"What will you do?" Bas asks now that the rough-and-tumble part of the entry is over. "Leave us and run?"

"You promised me a way to get back at the Amigga," Plake doesn't hesitate before replying. "We're seeing it through. I want those ugly things knocked down as much as you do."

"So you trust us."

"I trust what I can see," Plake replies. "The Vincere want you dead, which means there must be a reason. You two aren't smart enough to be thieves, so my guess is that you're a threat."

"We are always a threat," Sax says.

"Yeah, yeah." Plake sticks up one feathered arm, waves away Sax's words without looking at him. "I get it. The posturing. Oratus always have to be the deadliest ones in the room."

"Even when they're not," Agra-Red says from the back.

On the edge of the horizon, a dark pole appears, jutting up from the clouds beneath and its wide, flat top stopping well below the upper canopy.

Sax pushes away tempting thoughts of carving Agra-Red to fine, jelly bits and instead focuses on Plake.

"So you will not take us to the Chorus, even to hurt the Amigga?" Sax asks.

"Prove to me that's what we need to do and I'll think about it," Plake replies. "As it is, we're low on cash and I've still got all these supplies. You failed hard in that respect, Sax."

"Not our fault," Bas replies.

"Guess who doesn't care." Plake ruffles her feathers, then her long tongue wicks out of her mouth and brushes a few of them that didn't fall back into place. "Here's the plan. We'll dig around on Astre's Spire for a bit, see if we can't find out something on your missing commander. Agra-Red'll sell the supplies and Engee can make sure this ship isn't going to fall apart after the hits we took getting away from *Scrapper Station*."

"We're not much good at digging," Sax says. "It's not, as you say, what Oratus are for."

"Oh, I know," Plake replies. "That's why you'll be staying on board. Guard the ship, so that when Coorvin and I figure out where to go, it'll still be around."

"Guard it from what?"

Scrapper Station was lawless enough. How all these places continue to exist on their own, without the Vincere enforcing basic rules, makes no sense to Sax. Then again, if guarding the ship means he can spend the time threatening smaller, more pathetic species, he'll at least be entertained.

"How should I know?" Plake presses a hand on the terminal to her right and, immediately, the windshield covers the visible area around the growing Spire with diagrams, statistics, and news. "Read up, everyone, because in ten more minutes, this is going to be our new home."

Landing in Astre's Spire means doing some light dodging around the mess of cargo drones coming and going, ferrying raw materials to much larger ships that would break apart if they attempted to enter the atmosphere. Plake doesn't seem the slightest bit concerned as she weaves around the blocks and their big engines, and she settles the *Mobius* in with a half-dozen other passenger craft. Almost immedi-ately after, the captain and her crew disembark, leaving Sax and Bas alone with Engee, the Teven who prefers her endless experiments and her lab to interacting with the two Oratus.

At first, it's annoying being left behind. Sax burns to move, to get *going* after being stuck for so long. After an hour of watching ships come and go, and waving off the occasional robot asking if they have cargo to sell, Sax finds himself settling in, finds himself falling into a long conversation with Bas as the two of them stand at the base of the *Mobius'* entrance ramp. It's the first time in a long while they've been able to just be with each other for hours, and the time begins to whirl by as they walk back their memories.

Yet even when Rathfall goes through its deep night, with Astre's Spire lighting itself up in a bright blue glow to be more visible against the yellow murk, there's no sign of Plake, no sign of Agra-Red or Silver and Black, the two Flaum that vanished with them.

"Do we go after them?" Sax asks as Rathfall edges towards daylight, and their own exhaustion weighs heavy on their eyes. He's sad to ask the question, as it signals an end to what they've had, a return to the harsher realities of now.

"Plake said it might take a while," Bas replies. "And this is a large Spire. There's been no word of a fight, a kidnapping or anyone trying to take a ship who's captain has met a sudden end. Another day, then we look."

They wait one more round of shifts, another night under the halo lights in the bay as Rathfall's skies grow dark. In the morning, though, there's a sense that's something's definitely not right. Not a soul's returned to the ship, and nobody's tried to lower the ramp or yell for help.

"Doesn't make sense for them to pay for rooms in the Spire," Bas says what Sax is thinking. "Not when their quarters are here."

"But for all of them to vanish at once?" Sax replies. "That would mean a concerted effort. Who would care that much about a few worthless transporters?"

Bas punches the button to lower the *Mobius'* ramp. "It may not be Plake and her crew that are the target."

The two Oratus descend the ramp, claws out and ready, miners attached to tight holsters meant for smaller bodies. Sax wishes they had functioning masks, but such things are hard to come by without a Vincere operation behind you. As it is, they'll have to rely on their scales and a faster draw than anyone after them.

Outside, Astre's Spire continues apace. Ships come and go and various species mill back and forth through the docking bay. Nobody spares the *Mobius* a suspicious glance.

"Maybe they're all on a sudden vacation? Celebrating a successful sale somewhere?" Bas wonders after no threat presents itself. "Too much to take, and they decided to stay in the Spire?"

"Can you imagine Coorvin doing that?"

The Flaum, who'd spent a very long time in crippling service to an Amigga, was both old and careful, not one to take his consciousness and throw it in a trash bin for kicks. Even if Plake and Agra-Red wanted to blur out their stress for a night, Coorvin would have brought them back safe.

There's a scrambling noise behind them, and both Oratus whip around, claws at the ready.

"Whoa, hey!" Engee, the short Teven, stands at the top of the ramp.

Her carapace is covered in small hooks, from which hang a cascade of tools and devices. Engee herself pokes her eyes out of a couple of holes near the top, while her padded feet emerge at the bottom. Apparently she's nervous, as her arms stay protected inside the shell.

"Want to say that there was a message waiting for us this morning. Sounds pretty strange! You want to hear it?" Engee practically hops as she finishes the sentence. "Vocal signatures don't match the records either, so it's a new species or someone wants to keep themselves a secret!"

Sax glances at Bas, then they both clomp back up the ramp, shutting it behind them—no reason to give stowaways or thieves easy access—and they head to the cockpit. There, blinking on a large terminal, is the yellow indicator saying something's waiting for them.

"Engee," the message starts, and it's a synthesized voice, mechanical and distorted. "It is unfortunate that you did not come into the Spire. I know you still have what I need, and you will give it to me. I've waited long enough. Come to the Wildfire, and make good on your promise, or you will never leave this place."

The two Oratus look at the Teven. "That was the most straightforward and dull threat I've ever heard," Bas finally says. "Who are they and what do they want?"

"I don't know!" Engee pips. "I'm as confused as you are! I don't know anyone who would threaten me!"

Sax blinks. "Then what could they be talking about?"

Engee's arms pop out and wrangle themselves together. "I don't know, Sax. Maybe they want something on the ship? Something I have?"

Sax glances at the message. Plays it again. Listens hard for inflection, for background noise and gets none. Whomever left it is taking care not to give themselves away.

"It's probably a trap," Sax says. "If they know where you are, and that you have what they want, then they would come here and get it."

"The *Mobius* does have some defenses," Bas replies. "Perhaps they're afraid."

"Regardless, they gave us a choice," Sax hisses. "Either we answer, and go to this place, or we stay here and wait for them to act on their threat."

"Engee, the voice spoke to you. It's your choice," Bas says.

The Teven doesn't look like she wants to decide. She scampers a bit back and forth around the cockpit, then stops. Turns towards them.

"I'll go. But someone should stay and watch the ship, in case this is a trick to get us away."

"You watched the ship on *Cobalt*," Sax says to Bas. "I'll take guard duty here."

Bas touches Sax's tail with her own in thanks. Neither of them wants to stay here, and they both know it.

"Perfect. Bas and I!" Engee announces. "Before we leave, though, we should probably get some gear. I'm not going to be caught unprepared like on Scrapper!"

Back on that station, the Teven had found herself accosted and unequipped with any defenses. Sax had stepped in, but before he'd needed to use his claws, Agra-Red had annihilated one thug with a hard blast from the Whelk's miner. Unnecessary, messy, and something Sax had quite enjoyed.

Wearing masks, which coat Sax's skin like light cloth, is second-nature. Wearing what Engee gives him, which amounts to a vest with four holes cut for his arms, feels heavy and strange. The vest is made from woven chrysalis fibers, a not-very-rare insect product from Dellis, and it's a silver-blue color that would be beautiful were it not marred by a thousand little gadgets.

Sax may be exaggerating, but that's what he thinks when he looks down at it. Each node dotting the vest ties to a specific sensor, linked by pinprick needles to Sax's nerves, and each of those sensors tie into the *Mobius*. Engee describes the vest as a connection to the ship itself —if Sax is frightened, or nervous, then the ship will engage various defenses and use Sax's own mind to target threats. To eliminate them.

The problem, as Sax sees it, is that he doesn't get nervous. He doesn't get afraid.

Bas laughs at this. "You might not say it, my pair, but you feel it. We all do."

Sax doesn't dignify that with a reply, and after a quick touch of tails and claws, the Teven and Bas depart for the Spire, leaving Sax alone with the *Mobius*.

This begins an even more boring exercise of watching ships come and go. Sax replays Engee's message a few times and hears nothing new. Then resorts his attention to scanning the news, hunting for signs of Evva. There's word of major Sevora military moves, but they're not heading towards the Chorus or any known world, so the Vincere aren't trying to stop them.

A Flaum on an old space station accidentally triggered self-destruction protocols and prompted an evacuation. A poison gas leak on a ship required an emergency landing. The Amigga are introducing a new version of the Fassoth, said to be more dependable and less aggressive.

All standard stories. All boring.

This is not the life Sax wants for himself. He ought to be on the front lines, in perpetual fights and dealing death with his claws. Or, failing that, somewhere like Nova, enjoying beauty with Bas. Not here in this dull cockpit, watching the little freighters play out endless monotony.

Sleep doesn't announce itself, but when Sax is leaning back in crash netting with nothing happening, when the boarding ramp's closed and the alarms are set, there's not a lot of reason to stay awake, so Sax drifts away staring at Rathfall's yellow sky.

And wakes up later to another blink from the message terminal. Outside things are deep dark. He's slept too long, then remembers the only thing he's doing is waiting. He reaches out a claw, presses the button for the message, expecting some sort of status update from Bas.

The filtered voice comes on again.

"Engee, you missed our meeting. I'm not playing games anymore. Not again. This ends tonight."

The message cuts there, leaving Sax looking at the blank terminal. Not again? Missed our meeting? If Bas and Engee didn't even make it to the Wildfire, then what's going on?

Sax jerks himself up from the netting, retracts it into the ceiling, when the *Mobius* bursts into harsh noise. Alarm lights in the ceiling flash orange, and the terminals in front of Sax swap into camera feeds from around the ship.

Looking at the gray-scale images, Sax expects certain types of intruders. The common species for break-ins and threats. He doesn't expect this.

Scattered around the ship are cargo robots, ones with sleds attached to help with moving large goods. Their magnetic coating lets them hover above the surface, and now they're sitting outside the *Mobius* like metal ghosts, silently ringing the ship.

The intercom next to Sax crackles to life, bringing the same filtered voice into the cockpit.

"Engee, are you inside? I hope so, for the sake of your ship, for the sake of your own life," the filtered voice announces, and instead of anger, Sax hears sadness, frustration. "I've sent some robots to gather what you owe me, and I expect you to deliver it. Or I will have the Spire's own guards take it by force. You have thirty seconds to respond."

What would Engee possibly have that would require a dozen cargo robots to move? Sax doesn't recall seeing anything of that size here. He wouldn't mind a fight, but starting a struggle against a force of Spire guards, who might decide to just blow the *Mobius* apart from afar, doesn't seem like a great idea.

So Sax hits the button to reply.

"Engee isn't here. She went to meet you at the Wildfire. I'm only watching the ship, and don't know what you are looking for."

Straightforward. Peaceful. Bas would be proud.

There's a moment's wait before the intercom crackles again.

"No games, whoever you are. I know the Teven landed with this ship, and I know she never appeared at the Wildfire. So I will take what's mine. What's owed to me."

"What is it then?" Sax tries. "I don't even know what you're looking for."

"Engee promised me a dozen crates of Ceres Crystals. They must be on your ship somewhere. Find them. Now."

Ceres Crystals? Sax hasn't ever heard of those before, but then, the Oratus don't need to be versed in commodities without military application. If the Vincere doesn't need it, Sax doesn't need to know about it.

Until, of course, he does.

The escape mod settles on its side and Viera, at a sign from T'Oli, presses against the handle and twists it open with a screeching thunk. The door swings out, and I breathe the air of my home for the first time in what feels like forever.

And it's terrible. It feels, tastes like I'm breathing in rocks and wood chips. The air scratches at my throat, makes me cough before I've even stepped out. My eyes water as they burn, and when I look at Viera to see if she's experiencing the same thing, her eyes are blood red, her nose is running, and she looks like she's about to throw up.

Even T'Oli, normally a creamy white, has splotches all over its skin. Yellow and blue-black spots spatter across its form. The Ooblot's eyestalks shrink down and nearly close.

"This is quite the hostile environment," T'Oli says, before scurrying back into the evac mod.

"This isn't our home," I manage. "At least, not what it should be."

I'm trying to cover my face with my hands, and I hold cloth up to my mouth and wish I still had the mask. After the fight escaping Vimelia, our masks were fractured and broken, and we left them on the shuttle. As it is, I stumble back against the escape mod, try to stuff my face into my loose, makeshift robes, and know that we'll never survive any kind of journey in this air.

"Here," T'Oli announces, coming back out. "There's filters in the mod. They're adaptable."

The Ooblot's holding—in hardened grips of itself—a pair of what look like translucent spiderwebs. Viera and I don't hesitate. Even if this things are meant to kill us, breathing this air seems a more terrible way to die than anything these filters could do.

They're cool to touch at first, and slightly wet, as if grabbing a damp rope. I hold it up to my face as T'Oli says they belong over where we breathe. As if sensing my intention, the filter squirms in my hand, reaches out and grips my cheeks, my chin and my forehead. Pulls itself to me, then flattens against my face.

I can't see what it's doing, so I look at Viera, and over where she breathes—her nose and mouth—the filter glows bright white for a moment, and when the glow recedes, there's a solid pearl coating. The filter feels like wearing paint, but it works; I'm breathing in and out and there's no scratch, no choking weight of decay and ash.

The filter glosses my eyes too, at first making it seem as though everything is now just a shade lighter than it was—the black ash now looks gray, and T'Oli is closer to the snow I've seen on the tops of far away mountains than the milk it used to be.

"How are you handling this?" I ask the Ooblot.

"We breathe through pores in our skin," T'Oli says. "It's about calibrating myself to catch the particles I need and kick the others."

Already those yellow spots are shrinking as T'Oli does what it needs to do. I suppose if an Ooblot can harden itself, it might be able to do that on such a fine level as to block out the same things the filters do for us.

Turns out Ooblots are hardy creatures.

Now that we're not dying as we breathe, I actually take a look around where we landed. The foggy ash makes it hard to see far, but what's there looks like the aftermath of a fire. A vast plain coated in the flaky stuff.

During dry summers, I'd seen fires tear through the plains west of the jungles—their devastating journeys given away by the massive plumes of smoke—and my father had taken me once to see what they left behind. This scene matches those childhood memories, but what's confusing to me is that life comes back after a fire.

Ignos renews, after all.

Here, though, there's no sign of that. No plants poking back up through the grit, no weeds trying to make a start. It's as though life here has given up.

"What happened?" Viera asks the air and, so far as I can hear, she receives no reply.

"Let's go west," I announce. "That's the way towards our home, even if it's going to take us a long, long time."

"There are rations in the escape mod," T'Oli says. "Don't know how long they'll last for humans, though."

More nutrient goop, and the packets come in a variety of flavors with names I don't understand. We haven't eaten since Vimelia, since leaving the Clarity's Dawn hideout deep beneath those pipes, so Viera and I take a moment to devour packets of chalky slime.

The filters, as if sensing the motions of our mouths, peel back their layers while we suck down the gel. T'Oli, for its part, smears a packet on its skin and, like water disappearing into a cloth, the Ooblot absorbs the meal.

"You're really weird," Viera says to T'Oli.

"I get that a lot."

"Are you, uh, typical for your species?"

"I don't know," T'Oli replies, its eyestalks twisting into a slant. "I've never met another Ooblot before. I think I was the only one on Vimelia."

"You didn't grow up with any?" I can't help but ask.

"Grow up?" T'Oli does that weird Ooblot laugh, with its skin slapping against itself. "I was grown, Kaishi. Made right there in Vimelia off of Sevora samples. They tried to host me, but I'd just melt away any openings. So then they threw me away."

"That's awful." It's all I can think of to say. "No wonder you wanted revenge."

"Revenge?" T'Oli laughs again. "I just wanted purpose. Something to do, something with meaning. After slinking around the tubes for a long time, I found Clarity's Dawn and they offered me a job. That's all I wanted—to feel worthwhile. Don't need more than that."

We climb through the ash westward for hours. There's nothing much we see, aside from the odd two and three-meter black pole. They stand as silent watchers, and while at first I think they're trees—long dead, but still—when we happen to pass near one I take a closer look, brush away the thick grime coating it.

"Metal."

T'Oli, who's turned gray-black as the ash sticks to its flowing form, just blinks at the discovery. Viera, though, gets what I'm after.

"People lived here, once," she says.

"Something did, anyway," I reply.

But there's no further answers waiting in that single pole, so we move on. Keep going until the ground dips and the ash, if anything, gets even thicker. Up to my calves now, and I'm noticing that it's not all soft flakes. There's bigger chunks brushing by my legs, and I slip every now and then when my foot lands on something not quite broken down, like stepping on a log hidden by forest leaves.

After the pole, Viera keeps her miner drawn, her head on a constant sweep around us. When I ask why, she says it makes her feel better.

Makes me feel better too.

Especially when we see the shadow in front of us. More a swirl of disturbed ash than anything, the distant cloud marks a line ahead, a trail where something passed.

"Could be a small breeze," T'Oli says.

"No breeze is that small." I start moving towards the trail. "Come on—if there's something out here, I'd rather find it while it's still light out."

Viera agrees and the two of us break into a stumbling run, chasing the line of falling ash. I hope T'Oli's following, but the Ooblot doesn't make much noise, and it's so much slower that I don't even try to wait.

We're kicking up so many of the gray flakes that T'Oli shouldn't have trouble following anyway.

The trail leads us to a pit. Or a crater. It's large enough, either way, for the far edges to disappear behind the fog's obscuring mists. But we can see plenty of what's below.

"Well there's your proof," Viera says, and we stare for a long moment at the alien structure nestled in the ash.

From what I can see, the building sprawls out in rounded fashion. A front portion angles towards us, with enough ash dug up to provide something of a stair from the pit's edge down to what might have been a door once but is now a rusted portal to who knows where.

Beyond that opening, the building billows out, approaching and disappearing into the edges of the crater, though the ash covers so much of the structure that it's hard to know how much of it is simply mounds of dirt.

Put simply, I think it's huge. Bigger than the Vaos. Taller too. And it had clearly been the target of someone's wrath.

The walls and ceiling we can see are pitted with rust, with chunks blown apart or missing altogether, as though bitten away by sharp teeth. Or burned off by a miner.

"Who do you think made this?" I ask.

"Being an expert on all things alien," Viera says, "I have no idea."

I crouch, give my legs a breather after the run. We don't have unlimited rations. Taking the time to explore the building would put us even more at risk for getting anywhere habitable before we starved.

"Well that's certainly unexpected," T'Oli says as the Ooblot flows up behind us. "More and more mysteries. Have to say, this is all much more interesting than Sevora sewers."

"T'Oli." I brush off the Ooblot's meandering words like a fly. "How long do you think it would take us to make it halfway around a planet Earth's size?"

"At the speed we're going?" T'Oli blinks its eyestalks. "We'll be long dead by the time we get close to where the Sevora are."

I nod. That's what I needed to know.

"Then we're going in there. Might be something we can use."

"Might also get us very dead." Viera shrugs. "Then again, I've been expecting my sudden demise for so long now that it's not even scary anymore."

"Happened to Malo," I reply without thinking.

Viera only nods at that. I shut my eyes for a second. Take a slow breath.

Now's not the time.

"Let's go."

So I jump off the edge, land on the ashen slope and skip along, feet remembering what it's like to find holds and lose them again in a moment. There's a certain joy to moving fast under my own power and it's been too long. Even here, in this gray desolation, I manage to crack a smile and forget all the awfulness behind and ahead.

Only for a moment.

Viera yells for me to be careful, but I'm in my run and to the door before she's started her descent. I look back, flash a smile, then wave for them to come down. Nothing's jumped out of the door to scare me yet, and inside is only deep dark, so it's obviously safe.

Or maybe, at this point, I just don't care. T'Oli's saying we're going to starve long before we make it home, and everything around me is ruin, so I decide that I'm going to spend my last days smiling, laughing, trying to dig up what joy I can.

Malo would want that, I think.

T'Oli follows Viera, using the rivets made by the latter's feet as pools to guide it slime-run towards me. Eventually, the three of us form up again outside the door, a rusted, bent thing that's lost any element of security it once provided to this place.

"How about next time we go together?" Viera says. "There could have been something waiting here."

"Then I would've taken care of it," I reply, holding up my hands. "I know how to fight."

Viera pats her miner. "Trust me when I say shooting's much more effective."

I shrug. "As the Empress, I declare my opinion correct."

Viera rolls her eyes, but doesn't argue the point.

Sometimes, authority has its benefits.

"Anybody have a light?" I ask, staring into the deep entry. "I don't think Ignos is going to get much beyond that door."

The great god isn't keeping this side of the world bright anyway—the gray fog covers most things, and it's been getting steadily dimmer as the day goes on. None of us are under any illusions that we'll be spending the night somewhere in this blasted land, and all of us—T'Oli possibly excepted because Ooblot minds are, well, different—are hoping there'll be somewhere in this building we can use for shelter.

But nobody's eager to embark on a pitch-black chase after an unknown creature.

"I'll lead," T'Oli says. "I won't be able to see any better than you, but I'm very hard to kill."

Viera snorts, but we give T'Oli's plan the go-ahead and the Ooblot doesn't make anymore words about it, and slides into the door.

As the Ooblot moves, T'Oli describes the surroundings, remarking on the cold flat floor, the constant broken glass, swept-in ash, and evidence of long-dead devices now taking up their decaying places along the sides.

Viera and I—with me in last place—step slowly behind the Ooblot, following its directions as our sight gradually decreases until all I've got is a right-hand grip in Viera's own to guide me.

The sheer darkness calls me back to the moments before Ignos entered my mind for the first time, and I almost laugh at the contradictions. There, then, I was expecting to meet a god or his gift, find a way to save my people or bring them prosperity. Here, I'm marching with fatal determination, moving forward because staying still means a slow, pointless death.

"This remind you of home?" I ask Viera, remembering that the Lunare came from beneath the mountains.

"Our tunnels aren't dark," Viera replies and her voice sounds loud in the quiet hall. "We plant glow-worms, and feed them. The way their light reflects off of the rocks and pools of water is beautiful, fascinating. I miss it."

As if responding to Viera's remembrance, we turn a corner and notice wisps of light in front of us. Blue curls coming out of a round door not far ahead, ones that silhouette T'Oli's twin eyestalks and make it seem as though we're walking towards some portal to a dark beyond.

A person stands in the middle of the domed room. They're the source of the glow—or rather, a sapphire light beneath them is. It's a man, wearing what seems to be a series of striped bands all across his body. Because everything is in that blue color-scheme, I can't tell if the man's outfit is supposed to be a rainbow display or a black-and-white affair.

Which is good, because there are other things I ought to be focusing on. Namely, why the man's right eye seems to have slid down his face, so that it rests just on top of his cheek. He only has one ear—the left—though I don't see any evidence of a scar. Thick hair covers his head, unmoved by the subtle breeze slipping through the place.

"If you aren't the ugliest man I've ever seen," Viera announces as we head into the room.

She's already drawn her miner, aimed and pointed it at the man. I think she's happy we're facing, for once, another human. An enemy she knows.

"Hello," the man says, speaking in the same universal language as everyone else. "Welcome to my home."

Malo's Charre lingo, apparently, didn't make it to this side of the world.

Otherwise, the man's voice is an even-keel, though it fuzzes at the edges, as if someone ran the ends of his words through a rushing river.

"Your home could use some cleaning," I say, stepping into the room around Viera, who's slips me a 'stay-back' look that I ignore.

The man doesn't seem to have any weapons, doesn't look aggressive with his smallish hands by his sides. And with Viera covering him, I can't imagine anything he could do that wouldn't end in his smoking corpse on the ground.

Until I notice that his feet aren't on it. The ground, I mean. The man's floating a little above the floor. I check his shoes—but his feet are only wrapped in those same bands. None of the magnetic flying boots used by the Flaum back on Vimelia.

"It's an image," T'Oli says. "This thing isn't really here. Which, all things considered, seems like a smart decision."

The man's head swivels towards the Ooblot, and his face shifts into a sad, if disturbing, smile. "I haven't really been here in a very long time."

Behind the man, spaced out around the room, are piles of broken equipment. Shattered glass and bent, burnt metal couple with deep grooves in the stone floor to tell a story of disaster. The filter keeps me from knowing what it smells like down here, for which I'm thankful. Wreckage like this usually means death, and bodies left to rot tend to make unpleasant finds.

There are, however, two other doors splitting off to parts unknown.

"Looks like you're here right now?" Viera's asking.

"It's like Nasiya," I say. "Just a picture. The real question is, where are you?"

"Dead," the man says. "I've been dead for far longer than you've been alive."

There's a brief second of silence, before I bust out a long sigh. "Of course, after everything we've seen, why not a ghost too?"

Ignos, my god, supposedly casts reflections at times, sends back past relatives to glimpse the present, to meet with their chosen family and pass along wisdom. Not something I'd ever experienced, but seeing as the priests claimed Ignos sent these visions along in times of need, getting a ghost for myself now would make sense.

"A ghost?" the man shakes his head. "No. Merely a recording. For any who survived the cancellation."

"You're throwing terms out there without a lot of context," I say.

"You don't know?" The man doesn't put any shock into his voice, but I gather he would if he could. "You are not survivors?"

"We are," Viera says. "We'd like to stay that way, too."

"Then you should know that this place is not safe," the man replies. "You are at risk, here. And you should leave."

I gesture at the other doors leading further in, "We need supplies. A way to get to the other side of the world. You have that?"

"My data has been corrupted, survivor," the man says. "I have no inventory to give you. If, however, you helped me, I could perhaps find you a way."

Being told by a shimmering, distorted mistake of a creature that our survival depends, maybe, on helping it is not on the list of things I want to hear. I'm the one, no, we're the ones that need help, not some avatar that freely admits it's dead.

But what choice do we have? Say no? Venture back into the ash lands and starve slowly in the choking gray?

"What do we need to do?" I ask, T'Oli and Viera apparently deferring to me for once.

The ghost turns and gestures with its right hand, and from it leaps a series of small stars stretching forth to the closer of the two doors. The line hovers at my eye line, their blue sparks twinkling motes of fire.

"Follow them," the man says. "Find the core, and open the vents."

"Well, if that doesn't clear things up," Viera mutters, and we start off.

The blue line peters out at the edge of the room, not even lasting us past the door. I glance back at the man, wondering if the ghost realizes his guide-posting is rather lacking, but all I get is a blank stare.

"Guess this is what we have," I say and down we go, once more into the dark.

T'Oli again assumes its leadership role, courageously descending us along a wide, flat ramp that curls, every so often, back against itself as it winds further and further. Viera remarks that stairs would take up less space, and I'm inclined to agree.

"Not every species can step." T'Oli makes the observation in the same slap-tone it always does, as if unaware of what it's saying.

T'Oli's remark, though, cracks a certain code. I'd not thought of another alien species making it to Earth until that moment. That one might have been here far earlier, might have made this whole structure answers and creates questions at a rate that threatens to overwhelm me.

So I consider reaching out to the Cache, that all-knowing bracelet given to me by a Sevora when it first crashed outside my village, and rub the cool, hard surface. I want to check, to see if it knows anything about what's happened here, whether Earth's part in the galactic chaos comes earlier than my own dalliance with dominating parasites.

The Cache, though, is like walking into a dream. It takes all my concentration, and while reading its lines I'm going to be useless to Viera and T'Oli. In a place like this one, with who-knows-what around the corner, blasting my mind into purgatory isn't a safe move.

There's other ways of learning things, though.

"What do you think would use a ramp like this, T'Oli?" I ask the Ooblot as we continue through the dark.

On either side of me I can feel the walls close in, and I reach out to brush them every now and again. Cold metal, generally, though often pocked and scratched. T'Oli's been calling out to us whenever it hits debris that we have to blindly climb over, and a few times it's noted other doors, but I figure the ghost would have told us if the path branched at all en route to our destination.

"Like this one?" T'Oli muses. "Whelk certainly wouldn't mind it, but it's too wide for them. Or for other Ooblots, though there are other signs this isn't of our making."

"Then whose?"

"Oh, there's really only one species that would make a place like this," T'Oli says, and I can feel Viera stifling a sigh. "Amigga."

Sax glares at the intercom. Then heads out, jumps down to the loading bay and hits the button that lowers the boarding ramp. As he does so, one of the cargo robots shifts in front of the ramp, the small intercom on the thing's block-like body crackling to life.

"Where are the crystals?" the filtered voice, via the robot, demands. "I don't see any."

"Search the ship, if you want them," Sax hisses, stepping right around the robot.

The robot turns, as if it's going to follow Sax. "Where are you going?"

"Engee didn't show. My pair was with her," Sax replies, glaring back at the floating metal sled. "I'm going to find them."

As Sax walks away, though, his vest blinks red. The *Mobius'* ramp suddenly retracts, closing off the cargo bay and leaving the twelve robots without anything to do. Which doesn't bother Sax in the slightest. He's following the trails of light globes towards the Spire's center, towards one of the many doors leading inside.

He's nearly there before the entrances—wide, rectangular things with several layers—shift open to reveal a grimy airlock, coated with yellow pollen. Inside it, standing with two small miners in its hands, is a tall Teven.

Unlike the naked carapace so many of the species wear, this one is plated over with blue steel, and a pair of helmets house the creature's eyes through holes in its sides. Its arms, or legs—Sax isn't sure what is what when it comes to Teven—leak out the top of the carapace, two holding the miners, one free, and the fourth hanging on to what looks like an energy knife.

What's more fascinating though is what the Teven's done to its base; instead of leaving it open for the creature's legs, this one's gone ahead and attached a magnetic circle to itself, allowing it to float over the floor. Useful if you live on a metal construct, perhaps, but entirely pointless in the wilds.

As Sax starts into the open airlock, the Teven tilts back and, with its magnet, glides away from Sax towards the rear of the space.

"Stay right there, Oratus," the Teven says.

"Why?" Sax replies, and keeps moving forward. "You think you can hurt me before I tear you apart?"

"I'd aim for your eyes!"

Sax opens his mouth, shows off the teeth. Breathes deep through his vents and exhales in a loud hiss. "I don't need those to end you."

"But they'd help if you want to find your pair, wouldn't they?"

And there's the clue Sax needs. This is the filtered voice. Which means he's not wasting any more time. Sax digs his talons in and leaps high, over the Teven, and as he goes, Sax whips his tail down, knocking the miners from the creature's hands. As soon as the Oratus hits the ground, Sax digs in his claws, flips directions, and tackles the Teven, driving the yelling alien to the floor.

The airlock doors shut behind them as Sax looms over his victim.

"Tell me where they are," the Oratus says, making sure to open his mouth good and wide so the Teven can use the full power of his imagination on those razor teeth.

"I don't know," the Teven's voice is reedy, indignant. "They never came to the Wildfire."

"Then you have a problem," Sax says. "Because they were trying to get to you, and if something's happened to Bas, you're the one I'm going to blame."

The Teven squirms as the inside airlock seals shift open, leading to the interior of Astre's Spire. Here at the top, the walls are plastered with various terminals and vending machines for nutrient goop, water, and the various types of licenses and passes for cargo shipments. The center of the space is a series of inter-locking elevators, with large ones for cargo and smaller ones for passengers.

Sax stands and hooks a mid-claw around the Teven's carapace, lifting the lightweight creature and carrying him out of the airlock.

"You don't understand," the Teven's wailing. "I wouldn't hurt her! Or her friends!"

"Doesn't sound like your message," Sax says, looking around. "You made a clear threat."

There's not many other species on this level at this time of night. A few are set up around a vending bar, where drinks and other substances are provided purely by mechanical means. A big terminal scrolls through news sources and plays soundless video. Four Flaum are tugging a cargo sled out of one of the elevators towards another airlock.

Nobody pays them any attention.

"I know, I know, but I need those crystals, and Engee too," the Teven says.

There's a flutter around the Teven's words that catches Sax's attention. He's heard that lilt before, from Bas, from himself.

"Are you and Engee together?" Sax asks.

He's not sure how Teven mate, if they mate. Sax isn't sure if they lay eggs, if they replicate, or if there's some complex ritual involved.

"Well, no," the Teven says. "Not yet, anyway. That's why I need the crystals! To earn her love!"

"You're threatening Engee to get things from her . . . to earn her love?"

"I wouldn't expect an Oratus to understand." The Teven squirms hard, kicks that magnet bottom of his and shoots out of Sax's hand.

The Oratus lets the Teven go. Sax can catch him again if he needs to, and without his miners, the Teven's not exactly a threat.

"I don't really care," Sax says to the Teven. "Just tell me how to find them."

"I already said! I don't know where they are." The Teven searches, sees where his miners lay on the ground, just past the shut airlock door.

Sax leaps to them first, slips the small weapons into the many holsters on his waist. Vincere principles call for leaving extra space in case of useful finds, and just because Sax isn't part of the military anymore, doesn't mean he's not going to keep good habits.

"Then you're going to help me find them," Sax says as the Teven stares at his stolen weapons. "What's your name, Teven?"

"Nobaa," the Teven replies. "And you, Oratus? Should I call you Deathclaw?"

"Sax is fine."

He, Nobaa tells Sax while they wait for an elevator, is an engineer. He met Engee when they were both in school, and, like her, he's been fascinated with self-augmentation ever since. After achieving their degrees, they both came here, until Engee declared the noxious yellows of Rathfall some sort of creative killer and left when Plake offered her a job.

"I agree," Sax says at this part, as an elevator pings open in front of them and they step into its ad-blasting confines; shifting images with Flaum hawking various restaurants, hotels, and other products on Astre's Spire.

Sax is expecting a single-button stop, right to the Wildfire, but Nobaa uses the terminal to select more than a dozen points.

"You agree with what?" Nobaa says, tilting an eye in his dark blue helmet towards Sax.

"Leaving here. It's a terrible planet," Sax narrows his eyes at the Teven. "Why did you pick so many stops?"

"You don't know where they are, I don't know where they are, so they could be anywhere!" If Nobaa's expecting Sax to do something with this statement, the Teven's bitterly disappointed. But not for long. "Engee and I worked on Astre's Spire for a while—I might as well give you a tour, and maybe we'll run into them!"

"I'm not here for a tour."

"Oh, I know. Neither am I!" The elevator dings to its first stop as Nobaa speaks, and the doors shift open to reveal a dark and damp space.

There's no walls Sax can see, and the only light comes from floating motes—likely tied to robots—drifting around in the distance. From what illumination spills out of the elevator doors, Sax sees thick green fronds sneaking into view. The air's thick with the smells of flowers and fertilizer.

"Every Spire needs a greenhouse," Nobaa says as the elevator's doors shut. "We make sure Astre has fresh food, and that nobody's starved for something natural!"

"Stop it," Sax takes a long step over to the panel, pushes the Teven out of the way, and hits the emergency stop button. "You're going to tell me what you're doing. Now."

The elevator judders to a sharp halt. Sax glares at Nobaa, whose four hands wrangle their fingers together. The Teven's eyes bounce past Sax to the terminal, something the Teven's not going to get near again.

"It's true, I swear! All of it!"

"Talk straight," Sax replies. "Tell me where they are, or I'll cut you apart right here and take my chances."

"I don't know, uh, exactly where they are," Nobaa replies. "And I'm not the reason they're gone! I wanted to meet them at Wildfire, honest!"

"You're not helping."

"Right," the Teven takes a step back, but the elevator's not large. No move is going to buy Nobaa more than a half-second of time before Sax takes his due. "See. There's a lot of money on your heads, you know? Not just you, but the whole *Mobius* crew. I just wanted my crystals before you all wind up dead."

Sax takes this in like he does everything else—with shrugging resignation. The galaxy's never made things easy for him, why start now?

"So the Engee thing was a lie?"

Here Nobaa actually looks distressed. "No, no, that's all true! Yes, I want the crystals, but Engee's a friend. I was hoping she'd come to Wildfire, and then I'd find a way to keep her out of this. With the crystals, of course."

"Such a romantic," Sax throws some extra venom into the hiss. "This Spire isn't that populated. Who here is going to risk fighting us?"

The Teven nods at the elevator panel. "Can we go? I have a place. It's not big, but it's more secure than here. People might be listening."

"If you're trying to trap me, Teven, know that I'll kill you first."

That fact delivered, Sax steps aside and lets Nobaa adjust the elevator's destinations. Takes Sax deeper into the Spire, to one of the residential levels. If Sax is calculating correctly, it's right in the middle of the thick lower cloud, which means Nobaa's not among the power players in the Spire.

If the Teven doesn't have resources, then Nobaa had better have information, because without it, he's wasting Sax's time.

And Sax is not a patient person.

Nobaa's apartment is little more than a single room with a food dispenser and an info terminal where the window would be, if there was anything to see other than flowing mustard-yellow gas.

"It's not much, but then, I don't need much," Nobaa says, pointing one of his small arms at the soft-box in the middle of the floor.

Full of what looks like sand, it's where the Teven would sleep. The grit keeps the Teven's carapace centered and straight, while providing a comfortable space to thread limbs if Nobaa wants.

Overall, the whole space isn't far off from what Sax would have on a Vincere ship.

"Don't care," Sax hisses. "Tell me what you know. Now."

"Sure," Nobaa says, floating his way into the soft-box. "Here's the thing. You're all wanted by the Vincere and the Chorus for an amount that's, frankly, obscene. Only there's not many on the Spire that read those alerts and fewer that can act on them."

"Get to the point." Sax folds his four arms and lets his tail curl around his legs.

"As an engineer, I did some work for the group I think took Engee, and probably the rest of your friends. A Vyphen, goes by the name of Frayk."

"He runs the shipping around here?"

"That's the weird thing," Nobaa replies. "Frayk doesn't run anything, far as I can tell. His name isn't on any company, he doesn't show up to big ceremonies, and nobody talks about him. The only way I knew this store I was designing connected to him was because he stopped by once and you could tell, oh you could tell; there wasn't anybody in that place who didn't stop what they were doing and wait for him to stay something."

"So you think this Frayk is doing this for money?"

"I, I'm not sure," Nobaa says. "I don't think Frayk needs the money. I'd say he's doing it for something else. A favor, maybe? Get the Vincere or the Chorus to allow something?"

"Like what?"

"No idea! I'm not a detective, Sax. I'm an engineer! I make things!"

"Sure," Sax says. "How do I find the Vyphen?"

"No idea. You might be able to try the place I worked at though? The one I designed?" Nobaa waits a second. "Guess what it's called?"

"The Wildfire?"

"Wow! You're good. You're really good. I can see why the Vincere is all your species now, scary *and* smart."

Sax puts up with the Teven long enough to get the Wildfire's location, then ditches Nobaa in the apartment with a warning not to touch the *Mobius*. The Oratus heads back to the elevator, taking off Engee's vest along the way and tossing it into a trash bin. It's annoying to wear, and Sax isn't going back to the ship without his pair, without the crew that's been taken.

The Wildfire is on the fiftieth level from the top of the Spire, in the heart of the restaurant series. Sax gets off the elevator into a shifting crowd of night-cappers. It's well after dinner and the ones roaming the ring, drifting in and out of those few places still open have left sense and sensibility long behind. They barely glance at the walking array of weapons that is Sax, and those that do regard him like he's a dream.

Sax doesn't care. He's focusing on the luminous red display in jagged font screaming his destination. The nameplate sits above a broad opening flanked with billowing flames—not real ones, as fire in sealed environments can cause . . . problems. Regardless, there's an empty stand for visitors to check in and see available spots, unnecessary given the late hour, and past that a broad array of tables and seating areas bordered with walking isles marked by red-orange metallic paint.

The lighting in the place evokes the fires too—hitting the same color notes as the floor and doing so with strands of laser-wire hanging from the ceiling, as if it, too, is aflame.

There's a single many-armed, no-eyed robot bartender serving a half-dozen species around a central ring bar. Sax steps his way up to it, signals the robot for a glass of water and a packet of nutrient goop. Hardly an exotic order, but when a greased-up, working Whelk slides his wobbly eye over to mock Sax, the creature realizes who it's about to insult and quickly withdraws.

Sax can't see anyone else in the restaurant, and there's no visible signs of struggle. So either Engee and Bas didn't make it here at all, or someone talked them into leaving.

"Who's the manager?" Sax asks as the bartender delivers the goods.

"Currently?" the robot replies. "Or during the day?"

"Now. I want to speak to them."

The bartender turns and presses something beneath the bar. "They'll be out shortly."

While he waits, Sax glances up at the screen. There's an array of sports scores for games Sax neither knows nor cares about. Some talking-head Flaum blather on for a moment, before, at last, things shift to a galaxy update.

"The Chorus are responding to increasing unrest led by a pair of rogue Oratus, Evva and Avan, whose whereabouts are sought by the Vincere. After accusations emerged that the Chorus may be engaging in wholesale manipulation of civilized races, the First Chair denounced the assertions and laid out a long series of points purporting to show how the galaxy has improved under Chorus and Amigga control." The gray-black turns to his partner, a golden-haired, smaller Flaum. "Do you think that'll be enough?"

"It's ludicrous to go against the Chorus," the golden one says. "They've done too much good, and even if you don't agree, they control the Vincere. Anyone seriously opposing them is just going to wind up dead, so what's the point?"

"What's the point? Indeed. Inspiring stuff, as ever," the black Flaum replies.

Sax looks away from the screen at the sound of approaching wheels. The manager's here.

A Belloch. Thick, yellowed, and with eight thin arms of varying lengths wrapping around its curving bow of a body, the creature sits in a concave chair tied to a pair of treads trundling across the floor. At the top end of its body, the Belloch has a bulbous eye cluster, deep red and dark, and a slit that, Sax knows, can open to reveal its goop-sucking proboscis.

Sax recoils, though, presses back against the bar with his nutrient packet in one foreclaw and his water glass in the other. Bellochs are mistakes, Amigga errors long-since stopped, but with enough lifespan to keep on going. There's rumors that the species has found a way to reproduce, but Sax hasn't seen evidence.

He hopes he never does.

"You're not what I expected," the Belloch says, its voice nasally and full of mucous. "Usually, an ask for a manager is a complaint waiting to happen. You, though, don't seem the type."

"I want information."

"Yes. Who doesn't? Perhaps I can help you, perhaps not. The question really becomes, then, why?"

This is why Sax hates Bellochs. Why, he thinks, the Amigga gave up on them. Their reasoning is always circular, always angling for an advantage. Mostly, the things talk too much.

"I'll kill you if you don't," Sax says. "Do the galaxy a favor."

"Oh yes, another threat. I don't have any choice as to what I am, Oratus. Consider that before you snap your mouth at me."

"Consider my threats mercy, then," Sax says. "I'm looking for a Teven with another Oratus. A pink one. They were supposed to be here?"

The voices on the screen go quiet, and Sax is aware of the other bar patrons staring at them, pacing their conversation. As far as eavesdropping goes, they're not trying to hide. So Sax starts to plan his attack.

"Two Oratus in one night?" the Belloch clasps all eight arms in front of it, each eight-fingered hand entwining with another. "That would have been truly memorable. So I'm sorry to say such an event has never happened here. You are the only one of your species to grace the Wildfire this evening."

Sax takes a final slurp of the nutrient goop and sets it on the bar, where the robot scoops it up immediately. He slips off the chair, keeping his claws ready, and swishes his long tail across the floor. Have to make sure everyone here knows an Oratus isn't easy to kill, isn't worth even trying.

"Do you know what happened to them, or not?" Sax hisses.

"Do I know? Why would I? I'm only a simple manager of a simple restaurant catering to fine souls like yourself."

"You must have recordings, though," Sax says. "That would show what you say is true? If so, then I'll leave."

"Alas, my security is broken at the moment. It's why I retained these helpful friends to keep things civil. It can be rough out here, as I'm sure you know."

The Belloch doesn't seem concerned in the slightest, but Sax is picking up plenty of nervous scents from those behind him. Hard to tell whether the nerves come from their boss lying, or just from an Oratus standing battle-ready.

Time to find out.

Sax whirls away from the Belloch, jabs a foreclaw towards the Whelk that was, moments ago, so unnerved by Sax's presence. "What do you think, Whelk? Is the Belloch telling the truth?"

The alien can't even speak. The Whelk blubbers out some unintelligible garbage, stops, and takes a long sniff of the powders set in small bowls before it. The creature's color changes from a lime-green to a soft blue, and the Whelk's jelly body shivers.

"Now that you've got your courage," Sax hisses. "Try again."

"Yes," the Whelk blurts out. "Yes they were here. But not anymore, not anymore. I swear it wasn't me!"

There's a reedy sigh from the Belloch. "Whelks. Always prone to failure."

The Belloch acts first; throwing his tread-chair into reverse and zipping away from Sax even as stools topple and the Belloch's muscle makes their move. The blue Whelk imitates its employer as Sax takes stock of the opposition, squishing away from the Oratus and letting a Flaum trio, paired with a couple of ragged Vyphen missing most of their feathers, take front stage.

"Really?" Sax hisses at the group. He's not seeing weapons, while Sax himself has a couple of miners and plenty of claws ready to work. "You want to die for that one?"

"Acton pays," the center Flaum, mottled brown and white, says.

The five attempt to fan out around Sax, who keeps the bar to his back. Their eyes shift between the Oratus and each other, and it's obvious they're waiting for a signal.

Sax decides to give them one.

He springs to his left, towards a gray-black Flaum whose raised claws mean he's not caught entirely by surprise. Not that it matters. Sax catches the Flaum's hands with his foreclaws, then uses his midclaws to grip the Flaum's clothing and smash the creature into the bar. Once, twice and then he drops the limp alien to the floor.

A couple of clacks sound as the brown Flaum gets close, but a whip from Sax's tail sends that one flying into a table, denting the metal furniture. Sax pivots around in time to see the first Vyphen's strong tongue as it lashes out, grabs ahold of Sax's left leg and sweeps the Oratus' talons out from under him.

Another species might be troubled by that, but Sax catches his fall with his tail and boosts himself forward, leaning onto his claws and closing his mouth over the Vyphen's retracting tongue. Sax bites in just enough to stop, not enough to snap—eating through a Vyphen's tongue would probably mean death for the creature, and Sax doesn't want to kill.

Not yet.

The last Flaum and the other Vyphen see the stalemate and hesitate. The first smart decision they've made, and a sign that Sax can still make a deal with them. An employer that pays doesn't mean much if you're dead.

Sax thinks the Belloch's run away, which is why it's a surprise when the blue burning bolt from a miner hits Sax hard in his torso. His jaw goes numb, lax, and the captive Vyphen yanks its tongue back home. It's a powerful stun, meaning it's not coming from a handheld, small miner. Sax crumples to his side, manages to see the Belloch, holding a large assault miner and rolling back between his thugs.

"Always keep one around," the Belloch sneers. "Nobody ever

checks the chair. It's remarkable, really. Thanks for not ruining my friend here. For that, I'll let you in on a little secret."

Sax tries to move, but it's like there's a stone block between his mind and his body. No connection. No way through.

"You and your pair are only leaving this Spire one way, Oratus," Belloch continues. "In a prison prism."

The Belloch raises the miner a second time, fires it, and in a wash of blue, Sax ceases to think.

I find a wall to lean against in the black stairwell because, for the moment, I want a chance to breathe without wondering whether my next footfall will plunge me into some nether abyss.

Amigga. Of course it all comes back to them. Despite all the claims about how evil the Sevora are, the nightmares I keep having all revolve around the tests on *Cobalt*. The carousel of terrors that Dalachite subjected me to under some pretense of 'study'. As if I, and, by extension, our entire species is an experiment whose results are, as yet, unclear.

Courtesy of Sax and a miner, we cleared it up for that Amigga, at least.

"Doesn't matter," Viera says. "What the Amigga care about isn't our problem right now. It's damn dark in here, I'm cold, and we're still stuck on the slow track to starvation, so let's keep moving."

Right. Focus.

T'Oli, as usual, proceeds on in glib apathy, gliding down the ramp and calling out obstacles as they appear. Eventually the path straightens and, because my arms no longer hit hard metal when I reach out, I know we're at the bottom, and in a large space.

"Wait here," T'Oli says. "I'll scout around."

Viera and I take a seat at the end of the ramp, though I can only tell she's close by the sounds of her breath.

"This wasn't the homecoming I wanted," Viera says after a second. "Thought, maybe, I'd actually get home."

"Dumb of us to hope," I reply. "Nothing I've planned has worked out in a long time."

"We made it off of Vimelia, didn't we?"

"Some of us."

"That's how Malo would've wanted it," Viera says. "He was always looking for ways to give himself up for you."

"I never asked for that."

"That's what loyalty means—you don't have to ask."

I blink away a tear that's threatening to escape. Malo was loyal. To a fault, really. We'd left the hierarchy of Damantum, gone into an alien society where grit, strength, and knowing how to fight seemed to be the main link between life and death. That's where I should've been tossed aside—Malo, the warrior, ought to be sitting here now, ready to come back and lead our people in desperate battle against the Sevora.

"You think, if we make it back, that humanity's going to survive?" I ask.

"I'm not even worried about that," Viera replies. "You know us. We're like bugs—we'll scramble and find some way. Maybe not all, maybe not even most of us, but someone's going to make it out the other side of all this."

"I'm betting you will."

"Because I'm so good with a miner?"

I laugh. "No, because you're willing to do what it takes to win."

"It's not about winning, but about living to see what happens next. I'm too addicted to life to leave it."

There's a scuttle from the far end of the room, then a burst of orange.

The light leaks up from the apparent back wall of the chamber, central. If I'd run straight from the ramp across the space, I'd hit where those orange lines are crawling up the wall, to where they're now spidering out through the sides and up onto the ceiling.

T'Oli, shadowed by the glow, has formed up into its usual ball-and-stalk shape next to what appears to be a very crusty lever.

"Vents," T'Oli announces as we look over to it. "Simple stuff. Would've expected more from Amigga, but if you're lookin' to grab and throw heat, this works."

Viera and I glance at each other, then back at the lines of energy. They're moving slower now as they extend towards the ramp. Towards us. As the lines get closer, it's clear they're not a pure orange but instead a roiling cluster of reds, oranges, and deep yellows that swirl around and back on each other.

Like fire.

The lines, though, stop well before they reach us. Fade out, with licks occasionally popping further along before falling back.

"The thing upstairs said we had to open all the vents," I say, standing and, now that my pupils have adjusted to the shock of having actual light, following the dead remainder of the lines along the ceiling.

They keep flowing to the ramp and then up the walls alongside it, where they vanish into the dark higher up.

"If it lets us see, then I agree with the monster," Viera says, then she nods towards the circular door onward behind T'Oli. "Guessing there's more of these?"

"If I had to guess, which, cause I don't know, I have to," T'Oli muses, its eyestalks swiveling along the lines, "what we're getting now is only a trickle of what a place like this would need to run. Clarity's Dawn, down in that rusted sewer, took a lot more energy from the Sevora than this vent is giving here."

"Then we go?" Viera looks at me.

"We go," I reply.

Before we leave the room, though, I walk over to a pile of bent and broken metal. Unlike most of the other debris we've seen, this doesn't look burned but smashed. Someone deliberately beat what-ever this was to pieces, but as their efforts give me a good meter-long stick of hard, splintered metal to wield, I'm not mad about it.

Both T'Oli and Viera are staring at me when I turn around, the short staff in my hands.

"What?"

"Nothing." Viera smiles. "Glad to see you'll be able to fend for yourself."

"I'm only taking this to hit you when you're annoying," I wave the stick towards her. "Like now."

"Humans are a strange species," T'Oli burbles from his corner.

"You're one to talk." I swing the staff towards the Ooblot. "Lead on, slimeball."

T'Oli oozes forth, though one eye turns back towards me, and its back half ripples out another reply, "If only I could. The best Ooblots can turn themselves entirely liquid."

"Of course they can," Viera mutters as we follow beneath the orange lines. "Why wouldn't they?"

I'm expecting another ramp but instead we get hallways. So many hallways. It's not a straight line anymore either—we've reached a basement warren. As big as the building looked from above, standing on the lip of the ash pit, it feels bigger now as we follow T'Oli through one turn after another.

Viera and I only know we're shifting because T'Oli tells us, with short 'Rights' and 'Lefts' when a turn comes because those orange lines die out a few steps beyond the room, returning us to dark. I let the meandering go for a bit before I ask T'Oli to stop.

"How are you choosing where to go?" I ask. "And I'm going to be upset if you say 'at random'."

"The energy we're unlocking comes from below," T'Oli replies, though there's something different about its voice—it's off, though I can't figure out why. "The vents control access to lines that channel this energy, and it's hot. Keep your hands on the lines and you'll feel a little more heat from the right direction, where the energy's coming from."

"But the lines are above us?"

"At first it's not comfortable, but an Ooblot can get just about anywhere, even up."

Now I get what's different. T'Oli's talking down to us from the ceiling, where it's somehow attached himself.

"Remind me not to underestimate Ooblots," I say.

"I will."

Our line-tracing continues a little longer until we reach another room—identified as such because T'Oli announces it. Viera and I take up leaning on walls at the entrance while we wait for T'Oli to find the vent. But instead of the shunting of a lever, the next thing we hear is a series of rapid clicks along the floor behind us. Clicks I recognize.

"Claws," Viera and I say at the same time.

I hear my friend draw her miner, though I'm sure she can't see anything to shoot at. The claws click again, closer, and I try to remember how many turns took us here. How many possible ways a monster could find us.

"T'Oli? The vent?" I'm proud to say my voice only jumps up a little bit.

"Working on it!" the Ooblot's reply is maddeningly cheerful.

As if she's encouraging the Ooblot, Viera fires her miner. The bolt is bright, blue, and blinds me for a second before it buries itself into a wall. The hallway back the way we came, though, is empty.

"How many shots do you have left?"

"No idea," Viera says. "Never really learned how to read these things."

"Rackt didn't teach you?"

The Vyphen fighter back on Vimelia had given Viera that miner, had taught her how to shoot.

"There's a bunch of different options, Kaishi. If we need to kill someone, I'll figure it out." Viera stops talking for a second and I wonder why, until I catch the clicks again.

They're close. In the room.

I whirl and swing the piece of metal out behind me. Hit nothing, but I'm so juiced up at this point that I keep whirling and clang the bar off the wall to my right. The ringing noise echoes around the room, I wince, and then T'Oli finds the vent.

Orange bursts forth on the room's far side and we get our first look at what's following us, what's coming at me in a whirl of claws.

"Oratus!" Viera shouts, and on one hand, she's obviously right.

On another, I don't think Sax would call this thing one of his own. The same breaking orange light that lets me see the Oratus only has three arms left—the fourth, its left foreclaw, is nothing more than a shoulder stump—and less than half a tail, causes the Oratus to pause, snap its head back towards T'Oli.

Viera fires again.

She doesn't miss.

The blue bolt crashes into the Oratus' chest as the creature registers T'Oli's an Ooblot and, by the way it keeps its claws towards us, decides the slimeball isn't a threat. Viera's shot gets a hiss, a slight stumble, but the Oratus doesn't fall.

So I try my stick.

The Oratus is taller than me, so my strike heads in for the thing's waist. It notices, bloodshot yellow eyes glaring at me as its midclaws catch my metal bar, as they tear it from my hands and break it.

"Next shot kills, Oratus," Viera says. "Don't move."

The Oratus glances at her. Pauses with my bar in its claws. Opens its mouth with a long, angry hiss, "You should not be alive."

We're staring at the Oratus and it's staring back at Viera and I, claws out and ready, though it seems less bloodthirsty than before. Maybe that's what happens when you've got a miner pointed in your face, maybe that's what happens when things you think are long dead suddenly show up again in front of you.

"You're better than you were," the Oratus hisses. "More perfect. More as they intended."

"Yeah, you keep talking in riddles like that and we're going to get along just fine," Viera says. "How about you explain why you're hiding down here in the dark?"

Though, I think, it's not dark anymore. The roiling orange is all through this room now too, and the lines burn bright back the way we came. That whole network of hallways we stumbled through is probably all lit up now, which makes me wonder what we might've missed.

No. We're not here to explore. We're here to get home.

"It's been so long," the Oratus says, then looks at itself and shakes its head. "I was young then. My first assignment, to come here and oversee the deletion of a project."

"How about we start with your name, and then we can get into the messy details?" I offer.

T'Oli, meanwhile, has re-attached itself to the ceiling and has made it way above the Oratus. At first I don't understand why, but when the Ooblot shifts most of itself into a hard rock, it makes sense—a surprise, heavy dive bomb.

But Vee, who insists that his name is only one letter, decides he's not interested in fighting right then and instead, in a rasping, hazy voice, spills out one revelation after another.

Humans are, Vee says, simply one more experiment gone wrong. Earth, a habitable zone chosen because it would support the kind of life the Amigga wanted to grow. In fact, Earth already had most of its own life forms, plants and animals, so the Amigga didn't have to seed much at all to make it work.

Several Amigga began the project, which led to what we saw up above, a sampling of an earlier creation. Vee says he doesn't know much about what happened after the early humans were developed, but things went wrong soon after the Amigga gave us sentience.

"You're too hard to control," Vee says. "They wanted something pliable. Something more capable than Flaum, but less dangerous than us. What they wound up with had too much freedom."

Humanity pushed back. Fought against their creators for a chance at their own destinies. Which was when Vee arrived, along with other Vincere forces. They were told the Sevora had taken a species, told that humanity had lost itself and needed to be eradicated.

"The Vincere probably think they succeeded," Vee says. "I landed with another five Oratus. The whole engagement was kept secret, to keep other species from finding out what happened here." Vee snorts, laughs at this. "We were told it was to keep the fear of the Sevora in check—if the enemy destroyed a species, it might destroy others. But the real reason? To keep the Amigga's goals hidden from the rest of the galaxy."

Which is why, when five Oratus proved unable to wipe out the humans, the Vincere proceeded to obliterate the entire base from orbit. They fried everything for kilometers, burned the land to bury a species, to hide the Amigga's failure.

"Which is why I'm surprised to see you standing there," Vee says. "You shouldn't exist."

"Sorry to disappoint," Viera snaps. She still hasn't lowered her miner, and I'm not about to tell her to.

"Looks like you've got two choices, Vee," I say. "Either you prove, somehow, that you're not going to try to kill us, or Viera roasts you right here."

The Oratus keeps his eyes angled towards me, his half-tail swishing across the ground. "Do you know what it feels like to have your own people fire at you? Assume you're dead and burn the skies around you?"

"That's a hard no," I reply.

Vee laughs, but it's a broken thing. Nothing of the manic glee Sax had when he chuckled about his murderous rampages.

"It doesn't do much for loyalty," Vee replies, then gestures at himself. "I'm old, I'm breaking down. Nothing but hunting rats in the darkness and talking with that projection up there for far too long. You're offering a new life. Potential."

Something here, though, doesn't add up. What's an Oratus doing sitting here in the dark when all he has to do is flip these vents?

I ask the question. Vee blinks.

"Vents? I don't know anything about any vents," Vee says.

"Didn't the projection tell you?"

"We trade insults. I tell it stories and it listens." Vee cocks his head. "You, though, are something else. A human. Perhaps it trusts you more than the creature sent to destroy its civilization."

"Vee makes a good point," Viera says. "Why *would* we trust an Oratus?"

"I think I can help with that," T'Oli says. "If you'll stand still, Vee, I can give you a chance to prove yourself."

The Oratus starts, looks up, just as T'Oli drops from the ceiling. The Ooblot splashes onto Vee and flows around the creature's head, spine, and around his claws, becoming a robe, albeit one with a pair of eyestalks sticking out from the top, above Vee's head.

In a moment, the Ooblot hardens, locking Vee's claws out. Stiffening a hold on the Oratus' neck.

"There we go," T'Oli says. "Now, if you try and do anything, I can break all of your arms and your neck in a moment! Pretty neat, right?"

Vee makes a choking noise and T'Oli shivers the section around Vee's neck.

"A little tight?" T'Oli asks, and Vee tries to nod. "Sorry 'bout that. We'll just have to keep adjusting till we find the perfect fit between deadly and flexible."

Vee looks more than a little upset at the situation, his vents flaring, but when he notices Viera still hasn't lowered her miner, when he tries flexing his claws and finding the Ooblot really does have a hard hold on him, Vee sighs and dishes me a resigned stare.

"Think we can work with this, Viera?" I say.

"I'm not putting my miner down."

"Fine by me." I point towards the back of the room, towards another door heading deeper. "Guessing the third vent is that way. Vee, would you lead on?"

The Oratus doesn't fight this time and, with Viera behind him and me taking up the rear, we head on towards the third vent.

What Vee's saying, about humans being a failed Amigga experiment, I shuffle into the back corner of my mind. Even if it's true, there's nothing I can do about it. And there's something deeply satisfying about knowing we're an experiment the Amigga failed to destroy.

Unlike the first two, the third vent doesn't require a winding staircase or a hallway maze to reach. It's just a straight shot along a wide corridor, a gray one with thick doors spaced evenly on either side. Each door has a dead control panel next to it, and a range of numbers plated in tarnished bronze on the surface.

"What are these?" I ask Vee as we trod along.

"I don't know," Vee says. "By the time our force arrived, they had already sealed most of this base."

"The humans?"

"The Amigga that oversaw the experiment, the one they all said was the cause of the problems. It locked everything away. The only thing we found here were traps," Vee hisses. "Almost all of us were lost when we entered. Rooms sealed around us. Gasses and fire."

"How'd you survive?" Viera says.

"I ran. We realized what was happening, and it was my job to cut off the power. I wasn't fast enough."

I take a closer look at the plate of a door next to me. 50-75, it read. I trace the numbers with my finger. The grooves aren't precise. These were etched by hand, not by machine.

"Before, most of the base sat above this place," Vee continues. "I was so deep my mask couldn't send out any communication. Once the rest of the team was lost, the Vincere decided they didn't want to risk any more."

"So you hid down here while everything burned?" Viera asks.

Vee twitches his stump of a tail. Doesn't reply and keeps moving.

The third vent, on the other side of the corridor, is surrounded by dark terminals. Some sort of basement control center. Vee, at T'Oli's gentle instruction, flips up the vent and sends the orange bursting up the lines along the ceiling.

Around us, all those same terminals fly to life. At first the screens display blues, reds, angry reams of text flying around that I can't read before they're gone. Then they fade to a single logo, one I recognize because I've been taught to know it all my life. Taught to revere it.

A circular star, with a halo, black against a white backdrop, though I'm used to seeing it on stone.

Ignos.

Viera sees the icon too, guesses its meaning. T'Oli and Vee, though, stare at us like we've lost our minds.

"Something interesting?" T'Oli asks.

"The icon," I say. "There in the middle. What is it?"

"No idea," T'Oli says. "Vee? You can talk now."

I give the combo Ooblot and Oratus a side look as T'Oli, with a shimmer around Vee's neck, loosens his hold on the Oratus.

"I think that it's best to keep hostages on edge," T'Oli says at my look. "A tight throat means this Oratus isn't going to forget I can crush his neck whenever I want."

"I won't," Vee rasps, his hissing even more hoarse now. "As to your question, I don't know. These designs can mean anything."

Part of me wants to dive into the Cache then and there. I've never, I realize, actually looked for Ignos in the bracelet, never tried to find anything on the god my entire tribe has believed in. When neither Sax nor the Sevora that lived in my mind mentioned him, I figured Ignos simply wasn't followed in the wider galaxy.

And yet, here he is. I know that's the same design as the one carved into the top of my tribe's Tier. I want to trace the connection, to think about—

"Hey," Viera interrupts my thinking as she moves aside the sole exit door. "Something's happening."

Vee-T'Oli goes to peer out, then turns back to me. "The doors are open."

That's not all, though. I'm hearing a noise, one that starts low and grows, echoes off the walls and pours around us. A sound unmistakable and amazing.

Humans. Screaming.

"Go," I say after a moment. "Let's find them!"

With Vee-T'Oli in the lead, the three of us head out of the room, take the first left into an open door, into an orange-lit cavern where, piled on each other like the stacked full crates of nutrient bars in a shuttle, are dozens and dozens of tubes.

Immediately inside the door, there's a ramp leading to the base of the cavern, where the tubes rise three-deep, each one almost double my own height. They're filled with a black liquid, and all of them have red lights blinking on top. And a few, the ones from where the screaming pours, are open.

"No," I say, because I can't think of another word to describe the things hanging from those tubes, their harnesses keeping them suspended in the air.

They're not human, not really. Like the project in the upper level, these things are malformed. Limbs are in the wrong places, or have the wrong number. Too many fingers, too few arms. As if some child were building figures out of clay and didn't care if they misplaced bits and pieces.

"Maybe your people were right to bomb this place," Viera says to Vee. "This, this is terrifying."

The floor at the base is coated with spilled black liquid, a puddle that grows as more of the tubes begin to hiss and burst open. More yowls, hoots and strange hollers join the growing chorus as things better left dead find themselves alive.

"Let's go," I say. "I don't like this place."

"And leave them?" Viera says to me. "They're suffering."

"Do you have the energy to shoot them all?" I reply, motioning towards the tubes. "Or are you going to climb to every tube and stab whatever's inside?"

"I bet we could release them," T'Oli says. "Figure those consoles back there have a way. Usually how these things work."

Release them? I look from our door across the way to the closest tube, at a thing with three eyes, no nose, and a wide mouth open in a permanent scream. It senses my glance and meets me, and in those three eyes I see six deep blue pupils.

"I . . . " I have to fight down a sudden surge of nausea.

"Human," Vee hisses, and though I've never seen an Oratus look sad, I can tell this is it. "Now you see."

What I do see is that we need to get out of here.

"Come on." I lead the way out of the tube chamber, back into the hallway.

The others, thankfully, follow. I'm not sure I could've turned back after them if they hadn't.

As we go down the hallway, I glance at all the other rooms—now open—as we pass. They're also orange-lit, also filled with tubes and the crying of those within them. I start to run. Anything to get away from those screams.

We head through the second vent room, then beyond to the maze of corridors. Only now, with the orange lines glowing along the ceiling, it's not all that difficult to follow them and find our way through to the smaller room with the first vent, and the way to the stairs.

With the light, though, the dark hallways become storybooks, tales of horror, their walls lines with gouges, miner-caused blast marks, and unmistakable red stains. Metal junk couples with bits that look like bone, claws, or other parts.

Finally, when we reach that smooth stair up, I stop and breathe hard. Then turn to Vee.

"What happened here?" I ask. "This, this . . . I don't understand?"

"This was not us," Vee replies after T'Oli loosens its grip. "I told you, there was a fight. A push back against the experiments here, before the Vincere were called. War leaves scars, human, on all it touches."

"You can stop it with the philosophy," I reply. "If you came after the fight, what did you find? What was here?"

"As I said. Traps."

"But nobody fighting back?"

The Oratus shakes his head. "Other than those things, those failed experiments, nothing. Only the projection."

I lean against the wall. Vee said there were multiple Amigga here. And, apparently, plenty of humans, at least of one type or another. If there was a fight, and if nobody was left here, then what happened to the winners?

"Kaishi," Viera says. "As much as I'd like rest, I think we have to leave, as fast as possible."

She's right. But we can't just run. We'll die out in the ash lands too.

"The projection told us it would help if we opened the vents," I say.

"If you can trust it," Viera replies.

"We don't have a choice."

Stunned. Again. Sax is getting real tired of this. First Gar back on *Scrapper Station*, and now the Belloch, whose name he doesn't even know. It's sloppy, it's inexcusable, and it's one more tick on the long list of people Sax owes vengeance.

But now he's in a prison prism, surrounded by three glistening sheets of pure disintegrating energy on a wet floor. The water's licking at his scales, his talons. It's moving, and in one direction, which has Sax wondering for a moment if he's been dumped in a river.

Then he gets his head around. Sees the harsh reality. He's in a waste-water basin, and what's coming down his way is all the leftovers Astre's Spire doesn't use. The smell's more industrial than natural, meaning they didn't put Sax in the sewer, but instead where all the chemicals from the Spire's factory floors run.

The prism itself consists of four diodes, three on the bottom and one above, each about three meters apart from one another. They're connected by slim silver bars that Sax could snap in an instant if the act of doing so wouldn't start a chain of unstable combustion throughout his body.

More than one prisoner's been disintegrated that way.

Looking beyond his death cage, Sax sees the trough he's in is pretty small, and from the sounds of it, there are others near him, each with their own waste-water pipe sending fluid down to the purifier. Above, there's tiny lights casting a placid white, barely enough to see the edges of his cage.

Getting up takes effort, takes time. It's a puzzle re-assembling his nerves, though every connection made is a rush as senses come back online. When Sax finally crouches on his talons, when the slime's dripping off him to join the rest in its rush downstream, the Oratus blows out his mouth and vents with a hissing roar.

The sound echoes around the chamber—Sax has no idea how big it is—and, a moment later, it's followed by second hiss, this one lighter, surprised. Instantly identifiable.

"Bas?" Sax asks.

"I'm here," his pair answers from a few troughs away.

"Me too!" Engee announces. "They took you, huh?"

Sax expects Plake, Coorvin and the others to be here too, but there's no other responses. After a moment, Engee starts dishing the details of their capture. How she and Bas went to the Wildfire as promised, how it was absolutely jammed, and how, after queuing for a table, a green Whelk came their way and offered a special setting in the back.

"I was opposed," Bas clarifies at this point. "The Whelk seemed too nervous."

"But who doesn't want special service?" Engee says. "Although, perhaps it was suspicious. They shot us not long after we sat down, then we woke up here."

"The Belloch running the place knew I'd be coming," Sax says. "How?"

"Oh, they asked where Bas' pair was. I told them you were back at the ship," Engee chirps. "I mean, was that wrong?"

Teven. There's a reason the Vincere doesn't let them near the front.

"It's not worth worrying about," Bas says after a second. "We need to find a way out of these prisms."

Sax is about to say he has an idea when a doorway shunts open above them, blindingly lit, and several silhouettes come in.

"Find a way? No, no, there's no need," says a new voice, watery and thick. "Stay here, stay comfortable. You're much more valuable that way. Yes, yes you are."

Sax plumbs the air with his vents, catches a scent beneath the chemicals. Fresh-molted feathers, the tart smell of a Vyphen's mucous layer.

"Frayk?" Sax asks the shadow, which turns to one of the others.

"How does it know my name? It shouldn't, shouldn't know that," the Vyphen says. "I don't want it talking. Not at all, at all."

There's another flash, then. Bright and overwhelming.

Sax wakes as he falls. It's a second blind panic—his muscles still stunned and the only thing around him is black and bang, Sax hits a wall. Rolls as watery chemicals flood over him, push him on. Sax can't feel his claws enough to try and grab on.

The Oratus rockets around another bend before his stomach falls out as he plummets long seconds in the dark, not knowing if he's going to live or die or what when *splash*. Sax sinks beneath the oily surface, and he's piecing his nerves together as he goes, gets one swing of the tail, a couple pushes of the talons and Sax is almost out when he's sucked away again.

It's a fight to keep his chest above water, to suck in the stale, briny air through his vents. Those moments come in flashes as Sax thrashes his way through the pipes.

Until, at once, it's over.

Sax catches a glimmer of dense yellow and then the pipe ends, launching Sax out into the air. The Oratus crashes down, splashing into a deep and, as he gets his head above the surface, small lake.

Thick yellow-green gas obscures a lot, but Sax can still see the lake itself is a bubbling concoction of chemicals, and it's cleared away a zone of rock around the shores. Beyond those few meters, though, Rathfall's true rulers begin.

Arcing roots and leafy tendrils swoop and dance with each other in a tight maze, the very tips of petals, larger than the *Mobius*, coming into view like blades from a massive fan.

Sax turns and swims back towards the pipe and the shoreline beneath it. He's hoping the Spire's right there, that he might be able to climb it or find an elevator, but there's nothing more than the long, thick pipe rocketing back into the undergrowth and out of sight.

Once Sax gets himself on land, he has to deal with the air. It's thick and scratchy, like breathing smoke, only the smell isn't of ash— it's pollen, heavy and stuffy. Rathfall's air by itself won't kill him right away, but the pollen's going to clog his lungs eventually, leaving Sax without room to breathe in what he really needs.

That's only one of his problems, though. Sax watches the pipe's end, hoping Bas or even Engee's going to pop out and join him down here, but nothing comes except the endless sludge. Eventually, Sax will have to move or he'll die here, one more pile of waste.

If that happens, Sax won't find Frayk. Or the Belloch.

Can't leave a list like that unreconciled.

The only way he knows to go is along the pipe, so Sax forces himself to his feet and begins to claw his way into the wilds. The tendrils are hard and bulky, and every claw swipe that clears a root or stalk coats Sax in sticky sap. Pollen clings to him, along with bits of dirt from the ground, and soon Sax can't even see his own gray scales. He's all rotting yellow.

The pollen doesn't just affect his looks either—it keeps sticking to him, to itself as Sax forges on, weighing him down, pressing him closer to the ground until Sax has to use his tail to keep his balance. And his anger to keep his energy. Few things are better Oratus fuel than a fiery desire to end an enemy. Sax keeps hacking, keeps pressing along with the pipe to his left. One claw, then the other, then the next and the next and the next . . .

The wind hits Sax hard. Pollen blows off of him in chunks as Sax struggles to open his eyes. They'd been covered too, in the end. All of him, every last bit stuck over with sallow golden fluff until he couldn't move anymore.

Only now it's going away, washing off his skin and floating or rolling into the plants around him. Nature taking pity on Sax, maybe?

"Look at this," says a voice that tickles Sax's mind. "Never expected to find him out here."

"Wasn't he supposed to be watching the ship?"

"Don't know what Plake told him."

That name gets Sax to open his eyes fully, to look up and see two Flaum, one pure black and the other a bright silver, staring at him through breath masks attached to full suits. Black, her name, wields a wide tube that links around to a battery pack on her suit—that's where the wind is coming from, and as Sax looks up, she blasts him in the face with it.

"Sorry, had to get that last bit off ya," Black chitters, her voice coming through a mesh filter in the mask she's wearing. "Would've looked funny with a yellow hat on your head."

Sax tries to stand up, but his muscles are weak. He can't seem to get enough air. His vents strain, cough, and Sax sees the poof of yellow-orange dust that comes out when they do.

"Rath-lung," Silver says. "Have to pump him clean."

"Whaddya think he'll do if I try? Claw me to death?"

"I bet he can't lift a single arm. But if we don't help him and his pair finds out, she'll make sure we're meat."

Black slots the tube into a notch near her waist, bends down and takes hold of Sax's foreclaws. Tries to pull the Oratus, and all Sax does is shift some dirt.

"That's not gonna work," Black says, standing back. "Any ideas?"

"We've got to bring the pump to him."

"Think they'll allow that?"

"We won't tell them." Silver points to Sax. "You think Sax won't pay us back in full? An Oratus out here ought to get us plenty."

Sax washes out of consciousness as the lack of oxygen causes the world to fuzz. He does manage to hear the soft sounds of wheels on dirt, though, and definitely catches the fizzing suction of a vacuum going to work.

Black's holding something like her tube, only smaller and targeted, with a funnel leading back to a large tank.

"You stay real still," Black says as she kneels down next to Sax. "Last reward I want for saving your life is a slit throat."

She sticks the tube up to, and then inside Sax's first vent. It hurts, it's stunning, like feeling Sax's insides roiled around, but after a few seconds she pulls it away and Sax can suddenly breathe. Yet before he's had a breath, Silver plants himself next to Black and, with a tube in both hands, spreads a gray ointment over the vent Black just cleared.

"Don't wait for me," Silver says to Black. "Keep going. I want to get this done before he really gets going, so we have a chance to run if he's mad."

"You think we'd manage to get away?" Black laughs in her suit as she suctions another vent. "I need to get you off the ship more. He'd run us down and have us carved for dinner before you manage a single call for help."

Breathe.

That's all.

Breathe.

Sax opens his eyes, and both Flaum are staring at him. He must have passed out again, but now there's strength in his limbs. His mind is clear, and the blurs at the edge of his vision have passed away into nothing.

A glance at his chest confirms it; there's seals over all of his vents now, and bits of yellow dust cling to them.

"It'll keep the pollen out, though you'll want to clean them off from time to time," Silver says. "Basically required for going out on Rathfall."

"Been wantin' to ask you," Black starts in. "What're you doing way out here without a suit? Any kind of mask?"

"Also, you smell toxic." Silver runs a glance up and down Sax's long body. "You may want to shower, or you'll find yourself with some tumors by morning."

Sax decides to give his voice a try. "Fraykt took me. Took Engee and Bas and sent me through the waste channels out here."

"Fraykt?" Black says. "Never heard that name before."

Sax gives the short version of how he made it here, and at the end of it both Flaum shrug.

"We sold the gel, but Plake said we weren't leaving for a bit, so Silver and I thought why not make some extra cash?" Black waves at the plants around them. "Bug catching's a valuable service around here."

"Only there's a condition," Silver says. "Once you rent the suit, you've gotta get enough bugs before they'll let you back in."

"And it turns out we're not very good at bug-catching." Black holds up her small claws. "These don't work so well at grabbing them, and nobody told us to get some better equipment."

"I said we should wait, think about it, but you wanted to go right away." Silver ends the sentence with a sigh.

"Enough," Sax hisses, standing to his full height. "Bring me back to the Spire. I need to find Bas."

The two Flaum look at Sax. "Problem with that, Sax, is there's no getting back to the Spire from here. Not unless we hit our quota," Black says, then she presses a button on her suit.

A blue projection springs up in front of Black, with an image of the three-carapaced flying bugs that call Rathfall home, and a fat zero beneath it.

"Help us get the bugs, we'll help you get back in," Silver says. "It's that simple."

Sax narrows his eyes. Looks at both of these insignificant creatures. "There's no other way?"

"None," Black says. "It's kind of the thing here. If you're not digging up ore, you're catchin' bugs. They make a lot of things out of those parts."

Well, at least it's hunting, and if there's one thing Sax is good at, it's a hunt.

Sax has seen plenty of bugs; the small ones on most planets that buzz around until he swats them away, the cloud-sized ones on Alnert that glide through the atmosphere and feed on kilometer-high geysers, but Rathfall's pollen-chasers are a unique kind of ugly.

Silver and Black lead Sax to their first view of one, sitting on a flower petal, apparently catching its breath after a pollen frenzy, seeing as its shiny lime-green heads are covered in the yellow fluff. The bug itself has twin heads, each with a dark eye cluster, connected by a long, oval body over which, now, fold a pair of wide, luminous wings. Six legs jut out from that oval, each ending in a barbed single claw that cuts through the flower petal and gives the pollen-chaser its traction. Beneath each eye cluster, as if embarrassed by them, the pollen-chaser hides a proboscis and a mandible quartet. The whole thing is a couple of meters long.

"Ugly," Sax says.

"You're one to talk, Oratus," Silver replies.

Sax has to hiss a laugh at that. It's true the Oratus aren't on many lists of the most beautiful species to grace the galaxy, but then, if you're designed to be perfect for a singular purpose, is that not beautiful in its own way?

"So how do we capture one?" Sax says.

Both Flaum glance at each other, then back at Sax.

"Hoping you would have some ideas," Black says. "We've tried miners, we've tried grabbing them, but they break and fly away as soon as we get close."

"And we don't need them alive?"

"This isn't some environmental project," Silver replies. "These plants are crawling with pollen-chasers. All we need are the wings and the mandibles."

Sax could ask why, but ... why? There's only one goal here, and that's getting back into the Spire. So he brushes past the two Flaum, stalks down and low, keeping one eye on the pollen-chaser. It's using the proboscis to lick the pollen off its own head, suctioning at it like a vacuum.

Sax goes under some vines, keeping close to the ground until, looking back across the thorny meadow towards Silver and Black, he can tell he's beneath the bug. Straight up, Sax can see the green bits where the pollen-chaser's feet have burst through.

It's easier to harvest components from a dead creature—they tend not to struggle as you take what you want. So Sax crouches and bursts up, tearing through the thick petal and getting his claws around the pollen-chaser's midsection.

Or, at least, he tries.

Sax's sharp claws slide against the pollen-chaser's green carapace, flaking off the outer shell but not biting in. For something that can tear through metal, can even get through an Ooblot, not being able to pierce the pollen-chaser's shell throws Sax into a momentary panic, one that only grows when he finds himself being lifted off of the petal by the very bug he's trying to capture.

The pollen-chaser's legs close around him as its huge wings unfurl into Y-shaped gossamer. They catch the filtered light coming this far through Rathfall's atmosphere and sparkle it out around Sax, like he's moving through a glistening nebula. It would be beautiful, except the ground is getting awfully far away now. Silver and Black have disappeared, and the only thing Sax sees beneath him is a vast blanket of dull yellow. The wings fan floating dust against his face as they rise, forcing Sax to close his eyes.

There's no sense killing the bug now—Sax would only plummet who knows how far. So instead the Oratus uses his talons, claws and tail to find grips and hang on as the pollen-chaser carries him through the sky.

The ride goes on long enough to fade into an almost-relaxing carriage. The cool temperature mixes with the steady wing beat, the background clicking of the pollen-chaser's mandibles; it's a pleasant trip.

Until the pollen-chaser decides its done carrying the Oratus. The bug's legs open wide without warning, stretching Sax as he keeps his claws clinging. The beating wings, though, slow. The breeze changes, and Sax feels the bug give in to the pull of gravity.

They're landing. The question is, where?

The pollen-chaser answers that a moment later when it breaks into a dive, angling towards a bulky mound that appears from the dust like a dream. The mound is coated in pollen and pocked with holes, and Sax sees plenty more pollen-chasers coming and going from it, like ships to Astre's Spire above.

It's a nest, and the pollen-chaser's taking Sax right to it.

As the bug nears its target entrance, Sax lets go. He doesn't know what's inside that nest, and being carried in without a chance to scout seems like a bad idea. Instead, the Oratus drops a few meters, smacks the side of the mound, which crumples in some at the heavy Oratus impact, and Sax rolls down until his claws and tail can bring him to a stop.

The mound itself feels like thick clay under Sax's claws. Unlike the bugs, which blaze green in the yellow, the mound is a dirty, dried brown. At first Sax wonders if the bugs are actually digging up dirt, but the mound has a distinct scent as Sax hunkers close to it. Thick, loamy and with a hint of lemon.

The flowers. The mound is built on picked petals, placed and pressed down over who knows how long to create this strange palace in a pollen jungle. It's obvious too that Astre's Spire doesn't know this place exists, or they'd have attacked it already; an easy way to harvest a horde of pollen-chasers.

Silver and Blake said the wings and mandibles are the only targets, the only valuable parts. A full-grown pollen-chaser might be a difficult catch, but if Sax is right, if that's a nest in there, then he might find an easier option.

Not that going into the nest of an enemy comes without consequences. Sax goes down first, descending the mound until he reaches the very bottom where it tangles with flower vines. There aren't any pollen-chasers down here, but a few holes remain. No doubt holdovers from the mound's earlier days. Whereas the ones above are large enough for Sax to walk through standing, these are partially collapsed, tight, so when Sax picks one to use, he has to get on his stomach and crawl.

Bas would laugh if she saw him now, squirming through dirt, brushing his filtered vents against crushed flower petals like Sax is some sort of snake.

Light disappears a meter into the tunnel and Sax has to rely on touch and the constant clicking of what must be a thousand mandibles to tell him how close he's getting. The tunnel shrinks more and more as he moves, until Sax is essentially digging his way forward. The chittering gets louder.

How sharp are those mandibles? Can they get through his scales?

When Sax manages to get his head through the last stretch of the tunnel, he has to blink for a while and stare. Yellow light pours into the mound from the wider holes above, angling down like miner blasts. The beams strike shifting hordes of pollen-chasers, their bright green bodies crawling over each other and the walls. Some skitter right by Sax without giving him the slightest notice.

Nearby, clustered along the bottom level, are large clusters of dim-red eggs. They're translucent, and Sax can make out squirming babies within. Clusters of yellow pollen sit around the hatchery, and, in the middle, looms the Queen. She's more than four meters tall and looks much the same as the pollen-chaser that took Sax all the way here, only if that same chaser had been twisted by some horrifying accident: the Queen's mandibles hang at jagged angles, and her—Sax assumes—wings stick out, bent and broken. Scars litter her darker-green shell, though the deep red egg sack hanging from her abdomen appears in good shape.

Sax can't fight this many, even he's not that confident. But there's a chance he could trade the location, give away the hundreds of pollen-chasers clustered here to the ones who would have the firepower.

Proof.

That's what Sax would ask for if someone promised him a treasure cache like this. Something that shows Sax isn't lying to get back in. A bug part wouldn't work, but—Sax notices the red eggs littered at the base of the mount—those would. The smaller ones would fit in a single clawed hand, too.

All Sax has to do is get across a swarming legion of pollen-chasers and he's set!

The Oratus clenches his claws, gets ready to dive and run across the swarm. Grab an egg and break for one of the larger tunnels, get out and . . . what? Run in a random direction?

No, he has to go back the way he came, the way the pollen-chaser flew him. If Silver and Black are following, they'll be along that path. Forging through the flowers.

Sax has a direction, now he needs a plan. The bugs would crush him, grab Sax and chew him to pieces if he tries to just run across them, which means he needs a distraction. He doesn't have any miners, doesn't have any tools aside from his own body, so Sax decides to make one.

Using his claws, Sax scraps off the flower-clay from the tunnel around him and presses it together into a tight ball. It's small enough to fit into his right foreclaw's palm, about the size of a pollen-chaser's mandible. Now all he needs is a target.

Sax creeps to the very edge of the tunnel, where the nearest pollen-chaser is within a meter, its big body sitting in what looks like sleep along the mound's floor. Sax pushes himself up on his midclaws, gives his foreclaws enough room to throw, and lets loose.

The clay ball flies towards the only target big enough to matter— the battered queen in the middle of the mound. Sax's missile breaks up somewhat in flight, with nothing more than a few pebble-sized fragments streaking into the Queen's face.

It's enough of an insult.

The Queen jerks towards Sax, that abdomen of hers shifting more slowly to follow. Her mandibles click, and the resting bunch of bugs take notice. They rise, start to shift towards the Oratus, when Sax makes his move.

The Oratus scrambles the rest of the way out of the tunnel, jumps and plants his talons on the closest pollen-chaser and leaps to the next one.

It's a frantic set of hops that bring Sax smashing into the pile of eggs beneath the Queen. The eggs, with their soft shells, are at least easier for Sax to climb than the hard green carapaces and he scrambles as the pollen-chasers wake themselves up enough to care.

The Queen's huge up close, her shell riddled with cuts and dents from a thousand fights. The egg sack pulses deep red, and Sax's talons pick up the constant vibration of a thousand unborn bugs quivering beneath him.

The Oratus has a moment before he's crushed by the Queen's protection. One chance.

Sax jumps. Leaps and grapples the Queen's body, scrambles around the joint between her head and abdomen until he's on the Queen's back. Which is where the swarm catches him.

The pollen-chasers follow their Queen's order to the letter; attack and destroy the intruder, tear him to pieces. Only Sax makes himself a difficult target and uses the Queen's bulk to send the biting bugs into each other, into the Queen herself. Bugs slam into the carapace around Sax, grappling for a bite before the next diving bug knocks them away.

Sax earns one cut after another as scrabbling mandibles and

claws find their marks, but the Oratus stays true to his goal; get the swarm around the Queen, get them attacking her as they attack him.

The Queen plays her part, shifting around and snapping at pollen-chasers as they bash and climb her to get at Sax. She's his own defense, driving away her defenders in a panicked frenzy to keep herself on top of the egg pile she's so committed to growing.

Sax feels a moment of chaos—when there's so many bug bodies pressing into him, smashing and biting each other more than the smaller Oratus—and enacts his escape. He's made steady progress down the Queen's body, rolling and slashing, kicking and jumping, that the large egg sack bulges out beneath him. Sax takes another three slashes across his back, feeling scales peel away, and presses through the bugs onto the sack itself.

And Sax goes through it.

Tooth, claw, and talon play equal roles in the digging, and Sax sates his own hunger in the brutal process. The egg shells form their own barrier as Sax works deeper and deeper, the broken, ruined eggs falling around him, burying him.

Protecting him.

The noise outside is terrifying; the Queen's found some way of working her mandibles into a constant screech, and the thunder of a thousand pollen-chaser wings rattles the mound. Sax only goes deeper, until he reaches the bottom of the egg pile and the hard ground beneath it. There, covered by meters and meters of unhatched pollen-chasers, he finally takes a breath. Listens to the chaos play out.

Without a target, the pollen-chasers and the Queen turn on each other, parlaying momentary slights and scratches into deadly duels that send the bugs careening into the sides of the mound and, often, into other pollen-chasers, turning two-bug slugfests into quartets of slicing, biting misery.

Sax sees it all through the smeary red translucence of the eggs, taking what breaths he can spare. Pollen-chasers who don't survive the fighting start to pile up on the bottom, on top of the eggs. A mortal tent for Sax to hide beneath.

Bas would be impressed.

Bas *will* be impressed when Sax tells her about this.

After he saves her.

The projection is waiting for us when we follow the orange lines up the ramp to its room. Its misshapen face grins as we walk in, though I wish it wouldn't. There's something about that eerie smile that suggests all kinds of unpleasant things.

"You've succeeded," the projection states. "Thank you."

Then it looks over my shoulder, to Vee-T'Oli, and here its smile vanishes.

"And you've found our intruder."

"He found us, really," Viera says. "Told us what happened here, too. Unlike you."

The projection looks towards her. Doesn't change from its flat expression. "I have parameters. My first priority is to open the vents, and to do whatever is necessary to accomplish that task. Now that it's done—"

"You'll tell us how to get back home," I interrupt. There's been enough long-winded speeches in here, and my ears are picking up a noise from below, one that sounds too much like the screams we left behind. "Now."

The projection seems to stutter, the light breaking for a second, before it snaps back to existence in the center of the room, its blue-white shades flickering as it turns towards me. "Apologies," the ghost says. "This data is somewhat corrupted. I have not accessed it in a very long time."

"That's not what I asked for." I slide my hand to my waist, a signal for Viera to draw her miner. "Our exit, please."

If the projection notices or cares about the weapon now pointing its way, the ghost doesn't show it. Instead, it motions to the left side of the room, where a sealed door suddenly blinks to life and shunts open.

"If there is still hope for you, it lies at the end there," the projection says.

Vee-T'Oli's already moving towards the opening, taking their cue from the definitely-growing chorus of noises behind us. I'm not waiting either, and, with Viera following me, all of us dash from the room into the new path.

"Thank you!" the projection calls after us, echoing with faint malice.

I don't have time to think about why the projection wanted all those disasters freed. It's not like there's anywhere for them to go, any food for them to eat, unless Vee left some nutrient goop behind.

Of course, they could eat us.

The tunnel, though, makes it hard to speed up. Like the other paths, this one is littered with debris, though not the smashed junk piles and bones, but instead patches of caved-in walls. Broken ceiling panels hanging low, forcing us to duck and weave our way around. The damage causes gaps in the orange lighting, making the run a sprint through a gauntlet of shadows.

"What do you see?" I call ahead to Vee-T'Oli, who, with the Oratus' legs, are moving faster than Viera and I.

"Nothing so far, the hallway simply continues," T'Oli calls back. "It's a weird way to build, if I'm being honest."

"The Ooblot talks too much," Viera huffs behind me.

I find T'Oli kind of charming, a welcome respite from the tense straits tightening the rest of us, but I don't bother saying that. Instead,

I jump over a collapsed beam, dance around a broken sidewall and the mound of rock and dirt that's poured through.

Keep on moving, keep on moving.

Because I can still hear those screams.

The corridor goes on for a long ways—though it's hard to tell distances when your only reference point is the flashing half-tail of an Oratus waving in front of you. I'm sweating, breathing in the musty air hard with every breath, but I'm not going to stop.

"They're still coming!" Viera says behind me. "Why are they chasing us?"

All we have to go on is their voices. That endless moaning and shouting. We're moving fast enough that, to my ears anyway, the things we set free haven't made up any distance, but it's clear they're in the hallway now.

"They want to say thank you?" I reply.

"Almost to the end!" T'Oli yells from the front, riding on the Oratus. "I would say another ten seconds or so and you'll make it."

Ten more seconds of side-winding, hurdling jumps, and ducking under collapsed crud has us making T'Oli's guess come true. The question, though, is where we've gone. My first thought, coming out of the hallway, is that we're back on Vimelia, at the spaceport. The chamber is huge, with a strictly arched ceiling where, in several places, torn holes have let rocks crumble.

The chamber's floor is one of packed dirt, and it holds two cross-shaped shuttles. Ships with bulky, circular middles sporting four branches off of the sides. Both are painted a glistening yellow, and both bear, on their fat sides, Ignos' black design.

"I think that's our way out," T'Oli says, pointing Vee towards the closest shuttle.

Except I can't see an exit. There's one wide tunnel that, I think, was meant to be the way out, only it's collapsed. Broken beams, rocks and deep brown dirt clog the way.

"Where would we fly it?" I say as I look around, hoping for an option.

"While you figure that out, we'll see if it still runs," T'Oli announces, then heads for the ship.

"Always taking the hard problems," Viera says, moving next to me. "Don't suppose you have a shovel in that pack of yours?"

I shake my head, not that it would matter anyway. "We wouldn't have time."

Viera takes a few steps into the vast space. Looks towards the tunnel, towards the ceiling. "How far up do you think this goes? Close to the surface?"

I don't know. "Probably?"

There's a hissing noise from the closer shuttle, and I look to see T'Oli-Vee bound up a lowering entrance ramp. If nothing else, maybe we could hide in there until the creatures went away.

"Come with me," Viera says. "Let's see if we can get the other one working."

"The shuttle?"

"Yes, the shuttle." Viera heads across towards the second one and, not wanting to be left to the encroaching screams alone, I follow.

From underneath, the shuttle's four wings reveal a series of four . . . holes on each. Metal slats cover each of them in a lighter gray that stands out against the flower-yellow paint. I'm trying to figure out what the marks do while Viera takes stabs at a clear panel on the front of three landing struts.

"Any ideas?" I ask her, throwing a look back towards the way we came.

No creatures yet.

"We should've asked T'Oli," Viera grumbles. "I thought it would be easier."

T'Oli and its captive Oratus are still in their shuttle, and the only thing I've seen them do is turn on a number of exterior lights, popping glowing white bulbs all across the craft. Not that I'm unhappy with the extra illumination—the orange lines coating every ceiling in this place are high above and things get dim on the floor.

"Let me take a look," I say, heading over.

Viera touches the panel as I approach—it's a little wider than her spread hand, bolted against the metal strut—and the screen flashes red at her pressure. No ideas come to me, but then, I have something on my wrist that can help with that.

"Don't let anything jump me for a minute." I raise the Cache, look at its dull green-brown surface, and focus.

There's a green flash, and then I'm inside.

I think of terms: shuttle, controls, boarding ramp and images flood the mental space around me. All kinds of different craft, terminals, and things I don't recognize flash and float. At first I'm lost in a sea of gray shapes, then I remember the paint. Take away the yellow, the black design, and look for the cross.

The Cache reads my idea and most of the ships disappear in a poof of nothingness, leaving only a few, one of which is the right shape and size. I focus on it and then it's just me and the shuttle in a vast emptiness. I bring back the idea of control panels and different sets appear, some on all three struts, some standing alone.

There's only a pair that apply to the front strut alone. I go for them, and narrow the choices to the one we're working with. From there, I think a single word.

Open.

Around me, through me, walks a generic gray Flaum. I step to the side and watch as it places its hand flat against the screen. There's a green flash and the ramp descends. Only, we tried that and it didn't work.

So the Cache starts again. Another Flaum, this one black, comes up to the control panel. This time, instead of placing its palm, the Flaum pulls out a miner from beneath its fur, sticks it against the panel. With its left hand, the Flaum turns the miner's settings to a low burn, then holds the trigger. Blue light splashes the front of the panel until the screen crackles, there's a pop and an acrid sting in my nose, but the shuttle's ramp descends.

Got it.

I shake my head, withdraw from the Cache, and blink my way into consciousness.

To see Viera, miner raised, aiming towards a growing group of monsters making their way into the docking bay, their mouths open in constant screams.

These things were frightening enough in the tubes, held back by restraints and glass barriers. Now, lurching in the open, one even crawling on three long arms, the 'humans' hit me with a combo of revulsion and fear that has me taking a step back, then another, until I run into the strut and remember what I'm supposed to be doing.

"I need your miner, Viera!" I call.

The Lunare hasn't fired a shot yet, and I think it's because the humans aren't coming towards us so much as T'Oli's shuttle. Which still has its ramp down.

"What?" Viera says without turning to me. "Why?"

"Because we need a way in!"

Now Viera gives me a questioning look, wondering, I bet, if I'm going to just shoot a hole in the bottom of the shuttle, but apparently my outstretched hand and pleading look work enough magic to get her to toss me the weapon. By some miracle of coordination, I catch the miner in both hands, turn and, twisting the power dial, jam its nose against the panel.

"T'Oli, you need to raise that ramp!" Viera's yelling as I pull the miner's trigger.

The weapon judders in my grip as its gasses ionize to their lowest temperature, as they spit electrical fire against the panel.

"Raise it, T'Oli!" Viera calls again.

Come on, come on. We don't have time for this. I risk a look to the left, see a half-dozen humans nearing T'Oli's ramp. See another three heading our way, one, leading the bunch, sporting a head with at least five ears. It would be funny if not for the mindless panic on their faces, the rattling, hoarse screeches coming from their throats.

The panel crackles, my nose gets the smell, and there's a ping from inside the shuttle. Bright and clean, followed by a hiss as the ramp comes down.

Ignos, the Sevora that took up residence inside my head, did a lot of evil things, but I still owe the creature my life several times over for the Cache alone.

"Let's go!" I flip the miner back to Viera and we both head to where the ramp's landing, when we hear a roar that cuts through all the other noise.

It's impossible not to look at what follows, at the terrible destruction of an Oratus unleashed. Vee, with T'Oli nowhere in sight, tears out of their shuttle and into the pack of grasping humans. His four claws rip and tear, his mouth bites and shreds, and the humans fall away before him. Vee, for his part, seems to delight in the melee, moving from one target to the next in a whirling, slashing tornado.

"Wow," Viera says, and I can only agree. "Sax and Bas always looked deadly, but I never saw them fight. Not really."

I'd seen Sax duel with an Amigga, but that was only one target, and the Oratus had been badly injured by then. Vee is old, Vee has scars, but Vee has had a long time to wait for this chance.

Still, no matter how many the Oratus cuts down, more of the humans pour out of the hallway. After Vee slices through the initial wave, more press on him, grabbing at his claws, falling against his scales or picking up pieces of junk to wield as clubs.

"He's going to get overwhelmed," Viera says, starting forward to help him.

She doesn't make it two steps before T'Oli's shuttle spools to life, a pyrotechnic whine filling the cavern.

I clamber up our boarding ramp as soon as it hits the ground. T'Oli's lifting its shuttle, gliding it over towards Vee, though I don't know what the Ooblot plans to do with it. At least until T'Oli rotates the craft, bringing the right cross-wing over some of the humans, where the jets bursting from those holes in the wing commence some instant cooking.

I don't bother watching that. Viera doesn't either. She's coming up the ramp with me into what is, thankfully, a familiar setting. A fat area with netting and handholds for flight, with the cockpit visible to the right.

"I'll figure out the door, you learn how to fly," Viera says to me.

"On it." I head to the forest of levers, terminals, and buttons that is the cockpit.

I'm about to look at the Cache again when something burbles, crackles and bursts through the speakers next to me.

"See you've chosen your own ride!" T'Oli's voice comes through after a moment. "How's it look over there? Our's is a bit beat up. Nothing like the Beast."

There's a big green bar beneath the speaker grille in the center of the cockpit's set of terminals, so I try a hunch, press it, and speak, "T'Oli! How do you fly one of these things?"

"You'll want to cycle the power supply first—hold on a second." The speaker goes dead and I stare around, looking for something that looks like a power supply, not that I know what that is. "Sorry, had to roast a couple aggressive-looking types. These are great ships for that, you know. Most—"

"T'Oli!"

"Ah, sorry. You're wanting to pull the big lever on the right. That'll release the emergency tank. Do you know that's the only hard fuel on these things?"

I don't know what T'Oli means by 'hard fuel', but I see the lever. There's no chairs, no objects to dodge in these cockpits other than the flying net hanging up above, so when the lever doesn't move, I'm able to stand in front of it, brace my legs, and press down on the bright red stick.

There's a shunting noise somewhere beneath me, and a brief whoosh of rushing liquid.

"What'd you just do?" Viera shouts from back near the ramp.

"No idea!" I reply. "You get the ramp up yet?"

"Don't want to talk about it!"

One of the terminals blinks to life as the bright red lever slowly rises back up to its set position. Thanking Ignos that the galaxy uses the same language we do, I read what it says. Which isn't much:

BATTERY PRIMER READY

START?

So I hit the big green triangle beneath the word, and the shuttle gets to work. I reach towards the communication panel, hit the button.

"T'Oli, I think I've got the primer going. What're you doing?"

"Seems like these things won't stop coming, so I'm picking up Vee. Then we're going to have to figure out a way to get above ground. These shuttles aren't meant, you know—"

"I know. But how?"

"Good question! I've been pondering that. Oh, looks like one of them found a way onto the ramp. I'll be right back, Kaishi."

T'Oli cuts off, leaves me staring at the terminals, watching the one lit screen display a bar across it that fills extremely, extremely slowly. I think I've seen grass grow in my village faster than this. I tap the green triangle again, see if that makes it go faster, but no luck.

"Kaishi!" Viera calls from the back. "Help!"

As I rush into the passenger area, I see Viera take the miner in her right hand, pull back, and throw the weapon down the ramp.

"Out of power," Viera says as I get close.

Three of the humans are at the base of the ramp, which, I notice, holds more than a few motionless, burned bodies. Viera's been doing work.

"I'll take them," I say.

"You will? With what?"

"Myself." I take two steps onto the ramp, to the space where the shuttle's doorway keeps my left and right safe, to where the only place the humans can get near me is straight on. "Go back to the cockpit, let me know when it's ready to go. And, if you see another weapon, bring it!"

Viera's departure comes through the steel clang of her boots, leaving me looking at a tri-armed menace loping up my way. I'm expecting to see hate in its eyes, or anger. But there's none of those things—only desperation, fear.

What would I be like, stuck in a tube, unconscious and kept alive through means I don't understand, and suddenly released into a wild world with a hundred others both like me and utterly different? If I had nobody to teach me where I was, what I was, who I was?

So instead of going for a crushing kick to the throat, I aim for the legs instead, crouch low and sweep my foot at the human's knees. Buckle them and trip the person back along the ramp, into the others until the whole array collapses at the foot of the shuttle.

This gives me a bit of time to look out across the bay, back to where Vee's taken a leap away from the swarm and, using his claws, hooked himself into T'Oli's shuttle, which is drifting our way now.

Our way.

"What are you doing?" I shout, though of course T'Oli can't hear me.

I feel a tug on my left arm—it's a vice grip, strong. Nails dig into my skin. The three-armed one is back, and I turn to its frightened face as it pulls at me, tries to drag me to its friends. With my right hand, I deliver a series of blows to its stomach and its face, pushing it away, though not breaking its grip.

"Let go!" I snarl, but the thing doesn't care, doesn't know what I'm saying.

My feet slide on the ramp and I fall back up, use my legs to kick the human off of me. It's an equal-opportunity snatcher, though, so it snags my foot once it loses my arm and now I'm in the same snarl as before.

When Vee, over the approaching drone of T'Oli's shuttle, makes his entrance. The Oratus pushes his way past the other humans, climbs the ramp, grabs my attacker and throws it away to the floor. Vee doesn't stop, either—pulls me and keeps going till we're both inside the shuttle.

Then the Oratus turns, presses a claw on the control panel inside the door, and shuts the ramp.

"Thanks," I manage to say.

"Save it for the Ooblot," Vee replies. "T'Oli's making the real sacrifice."

"What?"

"We're ready!" Viera announces from the cockpit. "And T'Oli's saying it knows a way out of here!"

I leave Vee to supervise the ramp's closure and head back to the cockpit, where T'Oli's intercom voice is giving extremely patient instructions to Viera on what buttons to push, what terminals to look at, and which levers to pull.

"This is not what I'm good at," Viera says as I walk in. "Slow down, T'Oli!"

"Would if I could," T'Oli replies. "But once you put your shuttle in the air, you have to fly it. Or else things won't go well."

All the terminals are lit now with a mesmerizing display of shifting numbers, graphs, and blinking things that, frankly, send my heartbeat into overdrive and nearly push me into a panic. How are we supposed to deal with all this?

"Kaishi's here now," Viera says as she punches at something that looks like a big circle. "Yell at her for a minute while I try to breathe."

When Viera hits the screen, the shuttle shudders. There's a muffled whine—the same one I'm thinking we heard when T'Oli took off, but here blunted by the shuttle's own walls—and I notice the orange-lit cavern start to shift as we leave the ground.

"Kaishi! How are you?" T'Oli asks.

"Been better," I reply.

"Who hasn't?" T'Oli merrily continues. "Can you press the bar there on your central screen that says 'Manual'?"

It's a red bar, and all the ones we've pressed so far have been green, so T'Oli's command makes me suspicious.

"You sure that's the right one?"

"If you don't, the computer's going to route you on an automatic path that doesn't exist anymore. You'll fly right into the wall. Which would not be good."

The Ooblot makes a convincing argument. I press the bar.

The base of the terminal pops and what looks like a tightly-wound, light gray coil shoots out, then unwinds into a tall, three-pronged stick with a number of holes along the sides.

"Something strange just came out of the terminal," I reply as both Viera and I stare at it.

"That's your flight stick! See those holes? If you had claws, or used shaping techniques like me, you'd be able to grip there. Cool, right?" T'Oli says.

"Right," Viera replies. "We're not moving anymore, T'Oli."

The cavern walls have stopped shifting. I'm guessing we're hovering above the ground. Which, at least, puts us out of reach of the things below.

"Not supposed to be!" T'Oli says. "Who wants to fly?"

Viera throws a glance my way and I remember that I'm the only one that's really worked with this stuff. Ignos, through me, piloted the shuttle away from *Cobalt*. It's not much to draw on, but it's something.

"I'll do it," I say, and step up to the stick.

When my hands touch it, the shuttle lurches to the right. Not much, but enough to get a small yelp out of Viera. I let go immediately and the shuttle settles back.

Somehow, we're not dead.

T'Oli proceeds to give me a slow rundown of the mess in front of me, rendering it from indecipherable, deadly chaos into a mushy spread of semi-coherent options. The most important thing, the Ooblot tells me, is the flight stick in my hands. The shuttle's going to go where I point that thing.

Though, right now, there's not many good directions.

"I'm working on that," T'Oli says when I note our limited options. "Hang on just a moment, and we'll have ourselves an exit."

I'm about to ask what T'Oli's going to do when the cavern fills with a roar. I twist the flight stick rather than pull it, which rotates the shuttle to the right, giving us a broad view of the human mass teeming beneath us, and T'Oli's shuttle as it points its nose towards one of the thinner, collapsed sections of the ceiling and accelerates.

I don't have a second to protest. No time to yell. Viera and I can only watch as T'Oli's shuttle bursts up, crashing into, and through, the rock and orange lighting. Sparks shower down, followed by the gray fog clogging the air around the pit.

"T'Oli made it through!" Viera says.

Another rumbling quake follows her sentence as the ceiling around the new hole starts to collapse. The humans beneath us sense the problem and begin piling back into the hallway, back to the base from which they came.

We, meanwhile, are stuck in a floating box that's getting hammered by falling chunks of metal and debris.

"We should go!" Vee calls up from the passenger compartment.

Oh yeah. Guess that's my job now.

I push forward on the flight stick, just slightly. The shuttle's nose dips towards the floor, and when I nudge the small lever to the left, what T'Oli calls the throttle, we head forward till we're beneath the new hole. Then I try to mimic T'Oli's maneuver, pulling back on the stick until the shuttle's pointing towards the sky.

"Hold on," I say, then shove the throttle up.

The shuttle jumps like a juar, roaring up through the hole before I can even blink. The pressure should send me flying back out of the cockpit, but the acceleration triggers the netting, which drops in a flash behind me and keeps me pressed against the flight stick.

There's a long moment when we're simply churning into the sky before I take a breath. Before I tell myself that we're flying. That I'm flying.

And we're still alive.

"Yes!" Viera cries once she realizes the same. "Amazing! You didn't kill us!"

"I thought we were going to die!" I reply.

"Me too!"

The giddy moment only lasts longer when the fog parts to reveal a brilliant blue sky, white clouds streaking across it like feathers. It's beautiful. Ignos, in his yellow majesty, makes me squint, but I don't care.

This is home. This is what I've been trying to find.

Until Vee brings us down with a simple question,"Where's T'Oli?"

8 / EGG TRADING

By the time Sax crawls out of the mound, an egg in one midclaw, there's not a single pollen-chaser interested in him. Most, including the Queen, lie dead in piles while others twitch and flit about in confusion. None even spare him a glance as Sax takes the red egg and crawls out of a larger hole halfway up the mound.

Back in the yellow cloud, Sax finds the impact from his first drop and tracks along the pollen-chaser's flight path. Every so often, Sax stops, takes a deep breath from his vents, and lets loose a loud, hissing roar.

A crude way to get attention, but he doesn't have other options.

Still, progress is slow and Sax burns his energy hacking through the vines all day. When nightfall approaches, Sax crawls up into a flower, sets the egg aside, and dips in and out of sleep surrounded by long stalks coated in yellow pollen.

He wonders if Bas is stuck in that same place, talons dipping in wastewater, with nothing more than the grind of machinery to pass the time. Not that Sax is in much better straits—he has no food out here, and the only sound is the whistling wind as it cuts through the vines. That, though, is enough to bring about fitful dreams to guide him through to dawn.

Midway through the next day, not long after another hissing roar, Silver and Black crash through the vines in front of Sax. The Oratus has never been happier to see a pair of Flaum in his life. And, once they see the egg and Sax tells them what it means—that there's a horde of salvageable bodies not all that far away—they're ecstatic.

Until Sax relays the rest of his plan.

"No, no," Silver replies. "You can't tell them what you've found. They'll take it, they won't give you anything. Better if we bring it back piece by piece, ensure we get paid the whole amount."

"I don't have that kind of time," Sax replies. "They'll let me back in the Spire, or they'll never find out where it is."

"They'll just torture you," Black says. "Force you to give it up. There's a method to these things, Sax. Being out here is part of the punishment—you're not supposed to cheat it."

"What are you being punished for?"

"Greed." Black doesn't look the least bit embarrassed. "We want the money, this is what's required to get it."

Sax looks at the two Flaum. Processes the nonsense coming out of their mouths. This is some kind of game? A machination for profit?

The Vincere never once mentioned money as the reason for a raid, for an intercept or an ambush. Sax has been to dozens of worlds, never once under the guise of revenue. Survival was always—is always—the reason.

"Where's the Spire?" Sax hisses.

"There," Silver says, pointing back the way they came. "Keep going and you should see it by nightfall. Like we're saying, though, you don't get in."

"That's my problem," Sax says.

He doesn't get more than a few steps, enough for the Flaum to realize Sax intends to do just what he's saying, before Black calls back to him.

"Hey! Where's the mound?"

"Follow my claws," Sax replies.

Then the Oratus breaks into a run, his talons chewing up the ground and his tail straight back behind him for balance. It's a freeing sprint, even with the dust clogging up his eyes. Sax holds his vents open and gulps in the filtered air, pushing it through to his muscles, juicing them for each and every long footfall. The kilometers vanish as Sax follows the trail blazed by the two Flaum, occasionally jumping over or ducking under a vine not quite cut. The pollen-chaser egg stays clutched in his right mid-claw, cradled against Sax's abdomen as he runs.

Sax makes the Spire well before nightfall, when the roiling clouds above are only starting to fade from brighter yellow to orange and dark gold. The Spire's base expands beyond what Sax can see, coating the horizon as he gets close, and the area beyond this partic-ular entrance is heavily overgrown. He'd have to work if he wanted to circle the structure.

Instead, Sax goes right up to the wide airlock and taps at the single-button panel outside. Nothing happens. The panel doesn't even turn on or acknowledge the press. Beyond the lines of the airlock door and the heavy metal and stone construct of the Spire itself, its ridged curves rising up into the dust, nothing moves.

"Whatcha got there?" grumbles a voice from behind Sax.

The Oratus turns, making sure to keep his claws in full view, and looks right into the small hovering camera of a microdrone. Simply a metal ball containing a battery, a camera, and a thousand tiny jets, the drone stays out of Sax's reach, but it's focusing on the egg.

"A trade," Sax says to the thing. "A pollen-chaser egg to get back into the Spire."

"We're after wings and mandibles," the voice behind the drone replies—Sax thinks it sounds like an old Flaum, but it's hard to be sure. "What're we going to do with an egg?"

"Hatch it, breed it, harvest the results," Sax says. "Or go for the hive, a couple of days that way."

Sax points, but not the way he came. Far to the right of it. Silver and Black are on Plake's crew, and the last thing Sax wants is to save Bas and find themselves stranded on this waste of a world because he annoyed their ride.

"You think I'm going to let you back in for that?" the voice says, but the drone belies the intentions, as it swings around for a different angle on the egg. "Go get a few more and we'll talk."

"No," Sax says. "You'll let me in now. For the egg."

The voice laughs. "It's like you think you've got some power here, Oratus, but your Vincere buddies aren't on Rathfall. Don't know how you put yourself on the surface, but there's a price to get in this way, and you're not paying it with that egg."

Sax turns back to the airlock panel. It's a single-button, which means it's simple. Probably been here for some time. Sax isn't an engineer, but he's broken a lot of doors, and most of the locks come down to a switch. Connect the right wires, or break the right thing, and the door opens.

"What're you doing now?" the voice asks as Sax puts one fore-claw up to the panel. "It's not going to let you in."

"I'm going to tear it apart until it does."

The drone buzzes over near Sax's head. "You'll be trapping yourself, and everyone else, out here!"

"You'll be losing all your profits."

The drone hovers for another second. Sax drags his claw along the metal side of the control panel, letting the shriek sound long and loud. It blinks to life before Sax scrapes a single side.

"Good choice," Sax says, hitting the button.

The airlock shudders and opens slow, with dust cascading off the doors in yellow waterfalls.

"The egg, then," the voice says. "A fair trade."

Sax doesn't reply, but walks towards the airlock instead. The drone hovers close, dropping back only when Sax begins to enter the doors. Which puts the microdrone in the perfect position for a swat from Sax's tail that sends the machine careening into the ground, where it pops and fizzles into a hundred pieces.

The little robots are annoying.

The other side of the airlock shows that the Spire's ground entrance wasn't always a profiteering mess. Sax walks into a mostly-empty ring dominated by a central cargo elevator, and a smaller passenger version alongside it. Unlike the docking bays near the top, which hold an even assortment of small and large transports for goods and passengers alike, down here there's only a single option for him.

The rest of the level is smooth stone flooring and plain white lighting. Sax is almost disappointed that Fraykt doesn't have a squad of flunkies here for him to dismember; it's so dull. The cargo elevator tries to liven things up with rushes of rumbling action every few seconds, and the floor still reeks of pollen, showing that an airlock can only do so much when everyone coming inside is coated with the stuff.

Sax makes it all the way to the passenger elevator in three long strides, egg still in hand, and taps the request button. No lock on this one. No microdrone.

But there is the whoosh of an opening door, the humpf of a big, burly Flaum emerging from what Sax thought was a stack of old shipping containers but that, looking more closely, is a makeshift control room. This Flaum, though, makes Sax hiss in laughter.

Yes, the Flaum's holding an assault miner of a type banned for civilian use. Yes, he doesn't look thrilled—Sax figures the microdrone belonged to this angry furball. But the Flaum's also sporting a deep blue dye job, one that he's not been able to redo in a long time, as bits of bright tan fur are poking through at the roots.

"Laugh again and I'll shoot you right there," the Flaum barks in response. "You crushed my drone."

"Payment for wasting my time," Sax replies.

"I'll be wasting a lot more if you don't give me that egg right now," the Flaum says.

The Flaum's wearing a look Sax has seen too many times to count. There's a squint to his eyes, a set to his shoulders, and a tensing of the Flaum's muscles that says as soon as the egg makes its safe flight his way, the Flaum's going to be exacting a price of his own with the miner.

The predictability is boring. The results are not.

9 / JOY RIDE

Going down is far more frightening than going up. For one, turning away from Ignos means we're diving into a rippling, puffy gray expanse. For another, my stomach churns as we make the arc, the thought of that rocky ground we're now speeding towards tying my last snack into knots.

Several of the terminals start to blink, displaying numbers in increasingly large and panicky sizes. I'm assuming all of them are counting down the moments till we splatter against the rocks and die.

But T'Oli's the reason we're up here, T'Oli's the reason we're on Earth in the first place. I can't just leave, can't assume that the Ooblot's fine.

"Don't crash," Viera squeaks, pressing back against her netting as we dive into the gray.

"You may want to pull up," Vee hisses from the back. "You're coming in too steep."

Pull up. Right.

I move the flight stick back towards me and the shuttle responds, though it's hard to tell how much since everything I can see is just varying shades of foggy gray. Some of the terminals, though, stop yelling at me, so there's that.

"How are we going to find T'Oli if we can't see anything?" I ask nobody in particular.

"Get low, to the surface," Vee's voice is so close that I twitch.

The Oratus is up from the passenger bay, apparently willing to risk the journey while I'm piloting, which seems suicidal. Yet there he stands, his claws looped through my crash netting, those bloodshot eyes of his staring at the screens.

"Use the maneuvering jets," Vee hisses. "Not the engines."

"Yeah, that doesn't help me," I reply. "You know how to do that?"

"I'm not a pilot."

As not-a-pilot Vee keeps telling me how to fly, the shuttle coasts through the gray, and I start to see a darker shade below. Apparently we're still descending, because the shade resolves itself into the ashy ground I'd hoped we'd left behind.

I keep playing with the flight stick and the throttle and find that when I lock the throttle's lever into a central notch that the main engine dies away. This results in a momentary panic as our descent becomes a plummet, accompanied by our screaming trio—Vee's wild hissing doesn't harmonize, but I appreciate that the Oratus is as certain as we are about our impending death.

Then we bounce. Sort of.

It's like landing on a pile of grass—the shuttle catches itself as we near the ground, what must be the maneuvering jets finally finding enough pressure to keep us aloft. I take a huge gulp, stare at the ground around us, and thank Ignos I'm still alive.

"Intentional," I say a second later. "Completely intentional."

"Next time," Viera says, I'm riding with the Ooblot,"

The first signs of T'Oli come in the form of wreckage; a broken wing, a still-burning engine lying on the ash. We follow the debris trail till we find the main body in the middle of an ash trench dug by its own crash.

Now that I have a handle on the maneuvering jets, it's not too difficult to get the shuttle low enough to land. Actually deploying the struts, though, requires Viera slapping at terminals until something she hits works.

Vee takes the lead after we drop the ramp, and the Oratus doesn't bother waiting for us. He's loped through the ash all the way to the wreck before we make it to the ground.

"He makes me feel slow," Viera says as we move.

"We *are* slow compared to him."

"You're supposed to say we're just as good."

"Sax and Bas proved that's not true," I say. "At least, not when it comes to fighting."

"You think we're smarter?"

"I hope. Otherwise, we're going to wind up like the Flaum."

Humanity as servants, as playthings for the galaxy's more powerful species. I won't, can't accept that.

Vee's tearing away at the wreck, flinging bits of metal into the air as we get close.

"What do you think's happening on the other side?" I ask Viera. "Back home?"

"I think they're going to be gone by the time we make it there," Viera replies. "The Sevora will either take or destroy us all. I don't think Nasiya's going to accept an alternative."

"We'll stop them."

Now it's Viera who laughs. "Kaishi, when did you get to be such an optimist?"

"You told me I needed to act like an Empress, so I am. We have to have hope, Viera. If not us, then who?"

Whatever Viera's thinking of saying, it's interrupted by Vee's victorious hissing. With both foreclaws, Vee holds up what looks like a large lump of rock, complete with a pair of small stubs rising up from its surface.

T'Oli's rock skin is ash-blasted and burned, chips are missing and the Ooblot looks a far cry from the smooth puddle it often takes. The eye stalks, those two stubs, are more like stalagmites; solid black spikes emerging from a more mottled body.

"Is T'Oli still alive?" I ask as the three of us stand over the Ooblot.

We're back in our shuttle—ramp raised to keep any roaming creatures out—and T'Oli's sitting in the middle of the passenger compartment. It hasn't thawed, hasn't moved.

"Ooblots are difficult to kill," Vee rasps, then flexes his claws. "It would take me some time to carve through one."

"Never heard a better compliment," Viera mutters, then looks at me. "We can't just sit here waiting for it, Kaishi, if T'Oli's even alive."

"You're giving up quick," I reply.

"Every minute we spend here is one that we could be using to fly home." Viera points at Vee, who blinks back at her. "There are species on this planet that want nothing more than to kill us, or take us as living bodies. We have to get back, Kaishi. We have to help them."

She's right, but I barely know how to fly the shuttle, much less how to fly it where we want to go. And if I try anyway, choose wrong and wreck our one chance to get back?

"T'Oli crashed through the ceiling to make a hole, Viera." I crouch next to the Ooblot, place a hand on T'Oli's warm rock skin. "It's the reason we're here right now. We'll give T'Oli a chance. Besides, I'm exhausted, hungry, and it's almost night. Humanity can survive just a little longer."

That argument, at least, gets some support from my cohorts. We dig into some rations from our escape mod packs. The nutrient goop, preserved in sealed bags, tastes—as ever—like the dustiest of dirts, but my stomach isn't in a position to protest. The shuttle manages to have some filters that recycle water, and, Vee says, it even pulls moisture from the air, so we're able to quench our throats.

Night falls over the ash and at first we don't notice—the shuttle's a constant bright white inside. At least until Vee finds a setting in the cockpit that adjusts the spectrum so that we're sitting in twilight purple that gradually fades to a starry black.

"Why bother?" Viera asks as the lights shift around us. "Seems like a lot of unnecessary work."

"These are meant for survival on new worlds," Vee explains as we sit around T'Oli's rock-body. "The shuttles, I mean. Land, introduce colonization steps, and live here. It wouldn't help much if the colonists lost their minds, would it?"

"After seeing what they did here, I'm not sure." Viera takes a long look at her own hands, as if coming to the same conclusion I had back in the rooms with the tubes, with the experiments. "The Lunare always figured Ignos was a myth, you know. That we never came from some mystical god. Guess we were right."

She doesn't sound too thrilled about that. Go back not all that long and I'd press her, I'd defend Ignos with everything I had, but after this, after those things, I don't really have the energy.

"Congratulations," I finally say, and that's all.

"Gods are for those who need them," Vee hisses into the silence. "They're not right or wrong, they just are."

"Do you have any?" I ask the Oratus.

"The Oratus are weapons, human. We exist to serve a purpose, not to ask questions."

"I don't know whether that's a nightmare or a blessing." Viera stands, paces around the room. "Don't you ever get curious? Don't you ever wonder what it's all about? Why you're here?"

"We know why," Vee replies. "It's clear from the moment we are born."

I'm used to mornings starting with Ignos rising from the horizon, or, lately, the blinking on of lights in whatever dark metal structure I happen to be in. This one, this time I wake up to the sound of cracking stone, of flakes and chips settling onto the shuttle's floor in soft patters.

We're all curled up in the various netting, sleeping as best we can, so it's something of a mess as Viera, Vee and I scramble up and get ourselves tangled. We're able to see T'Oli shift back to its creamy white form, though—even its eyestalks shake off the coating, blink their way back to life.

"That took a longer nap than I thought," T'Oli announces, taking the rest of us in. "Is that how you all normally sleep? It seems uncomfortable."

I wrestle myself free first—a virtue, I think, of being the smallest one—and crouch next to T'Oli. Hunt for any signs of damage, like bleeding or scars, but see nothing. It's as if the Ooblot is perfect, even though it just crashed a ship through a rock wall, a ship that then exploded and fell into the ground.

"How?" I can only ask.

"Ooblots are very hard to kill," T'Oli says. "Shooting us into space works. As does concentrated miner fire. But an explosion? Especially if we have time to prepare? Not an issue."

"He's got scales, this thing can turn itself into a rock," Viera says, getting up. "How'd we get stuck with the fragile bodies?"

"Because the Amigga wanted something they could control," Vee hisses. "Something that would not be hard to kill should it prove a problem."

"Seems like we weren't as easy to kill as you wanted."

Vee hisses a laugh. "We underestimated your species. And the Amigga who very much wanted you to survive."

"What happened to it? The Amigga?" I ask.

Vee shakes his head, "I don't know. It was gone, with plenty of humans, before we arrived. They used shuttles like this one, I believe. Escaped to the far side of the planet. I don't know why the Vincere did not pursue."

I wait for Vee to say more, but instead the Oratus hunts for and finds a package of nutrient goop and starts tearing into it. Breakfast is a higher priority than information, apparently. So I switch targets:

"T'Oli, we need you to fly us home," I ask.

"Can't do that for a while," T'Oli replies. "I might look good, but it'll take another day or two before I'm able to shift cleanly again. You want to travel now, you're going to have to do the flying."

"You can guide me, though, right?"

"My speaking abilities are just fine, Kaishi." T'Oli swivels its stalks towards the cockpit. "Let me grab a bite, then let's see if this shuttle's still in good shape."

This time, when the shuttle clears the gray fog, I have T'Oli beside me yammering about what each and every little symbol means. This diagram shows the shuttle's orientation, that one shows the speed, and this last thing here is the fuel, powered by batteries.

"Batteries?" I ask.

"Big buckets of energy," T'Oli replies. "These were dead, which is why you needed to release the emergency liquid fuel to kick them up. I'd say we have a few hours of flight time before you'll have to land."

"Then what?"

"Either we get some place where the light can hit the shuttle's wings and charge it up, or we walk."

So I boost the speed, turn the shuttle west, and hope we can outrun the fog. Even with the time limit, flying above a gray sea doesn't do much for my attention. It's relaxing, sure, but T'Oli pushes me to let the computer keep to the course. Diversions waste power.

I take my hands from the flight stick and look at the Ooblot puddled up on the ground next to me. Vee and Viera are in the back, both catching naps after the initial excitement of clearing the clouds wore off.

"Do you think we can trust Vee?" I ask the Ooblot. "He was sent here to kill us, right?"

"If I had to guess, he'd rather be killing Sevora. Seeing as that's where we're going, he ought to be fine." T'Oli tilts an eye stalk. "Between you and me, who'd you be more loyal to? The group that left you to rot in that base for so long, or the ones that rescued you?"

"Oratus are strange, T'Oli. I don't know what he'll choose."

"They're strange, Kaishi, but they're not stupid. One thing I'm curious about, though, what's your place here? With the humans?"

We've got the time, so I tell T'Oli the story. The Ooblot's a patient listener, and I feel like I've gone through the tale enough that I tell it efficiently. Skip the boring bits. Though I find myself stumbling over Malo. He's only a character now. Someone that appears in memories and nowhere else.

T'Oli notices.

"Losing friends is a terrible thing," T'Oli says after I finish the bit about *Cobalt*, how we barely survived, when the Sevora in my head sent us to the place that would take Malo's life.

"I'm sure you've lost plenty." I wonder how many T'Oli's known, forgotten during the time spent with Clarity's Dawn.

"Gained plenty too," T'Oli replies. "You can't dwell on it, Kaishi. Otherwise it becomes all you are; a walking list of tragedies."

"That's what you think I am?"

"Not yet."

I laugh, sad and short. "Thanks. Guess a living puddle would know."

"Now there's an insult," T'Oli replies. "You know, I've heard that in most of the galaxy, Ooblots have plenty of power. We handle things the Amigga don't care to. I might wind up running this planet when we're done, and then we'll see what you call me."

I think it's joking, but there's enough in the Ooblot's words to catch my mind. Running this planet? Did that happen?

"What do you mean?" I finally ask. "Wouldn't we, humans, choose who's ruling us?"

"Nope," T'Oli says. "If you fight off the Sevora, the Amigga will come next. They'll give you a choice: annihilation, or joining the galaxy. And once you join, you're under their laws. Not so bad really —the Amigga mostly care about themselves and, after they've stripped your DNA of anything they want, they'll leave you alone. You understand, of course, I only know this secondhand, but everyone in Clarity's Dawn preferred the Amigga to the Sevora."

Two of the terminals are flashing by the time the mountain rises into view above the gray. T'Oli's calmly counting down the moments till our shuttle runs out of power and sends us crashing, Viera and Vee are all strapped into the netting for when that happens, and my hands are on the flight stick, holding it tight and wondering how much control I'll have when what amounts to a big metal rock decides to fall out of the sky.

"Can I land there?" I point to the mountain, whose frosted top rises out like the tip of my father's black-glass knife.

"Are there any flat parts?" T'Oli asks.

That's a no. At least, not above the cloud. The gray is thinner here—we've made progress and I'm able to see the shadowy outline of the rest of the mountain—and its shorter brethren—beneath the top of the haze. Maybe the shuttle could still get some energy under the lighter cloak?

In any case, it's not like I have a choice.

I angle the shuttle into a slow descent, aiming for the peak and hoping something resolves itself.

"If you crash us into the only thing above the clouds . . . " Viera says behind me.

"I'm trying to land us anywhere," I reply. "There's not a lot of options."

By which I mean zero, but I don't say that. All I do is continue sending us towards the mountain, lower until we're kissing the tops of the foggy clouds. The peak draws close, and I'm still not seeing anything.

"I would start going in," T'Oli says. "Staying up here much longer will make for a rough landing."

"Go in where?"

"Anywhere, really. Landing under some semblance of control is always better than crashing without it."

The peak is beautiful snowy obsidian and it glints in the noonday light as I start a long banking turn around it, dropping all the while. It's a magical last look at nature, something I've missed since leaving Damantum, since leaving home.

Then it's all gray. All fog.

"Push that there," T'Oli says, angling an eyestalk towards a circular icon split by various lines.

When I push it, the glass in front of me flashes and suddenly burning blue lines appear beneath us. At first I don't know what's happening, then I see a big line glowing to the left, right where the peak rises. Outlining the landscape.

"Easier than flying blind," T'Oli says.

"You could have told me about that," I reply. "I would've gone in sooner."

"But the view was wonderful."

"You need to work on your priorities, Ooblot," Viera snaps from the back, and I agree with her.

Regardless, we're now coasting over a rocky pattern of blue. The terminals now are all showing red, and I've noticed the lights inside the shuttle are shutting off.

"Non-essential systems shutting down." says a voice, a very non-living voice, from the speakers in front of me.

"Nice of it to tell me," I say.

"Focus on finding a place to land," Vee hisses. "I just escaped from that terrible prison. I'd rather not die now."

"Then maybe you should be the one flying," I shoot back.

So far, being a pilot is a terrible experience; I'm always under attack from enemies outside or from snarky passengers inside. I'm either breaking out of a buried spaceport, or crash-landing into nowhere.

Give me legs on the ground and a long march, and I'll be happy.

As if listening to me, a section of blue lines ahead flares bright white for a moment, and then a section the lines surround shades in with that soft white color.

"Going to guess it wants me to land there?" I say.

"You're learning!" T'Oli cries. "There is no prouder moment for a teacher than when their student acts on their own for the first time."

"Uh, thanks. Now, how do I land?"

T'Oli falls into rote instruction mode, rattling off buttons to press, angles to shift the flight stick, and, finally, when to shove the whole thing into neutral and use the maneuvering jets to settle down. It's all going fine until, when I activate the struts, all the terminals flicker and blink off. The jets die, and the shuttle plummets the last two meters to slam into the dirt.

But, somehow, nobody dies. The shuttle doesn't explode. I fall into my netting, T'Oli slides around, and Vee and Viera continue hanging, useless.

"That wasn't so bad?" I offer.

"Had better," Vee hisses. "But, I am alive."

"Kaishi, I'm never flying with you again," Viera says. "But, thanks for not getting us killed."

"You're welcome."

10 / CLIMBING THE SPIRE

Sax doesn't reply, doesn't clue the Flaum in except to take the egg in his right midclaw and toss it high in the air, almost to the level's ceiling. The Flaum tracks it, and Sax takes advantage. A one-two kick with his legs sends Sax flying across the floor and into the Flaum before the furry creature can react.

With his midclaws, Sax tears away the miner as his foreclaws pick the Flaum up—painfully—by the shoulders. Sax digs in his midclaws, piercing the miner's circuits and gas canisters, rendering the weapon a useless hunk of garbage. Then, glancing up, Sax swings the Flaum around.

"Catch," Sax hisses in the Flaum's face, and, to both their surprise, the Flaum actually overcomes the pain and shock to get his furry hands up and snatch the egg as it falls. "Nicely done."

Sax sets the Flaum back on the floor.

"A fair trade," Sax hisses as he turns back to the elevator.

The Flaum offers nothing in reply.

The elevator only rises a short distance before chugging to a stop, the panel blinking orange in the universal signal for remote override. Sax doesn't doubt for a second who's actually controlling the lift now.

Fraykt, or one of the Vyphen's cronies.

But he doesn't expect the doors to open.

Level 93 makes a greasy first impression. Chunks of half-refined ore sit immediately outside the lift's doors, and the mechanisms for turning dirt-covered minerals into usable metals lay further back, behind hanging sheets and exposed walls, as if someone wanted to hide their misuse. Light comes from the floor-to-ceiling windows that, as the day dims into evening, start to glow with their own stored energy. Not solar, not on a planet as fogged as this, but wind-driven. Molecules blown around and around, giving off low light only visible when other sources go away. Old tech, and inefficient, but given its place in the Spire, Level 93 might be very old.

So why's he here?

"Bring me to Bas," Sax hisses loud.

Anyone waiting for him on this level's going to know he's here anyway, and if Fraykt is listening, then Sax may as well make demands.

"You want, really want your pair?" the voice comes back at Sax from a speaker somewhere—maybe even multiple ones—throughout the level. "Then tell me, Oratus, tell me why you left your precious Vincere for our little, little Spire?"

"I didn't leave for your Spire." Sax gets around the chunks of ore and heads back through the sheets. "We left to find the truth. To find Evva and learn why she abandoned her post."

"What truth?"

Sax hesitates, then makes a cold calculation; there's no reason not to tell Fraykt everything. If the Vyphen is loyal to the Chorus and the Amigga, then he's probably already killed Bas, and Sax will destroy him for it. If the Vyphen's not, or has other ideas, then Sax proving he's not a follower of Chorus law—a statement that sounds weird anytime Sax thinks it—might lead the Vyphen to give in without a fight.

In that case, Sax might even show the creature mercy.

Maybe.

"The Chorus and the Amigga are after perfection," Sax says.

"Control. They don't trust us, or any species. We found one on a space station Evva sent us to, and it was designing biological servants. Replacements for us."

There's quiet for a moment, then a soft laugh comes through the intercom. "Replacements. Your friend Plake surely, must have told you how it feels to be replaced? To be told, declared you're no longer useful?"

Sax has no time for Vyphen pity.

"This is not the same," the Oratus hisses as he completes a circuit of the level. "The Amigga don't want to retire us, they want to eliminate us. Remove any threats to their power, their way of life."

There's nothing on Level 93 for Sax to use, nobody for him to kill. Though by the time Sax gets back around to the lift, its doors are closed. He punches the control panel, but gets no response. So Fraykt's trapped him here.

"What is your solution, your answer to this problem, Oratus?" Fraykt asks. "Slaughter them all? Use your claws in the only, absolute way you know how?"

"That wouldn't be the worst thing."

"This Spire and all within it survive, live because an order exists in the galaxy," Fraykt replies. "That order allows commerce, allows us to profit and, if not prosper, if not thrive, to make something of our lives. Removing the Chorus would thrust everything into chaos, disorder. Trillions would die as everyone scrambles for power."

"Better that than a slow extinction."

Sax looks up along the lift shaft to the level's ceiling. No obvious options. Except, and Sax turns to the chunks of rock, he could make his own exit.

"That's your thought, your opinion," Fraykt tries a comeback. "Some of us would prefer to enjoy our remaining lives, rather than spend them in your fight."

Sax picks up the nearest chunk of ore. It's heavy, and he's using all four claws to hold it. This would have been easier if he'd kept that

Flaum's miner, but Sax isn't good at planning for the future. He's much better at wrecking the present.

"Last chance," Sax hisses. "Open the lift and bring me to Bas, or I'll start breaking things."

"It's coming," Fraykt replies. "I also find it quaint you assume, you think your pair is still alive. We had the same conversation, her and I, and I have to commend you both. You're made for each other, both of you. Or were, anyway."

Sax hears the shuttling of the lift heading his way and drops the rock, makes a dash for the other side of the level, then leaps up into the crossbars from which those thick sheets hang. The lift settles into the platform and, with a chime, the doors open. As expected, two Flaum and two Whelk come out slow, miners raised and ready.

"I trust you'll let my friends continue our conversation," Fraykt announces, though Sax doesn't hear any glee in the Vyphen's watery voice. "You and your pair reached, clawed too far, Sax. Revolution doesn't need to be done in such broad strokes. Better to change the galaxy in small shifts. I am sorry, so sorry."

Sax doesn't believe Fraykt's sorry at all. The two Oratus are just another annoyance to be removed. Sax, though, has no intention of dying. Not yet, anyway.

The quartet split into pairs, a Flaum and a Whelk in each, with the furry ones taking the lead and sticking their noses in the air. Smelling for Sax, who, no doubt, reeks of pollen dust. With one pair coming towards him and the other breaking the opposite way around the central shaft, though, Sax has an opportunity.

Those lift doors are still open.

Sax bounces from his crossbar to another, then another, each landing causing a metal rattle as the bars bang against their settings. Flaum and Whelk cry out their alarms, but Sax has one goal, and with his claws and talons pushing and grabbing in unison, he skates into the open lift before anyone can pull the trigger.

Sax's tail slaps at the door panel and a moment later the lift's closed and rising. There'll be another override coming, but the Oratus is getting higher up the Spire. Getting closer to Fraykt.

His claws can wait for that.

When the lift judders to a stop after only one level, it's not exactly a surprise. Fraykt isn't going to let Sax come riding right to his floor, not that Sax knows where that is. Right now, the Oratus is trying to get back up towards the top, because everything about Fraykt screams that the Vyphen isn't much for bottom-dwelling.

The doors, though, don't open this time. Sax doesn't feel like waiting for whatever plan Fraykt cooks up, so he springs to the lift's ceiling, using his claws and talons to forge his own handholds in the smooth gray tile. There's a thick outline for the meter-long access hatch, with a small handle jutting out from the ceiling, marked with holes for easy gripping by small Flaum hands. Sax uses his right fore-claw to do the dirty work, grasping and pulling the hatch open. It swings free of its stuck sides with a shower of dust, and then Sax climbs through into the wide shaft.

As he's making his escape, Fraykt pulls his next move and starts the lift heading back down. Standing on top of it, Sax has a great view of the entire shaft, which launches up through the Spire like some strange tunnel. Neon blue lights line the shaft at four sides, casting a just-over-dim amount of glow into the wide space. The constant squeal of brakes and the whistling whoosh of other lifts far above echo around Sax.

Who jumps.

Thankfully, the walls of the Spire shaft aren't all that thick, and Sax carves himself an easy perch where he can see his former lift descending, and stopping a level below. When he sees the Flaum and Whelk head into the elevator, Sax realizes he forgot to close the hatch behind him.

Guess that makes things more difficult.

Fraykt's thugs aren't oblivious to the new opening above them, and they look Sax's way, bringing their miners to bear. So Sax decides to take himself where they're not, jumping across the shaft towards the other side.

And landing on the rapidly rising cargo lift that, at this level, takes up the rest of the shaft. Sax hits hard and rolls, barely managing to stop himself from skinning against the shaft's sides. The pressure from the throttling rise pushes Sax into the floor. The smooth walls blitz by him, making his peripheral vision a blur.

One thing's certain though—this lift will end, and soon. The shaft breaks into different lift setups as the Spire goes on, shifting from most of the space reserved for cargo to smaller, passenger-friendly lifts. Which is why Sax isn't thrilled to see the dark bulk of another lift heading down towards him.

Using his tail and his midclaws, Sax scurries out from under the approaching lift as his ride slows and eventually stops. There's a loud shunt as the cargo lift's doors grind open, and Sax takes the opportunity to stand as the smaller, higher lift settles to its own halt before a door one level higher.

There's a couple meters between the two, and Sax makes the leap, clawing up the side of the smaller lift and over the top as it starts to rise again.

He's done with the outside.

Sax rips open this lift's emergency hatch from above, then drops into the middle of a pair of uniformed Flaum, wearing dirty full-body seals coated with dust and oil. They both press themselves back against the sides of the elevator when Sax lands between them, and the Oratus gives them a feral grin.

"Stay there," Sax hisses, "and I won't maul you."

He looks at the panel. Level 68 and climbing. Looks like this lift is heading to the 43rd.

"Fraykt," Sax says, swinging his head to catch both Flaum in the glare. "Where is he?"

"Who?" says the Flaum on Sax's left, but Sax doesn't care, because the one to his right emits a high-pitched, incriminating squeak.

"You," Sax says, turning and looming over the smaller creature. Behind him, Sax uses his tail to press and trap the other Flaum against the lift's wall, keeping the furry critter from getting any stupid ideas. "Fraykt. Speak, and you both leave this lift alive."

"I don't know where he lives," the Flaum says. "Nobody does! But, but, I can tell you where you go if you want to see him?"

The Flaum hesitates, his small black beady eyes searching for some hope in Sax, that this nugget might be enough to earn him his life.

"Tell me, then," Sax says.

"39th level. It's a utility floor, but he keeps a shop there. In the back, near the generators."

Sax leans in close. Flaum aren't normally good liars, especially not with their lives on the line, but this one's had it rough. His gray-white fur is black-tarred and torn, one of his large ears is missing a chunk. A dangerous life breeds dangerous habits, like lying to an Oratus.

"You'll guide me, then," Sax says as the lift stops at level 43.

The doors open, showing a quiet residential level split into small apartments. No miners, no Fraykt guards waiting for him, so Sax uses his tail to push out the Flaum's friend, then, with his left midclaw, Sax punches the 39th level into the lift's control panel. The doors shut and they're off again.

"Are you fighting Fraykt? Are the Vincere finally coming for him?" Now the Flaum's got coy hint in his voice.

Information is as good a currency as any other, Sax supposes.

"I'm not with the Vincere," Sax says. "Fraykt has a friend, and I'm getting her back."

"You think you're getting her back?" the Flaum shakes his large head. "Even you, Oratus, aren't going to win a fight with him."

"His guards don't scare me." Sax watches the lift's counter tick down on the panel.

Almost there. Almost to Bas.

"No, not the guards. Fraykt himself. He used to be a commander, you know. Before?"

"That means nothing to me."

Sax, though, is lying as he speaks. There aren't many Vyphen commanders left. The Chorus had tried to kill them all when they removed the Vyphen from power, when the Oratus took their place as the officers in the Vincere. The culling had made sense at the time—these Vyphen knew the secrets of the Vincere fleet, of their strategies and ships.

Leaving any alive to be taken by the Sevora, even if Vyphen couldn't be controlled directly, presented a risk.

Sax, though, has never hunted one before. If Fraykt is truly an old Vyphen commander, then the fight would be a good one. If it ever occurs. Sax blinks his priorities straight as the lift opens onto level 38. He's not here to fight Fraykt. He's here to rescue Bas and, if possible, Plake, Engee, and Agra-Red.

We don't lower the boarding ramp so much as open the door. A few stones roll into the shuttle, and we actually step out onto the plateau where I managed to set down the ship. Aside from the usual clutter of gray and black rocks, flimsy grasses make themselves apparent too. They're light green and white, shivering in the cold wind whipping the fog around up here.

"At least there's life," Viera says as she stands next to me, keeping her hands close in to her sides.

I'm freezing too—our thin outfits aren't a match for this weather, and I'm about to suggest holing back up in the shuttle when Vee, exploring off the front end of the ship, makes a loud hiss and waves us over.

The Oratus is standing over a drop-off, though it's one I could see myself scaling if I had to; plenty of jutting cliffs and handholds. My hands ache at the thought of gripping all those icy rocks, but then, considering what we're looking at, I'll probably make them.

Because beneath our feet there's a particular orange glow. Not like the pipes back in that Amigga horror-base, but the calming flicker of something very human: fire.

"There's something down there," Vee states the obvious analysis.

"A settlement?" T'Oli proposes.

"Too small," I say. "There's not enough food, land here. Maybe travelers, someone who's very, very lost?"

"No." Viera joins us at the edge and, by the stunned tone in her voice, I get she knows something we don't. "This is one of ours. Mine, I mean. The Lunare."

"The Lunare?" Vee's confused.

"One of your caves?" I don't have the patience to give Vee a crash course on real human history right now. "All the way here?"

"It's possible," Viera says. "We've tunneled a long way. Always looking for more resources, for a places we can expand without the Charre, without your tribes in the way. But I don't think we've gone to the other side of the world..."

"The shuttle was flying fast," T'Oli adds. "We're much closer to your side of things than we were. I'm surprised the Sevora haven't found us, really. They should have shot us from the sky, or hunted us here."

"So you're saying we need to get off this rock as soon as possible?" I give T'Oli a bewildered stare.

"Oh, yes. The longer we're up here, the odds the Sevora blow all of us to pieces goes up exponentially. They would be certain to detect the shuttle's energy."

"T'Oli, next time you know these things, please tell us," Viera says.

"Teaching Kaishi how to fly seemed the greater priority at the moment. And after we landed, I assumed we would depart quickly. We are, however, moving slower than expected."

I shake my head. "Fine. Let's go."

We take a quick minute dashing back to the shuttle, stuff the emergency packs full of nutrient goop, and head back out. Vee offers to carry all the packs down the mountainside, for which I'm grateful, as the climb proves harder than I thought. Numb fingers, it turns out, make physical acts difficult.

T'Oli and Vee, by virtue of one being, effectively, a liquid and the other a four-armed physical freak, beat Viera and I down the cliff. I take my time, testing every rock before putting my weight on it, ignoring the constant ache in my hands until they finally go numb. It's not pleasant, but I'm making my way.

Until a cascade of red flashes splits the fog from above and an earth-rattling explosion pours over the cliff edge. Gouts of yellow-white flame followed by black smoke and flying chunks of debris follow, cascading over Viera and I.

Somewhere in there—I can't feel when—my fingers lose their hold on the rocks and I fall back, staring up and screaming as more red beams lance towards where our shuttle sits. I'm sure, certain, I'm going to bash against the bottom in a second and in that moment of certain death, I call out to the only thing that comes to mind.

Ignos.

And, despite everything I've seen, despite all the contradictions, my god comes through for me.

Vee catches me in his four arms, his legs squat down and his half-tail pressed to the ground so that I collapse into the Oratus' massive chest. Which isn't to say that the fall doesn't hurt—whatever air had been in my lungs takes the impact as a chance to flee, and my back blossoms into a new kind of pain as it crunches against Vee's bones.

The Oratus, too, gasps, Vee's chest vents blowing their own air against my face. The Oratus stumbles back, then half drops, half rolls me onto the ground. It's cold, hard, and wonderful.

I'm not dead.

The thought repeats itself a thousand times before I get around to thanking Ignos, before my heartbeat slows enough to check if Viera's made it down safe—she has—and to actually pick myself up.

"Thanks." It's the first thing I say, and Vee takes it with a slight nod. "Really. Thank you."

"There's no need for it," Vee finally replies. "The risk to myself was slight, the benefits to our expedition of your survival great."

"That's the Oratus-talk I'm used to," Viera says, before she steps up and wraps me in a hug. "Next time, Kaishi, I'll teach you how to climb like a Lunare."

I separate, stare her dead in the eyes; "I'm never climbing again."

"I suggest we get moving," T'Oli says, the Ooblot oozing its way over towards the glow. "Those blasts probably came from a Sevora ship, and they might decide to cleanse this entire mountain rather than risk our escape."

"They'd blow up a mountain to get to us?" I ask.

"Kaishi, they would cover this planet in ash and fire to destroy you. You are an existential threat to the Sevora. If they cannot control you, they will annihilate you. It's how they operate."

"Well, they've failed so far," Viera says.

"Let's keep it that way." I point at the glow. "Lead the way, Viera?"

The Lunare takes the charge, goes in front of T'Oli, and though we have no weapons—aside from Vee's formidable claws—Viera strides ahead tall and sure. I suppose, after surviving what we've lived through, there's a lot less to fear from a Lunare outpost.

So I catch up to her, and together the four of us leave behind the smoldering ruin of our shuttle.

The Lunare spread all over under the Earth's crust, spiderwebbing their way through rock to try and find resources, places to build cities or, the ultimate goal, to find a new surface that they could claim for their own.

"Until we found this," Viera's saying as we stand outside the tunnel entrance. "I'd heard about the fog, about how this side of the mountains was all covered in it, how everything was dead."

The cave is twice as tall as Vee, plenty wide for the four of us to walk abreast, though we haven't gone in because it's gated shut. Wood planks seal the way, with a pair of torches flickering in braziers on either side.

"Where are they?" I ask, nodding at the torches. "The Lunare who must be here?"

"I don't know." Viera walks up to the gate. There's no visible handle on this side, but she puts her hand on the boards anyway. "They might have sealed it after the explosion. Figured anything causing that kind of destruction was better left on the other side."

"Is there a way to talk to them?"

"They're listening now," Vee hisses. "I can smell them. They're afraid."

The Oratus stalks up the gate, next to Viera, and places a claw in front of her head. Then reaches with his left midclaw and taps it a half-meter to his own left. "Here, and here. I could break through this barrier and end them, if we want."

"No, no, that's not necessary." I join them at the gate, then raise my voice. "Lunare, I ask those of you behind this gate for help. We're lost, and without aid, we'll die. In exchange, we'll give you information. We'll give you hope."

There's a shifting noise from behind us, and the three of us—T'Oli doesn't turn so much as swivel—spin around to see a trio of humans rappel from the rock above. As soon as we turn, there's a creaking as the wooden gate slides up to show two more Lunare.

All of them are wearing thick fur jackets, and all of them wield the crude gray pistols Viera used to carry, the weapons I thought were the height of deadly warfare until I saw what true danger looked like.

"Hope?" says a burly man in the middle of the climbers. "How can you say that when you've brought one of those monsters here with you?"

That's when I realize all of their weapons are pointing at Vee.

"You know him?" I nod at Vee.

"Seen their kind before," the man replies. "Though not this one. Where'd you come from? Nothing lives out in the damn fog."

I think back to the strange humans stuck in those tubes. How there's plenty of them still wandering that base.

"There's more out there than you realize," I say. "We'll be happy to tell you about it, but first, could you lower your weapons?"

"Not till I get some proof that thing won't kill us all."

Vee bares his teeth. "None of you would be worth the effort."

The man laughs. "Insults aren't going to work, creature."

"I'll guarantee it. On my life." I move to stand in front of Vee. "He will not hurt you. And you will not hurt him."

"They couldn't even if they tried," Vee whispers to me.

"And who're you to make that guarantee? A scared, cold girl?" The man doesn't know who I am.

I relish the moment.

"I am Kaishi, Empress of the Charre people, and emissary of Ignos to Humanity." I announce with all the grandeur I can muster.

A snort is not the reaction I'm hoping for. But at least the man waves at the others to put down their weapons. "Empress? Guess it's worth taking you to Avril, then. She'll decide if you're telling the truth, and then she'll probably kill ya."

After that delightful opening, the man introduces himself as Diego, declares that he's the leader of the small band in charge of this outpost, and caps it off, as we sit around their small fire a little beyond the gate, by stating we've had the misfortune of arriving at the worst place on Earth.

"I think," I say after he finishes. "That is where we came from."

"Don't know where that is, don't want to know," Diego replies. "Because if it's worse than here . . . well, I have too many nightmares already."

Vee and T'Oli take the hint based on the wary eyes of the Lunare and sit off to one side, Vee calmly munching through a packet of goop while spreading some on T'Oli, who absorbs it all. Whatever urgency I'm feeling about getting home hasn't passed along to the two of them, and while it should irk me, all I really feel is jealousy.

I miss coasting through life without a world weighing on my shoulders.

"We need to get back home." I turn the topic to what's important. "I know it's far, but we don't know the way, and you do. If you or one of your men could guide us?"

Diego holds up his left hand, keeps his right near the pistol. "Hold on. I know what you said. Empress, right? We'll take you to

Avril, sure. But we're scheduled to run our term here for a long time yet. You want to get back earlier, you've got to give me a reason."

I take a breath. About to launch into the old story, when Viera takes over. She stands up—quick enough that Diego's men reach for their weapons and Vee drops his nutrient pack—and stalks over to stand above Diego, and stares pure heat at the gruff Lunare.

"Your reason is sitting right over there," Viera says, pointing towards T'Oli and Vee. "Your reason is back out that gate, up that cliff where the wreck that we flew, *that we flew*, is still burning! You say nothing lives in that fog but here we are—doesn't that make you think Avril ought to know what's going on here? Isn't your job supposed to be to watch for threats? Don't you think this is one?"

Diego for his part, takes a big swallow, which gives me enough time to ask, "Who's Avril?"

Viera dashes me a look that says she's got this, and answers me only after looking back towards Diego, "I'm guessing she's taken over? Always seemed like that'd be her final play. She used to run Lunare's biggest city. Reasonable, so long as your reasons go along with hers."

"Hey," Diego finally musters a spine. "She's kept us alive. Charre and Solare too, when they came running."

Now I'm on my feet too, though less in anger than from a desire to start heading home right now, this very second.

"Running?" Viera asks the question I'm too frazzled to.

"Why'd you think we didn't come out when we saw the red lights?" Diego sputters, Viera standing over him like she's going to kill him right there. "We know what they mean. They're everywhere back home. It's all we can do to hold the caves. The whole reason we're here is to keep this exit open in case everyone needs to run."

Nobody needs to ask what they'd be running from.

Later, after the fire's left to smolder and the wood gate's shut, with the four of us shoved into a side chamber with a bunch of food crates, I'm leaning against a rock wall waiting for exhaustion to find me. Thus far, it's failed. Thus far, my eyes have stayed wide open as I race from one idea to the next.

Damantum, gone. That's what Diego hinted at—my people, both the Charre and the Solare, have fled their homes against an impossible adversary and fled to an enemy who's done what? Provided refuge? At what cost?

"You should sleep," Viera whispers to me over Vee's hissing snores.

T'Oli doesn't make a sound, but it's gone all rock over in a corner. Continuing the healing process, apparently.

Viera, though, is lying down, propped up on one arm and keeping a weary face on me, "Cave crawling takes a lot of energy, and I bet Diego's not going to go easy on you."

"He won't have to," I reply. It's not my muscles, my bones that I'm worried about. "You know Avril?"

"She's been playing on the fringes for a long time." Viera yawns. "She never had the family connections to get up to the top, but your grand defeat of all the old guard in the desert probably left a vacuum."

"You think she cast them out?"

"I think my own people did," Viera stifles a laugh. "The Lunare don't hold much with the royalty idea. Families get power till they screw up, then they're torn down and forgotten. Someone else gets a chance."

"That's . . . very democratic."

"Sometimes it works, sometimes it doesn't, like everything else."

Viera's lounging pose finally convinces me to lay down my own bedroll. It's nothing more than a pad, scrounged from extras left at this outpost over the years. Turns a sharp rock from a stab wound into a bruise, which, out here, is about all you can ask for. I pile up some of the packets of nutrient goop as a sort-of pillow—I'd prefer cool grass, but the stone here is too much for me.

"You said you liked adventure," I say, because I'm not quite ready to go to dreamy oblivion. "I used to wish for it. Now, I don't know."

"Because of the cost?"

It's almost better conversing this way, when I'm staring at the craggy ceiling in the cool pink light of a patch of glowing moss. No expressions to read, just the tone, the in-and-out of breath between the words.

"Because it never seems to end."

"It does, Kaishi, but you don't want it to."

"I don't know how old I am anymore, Viera."

"What?"

"We count our age in seasons, but I don't know how long we've been gone."

"Not that long, Kaishi. Probably less than a season."

"So I'm being stupid?"

"You're being tired. Go to bed, Empress. We're going to need you thinking tomorrow."

Level 39 announces itself with a blast of steam as soon as the lift door opens. Murky red lighting lines the floor and walls, serving as guides for Sax and the Flaum as they move between huffing machinery and hissing pipes, with the constant low whine of electric energy coursing through conductors above and below them. The noise serves as more than a reminder of the multitude of actions necessary to keep Astre's Spire running on Rathfall; they serve as cover for whomever or whatever could be hiding around the next bend in the clogged level.

Which is why Sax has the Flaum lead the way, one midclaw positioned just so against the back of the Flaum's throat.

"I'm not going to run," the Flaum protests as they go. "I know you'd catch me."

"I wouldn't have to catch you," Sax replies. "You wouldn't make it a single step."

"Then how'd you know I was running?"

"I'd smell it."

Fear has a special spice to it, and the Flaum's drenched in a coating of his species' panicky pheromones right now. Without the leaden scent from the venting steam, Sax might choke on it. Flaums are legendary for their overactive glands, one of many reasons why Sax never commences an assault mixed in with the furry species; he could never concentrate under that olfactory attack.

The Flaum, though, is true to his word and navigates Sax through the winding maze until they end up at what Sax would take for an ordinary section of steel wall. The only thing out of the ordinary, really, are the spots of rust on the section they're looking at. A quick glance wouldn't give a moment's thought, but Sax is bred for pattern recognition, to find a weakness and act on it.

"Which one opens the door?" Sax says, gesturing with his left foreclaw to the seven spots arranged in a Z pattern.

"No idea," the Flaum replies. "If Fraykt wants to talk to you, he'll open up."

"That's not good enough," Sax says, and he's about to test his claws on the door when it swings open on hinges.

Actual hinges. The last time Sax had seen those was on some dirt-water planet on a mission he's otherwise scrubbed from his mind. Now he can't help wondering how old this Spire really is.

On the other side is a moldy, old yellow Ooblot. Patches of the creature are crusted over, revealing its age as far greater than Sax's own. It only has a sole eye-stalk, the other a rocky lump on its boulder-sized bulk, and it turns a red-washed iris towards Sax.

"Fraykt's willin' to talk," the Ooblot patters lightly. "Without that one."

There's no question as to who 'that one' happens to be, and Sax tosses the Flaum aside. The creature doesn't seem to mind, picking itself up on its claws and scurrying away back towards the lift.

"You're the guard?"

"I'm Dol, and I'm Fraykt's *partner*," the Ooblot says. "Don't make that mistake again."

"Are you threatening me, Ooblot?"

"Yes," Dol replies, then the Ooblot shuffles itself around and heads back into the recess.

Sax represses the desire to carve away at the big block of rock-

'n'pollen-yellow cream. Not only did the Ooblot mock him, but it turned its back. Insult after insult, but there's more important things here than Sax's pride, so he swallows it and follows.

Sax thought the munching machines made up the entire utility level, but the Ooblot leads him to a small room with a flat lift tied to a simple rotor. There's a set of terminals covering the damp wall opposite the lift's platform, a metal shelf serving as a shield from the dripping water plinking from a maze of pipes above.

At first Sax doesn't get where the water's coming from, and the Ooblot must sense his confusion, because it settles its bulk in front of the lift and turns its rotating eye towards the Oratus.

"You play claws and miners, you rake and take, the rest of us have to use the scraps," Dol says. "Set ourselves up in the ditches and dives your Amigga masters leave us."

"They're not our masters."

Before Evva, before *Cobalt*, Sax would have answered that question differently. There didn't used to be shame in the thought—the Oratus are weapons, wielded to their purpose. What does it matter who's doing the wielding?

"They're not? Then your species is even dumber than I thought." Dol slides onto the platform.

That's one insult too many. Sax takes a long step towards Dol, raises a warning claw, and hears a dozen sharp tines of miners powering up. The weapons' laser-red eyes peer at Sax from between the pipes, from beneath the terminals, and, Sax notices, from a dark cavity in Dol's own massive bulk.

"Not going to work," Dol says. "Fraykt thinks you're clever, that you might be worth saving."

That stops Sax. "Saving?"

The Ooblot laughs. Slaps a button on the lift, which starts a trundling ride up. "Better get on, lizard man, or I'll shoot you."

With all the miners around him, Sax doesn't want to call the Ooblot's bluff. He leaps, catches the edge of the rising platform with his foreclaws, pulls himself up enough for his midclaws to assist and then he's over, fitting in alongside Dol as the platform continues its slow rise.

"All this houses the cooling for the Spire," Dol says as they go up. "Fraykt and I built our little empire behind the scenes, because if we'd gone out in the open, you'd have murdered him. Probably would have killed me right after."

"Because Fraykt's a commander."

"Because you're all monsters." Dol changes and flips out a gooey limb towards the encroaching wall as the platform begins its trek between levels.

Sax doesn't get what the Ooblot is meaning till the tight squeeze becomes clear as the lift goes between the Spire's outer wall and the supporting floor between levels. Sax has to squeeze tight, draping himself over the Ooblot and curling his tail across his back to fit.

"We are what we are," Sax attempts to hiss, though he's having a hard time getting enough air with his vents compressed on the Ooblot, so it comes out as a harsh whisper.

"You've got a brain, haven't you? Or did the Amigga make you all instinct?"

Sax can't even reply. He wants to get mad, but the awkward position cuts the rage to nothing. The whole thing is too ridiculous. An old Ooblot ranting at him about the state of the galaxy? Why should Sax care?

"When Plake came to us," Dol says, and Sax twitches at the name,"we thought she'd been captured, that she was leading you and the Vincere right to us out of some trade. Turns out Plake's still her same sour self."

The lift finally gets to the next level, and Sax unravels himself off of the Ooblot like a blanket falling on the floor. His vents suck in air as the lift settles into a totally different place than before. One that's lit in the normal soft whites, that's marked with clean floors and walls, and that has a pair of Flaum that Sax recognizes from his trickery down below, holding miners, their eyes tight and their little fangs bared at the sight of the Oratus.

"What do you mean, Plake?" Sax manages from the floor. Even there, he's shifting his legs, getting his talons and tail ready to strike if the Flaum decide torching him is a viable tactic. "She didn't come back to her own ship."

"Precautions," Dol says, easing itself off of the platform. "Don't worry, they won't melt your face 'less I say so." The Ooblot waits for Sax to right himself, to fall in line behind it. "Plake's one of us, ex-Vincere you might say. Had to make sure she still holds the right loyalty."

"By kidnapping her?"

The two Flaum fall into step behind Sax and Dol as they head through another cramped hallway. One that opens, through a second hinged door, into a clean and bright living space. An apartment, going by the solid walled rectangle covered in screens showing what looks like an infinite flowing ocean beneath a clear sapphire sky.

"We live in deadly times, Oratus," Dol says as it moves into the room. "Trusting the wrong person means you wind up a corpse or worse, an Amigga experiment."

The Ooblot flattens out here, lets its yellow-creamy self relax in what Sax thinks must be Dol's home. There's not much to it—a simple nutrient delivery terminal, the image screens, and the wide open floor. But then, Ooblots don't need much. Even the two sisters running *Scrapper Station* didn't seem to know what to do with their luxury garden.

"You want them to lose, don't you?" Sax says finally. "You want the Amigga to fall."

"The Chorus are a bunch of overheated mudballs twisting the rest of us to pieces until the galaxy's theirs." Dol twitches and the screens shift to a sight Sax hasn't seen in a long, long time.

The Chorus live in a giant space elevator, a rising spike that lifts up from the surface of the Amigga's home planet, Aspicis—Sax doesn't know if that's where the species actually came from, or if they've adopted it. At the very top of the elevator is a round ball as large as a moon, with plenty of tendrils arcing out of it, some bristling with weapons and others with scores of antennae for sending and boosting signals. Further ribbons of red and orange light dance above the structure in what would be a pretty display if anyone else had made it—with the Amigga, the fanciful glimmers stink of calculation, an effort to dazzle the eyes while stealing the soul.

Beneath the elevator, down towards Aspicis' surface, the screens show the endless forest of thick vines, almost like Rathfall but without the pollen and extracted gasses. The day-night line, which moves ever-so-slowly on the planet, recedes away from the view, shrouding the right edge of the picture in pure dark.

"You can't mean to attack it," Sax says, and for the first time he can remember, he's quiet, in awe of the sheer audacity of what he's seeing. "You'll never win."

"It's not our idea," Dol says. "It's hers."

The central screen flips away from the Chorus and their technological wonder of a home to a feed—always pre-recorded to be sent across these distances—of a beaten, wounded Oratus who's nonetheless standing inside a large, decrepit room.

Her red scales stand out even in the low white light, which comes peeking through a hole and not through any globes. Junk scatters around her, torn curtains and broken walls frame her locked golden eyes. The scene is a far cry from every situation he's ever seen the Oratus in before, but there's no mistaking Evva.

"She's alive." Sax didn't really think she was, not anymore. Nobody survives an Amigga bounty like hers for long.

"She's more than alive, Oratus," Dol says. "She's fighting. We're fighting. It's time you joined in."

Fraykt waits in what's obviously another apartment but one that's devoid of living signs. There's only a table, too short for Sax, spanning the sole room and its white-washed walls. The walls have screens like Dol's, but they're off, leaving them blank and clear.

Fraykt himself, his weathered vyphen feathers clustered in his chair, offers Sax a dour glower as the Oratus follows Dol into the room. The two Whelk from Sax's evasion earlier stand near the table too, miners aimed. Which means there's now four weapons in the room ready to fire should Sax make the wrong move.

"So Dol told you everything," Fraykt begins.

"Where is Bas?"

"Gone," Fraykt says, the holds up a feathered hand. "Not dead, but gone. Evva's alive, our resistance is moving. We don't have the luxury of keeping lovers together anymore."

"She's my pair," Sax hisses out the sudden anger. "She's the other part of me. There is no task worth splitting us for."

"In your view, perhaps." Fraykt waves towards the table. "We don't have many Oratus on our side, so we have to use them well."

"Use us for what?"

"Sax, you haven't forgotten how the Vincere preserve their secrets already, have you?" Dol says, its bulk taking up a spot on the table's left side. "Need to know only, and right now you don't."

Sax settles his midclaws on the table. Tests its weight. Rathfall's not a small planet, and the gravity's going to provide some resistance, but Sax is pretty confident he can push this table hard and fast enough to smash Fraykt against the wall and splatter the arrogant Vyphen into bits.

"Evva wants you with her," Fraykt says then, and his words temporarily steal away Sax's murderous ideas. "They're coming close to being able to act and, in her words, they could use your talents."

Evva wants him? His commander?

"How would I even get to her?" Sax asks.

"Plake will take you. On the *Mobius*." Fraykt nods at the screen to Sax's right and it flickers to a camera feed showing Plake directing the unloading of cargo from the *Mobius* into the docking bay. "She's a good enough pilot to get you in."

"But Bas won't be coming."

"Like I said, she's gone," Fraykt replies.

"She wouldn't have left without me."

"Look around you," Fraykt says, his bulbous eyes tracking to the pair of Whelk and Flaum on either side of Sax. "Do you think we have an army? That we're ready to fight the Vincere and overwhelm the Chorus with hordes of vengeful species? We can't afford to keep you together. There is too much to do. Too many things that could use your pair's claws."

Sax is beginning to think this Vyphen won't actually bring him together with Bas. That no matter how much he pushes for details or presses to get Bas back, they're going to keep her hidden from him. Which leaves two options:

Believe Fraykt and Dol and go after Evva.

Or tear this whole thing apart.

"Why?" Sax decides to probe. "Why would you capture us? Send me outside if you needed my help?"

Fraykt settles into his chair. He thinks he's won the battle now. That Sax is coming over and there's only some formalities. Sax keeps his midclaws ready. One push, and Fraykt is gone.

"Plake promised you would both be ready to join," Fraykt says slow. "I didn't think that likely. The Chorus knows we exist. Knows that we would be tempted by a pair of Oratus so eager to help us. So I had to see whether you were true."

"By throwing me out of the Spire?"

"You were found, were you not? By Plake's own crew, who thought you would be less likely to attack someone you knew."

"They wanted me to gather pollen-chaser parts. For money."

Here Fraykt looks confused, and glances at Dol.

"It happens," the Ooblot says. "But that wasn't part of our plan. Silver and Black were to keep you occupied until we had convinced Bas. Plake said Bas was the more reasonable one, and she was right. We would have come for you eventually."

So the Flaum wanted a bit of money for their efforts. Sax can't blame them, really. Not that understanding will keep him from issuing a stern, slightly bloody warning to the two furry creatures when he next sees them.

"And the lift? Sending all of these?"

"As we said." Fraykt takes back control. "There was some concern you'd be aggressive. That you wouldn't take this well."

"I'm not."

Fraykt waves away Sax's words. "Stunning you first, letting you hear our story without the chance of spontaneous aggression seemed like the better course."

The room settles around him. It's time, now, to choose. Trust them, and go to Evva. Or fight them, and find Bas.

She came out of the jungle, down the tall pink flowers and into the forest. She carried Sax when he couldn't carry himself. Spoke the words he couldn't say. Gave him his life when he was about to lose it. So, so many times.

Sax pushes the table hard. It slides across the floor, shoves Fraykt back against the wall. The Vyphen chokes, coughs, but Sax didn't shove it to kill. In the space of that stunned moment, when everyone's looking to see if Fraykt is still alive, Sax leans right and sweeps his tail through the Flaum's feet, knocking both to the ground.

The Whelk manage to get their miners up as Sax reaches them, as Sax tears the weapons from their grip with his foreclaws and, getting his midclaws on the triggers, fires them. The miners aren't designed for Oratus and his shots aren't accurate, but that hardly matters when he's centimeters from his targets. The blue bolts flash and both Whelk quiver and slide into mush.

A single shot manages to miss Sax, fired quick by one of the Flaum, and the Oratus makes them pay for their haste with two more blasts, knocking out, in the span of four seconds, all of Fraykt's guards.

Sax levels the miners at Dol. "Tell me where Bas is, or I'll end every last one of you."

Dol doesn't look the least bit panicked. The Ooblot has a pair of miners leveled at it, and following them, an Oratus with plenty of claws, but the only thing Dol does is shift its bulk to give Sax an even clearer target.

"You can't threaten people whose lives are already forfeit," Dol replies. "We've been working since the Vincere removed us to overthrow the Chorus. We're closer now than ever before. You kill us, maybe Evva succeeds anyway. Maybe she doesn't. We've given our lives to this cause, whether it's now or later."

"You'll die to keep me from my pair?"

"Dol," Fraykt burbles from the back wall, a watery gasp of broken ribs. "Tell him. Tell him where."

Dol's hesitation shows whether its debating whether Fraykt's life is worth giving up Bas, which in itself makes Sax even more angry. Not only did they send Bas away from him, they put her in so much danger, in such a secretive, high level mission . . .

Sax can't help himself. He pulls the trigger on the miner in his left foreclaw. Sends the bolt into the wall behind Dol.

"You heard him," Sax hisses.

Ooblots can't really sigh. Not audibly, anyway. Instead, Dol collapses, spreads out like a melting ball of wax.

"Fine. You want to chase after Bas? You want to jeopardize everything?" Dol says. "She's going back to your home. To where the Oratus are made."

"Why?"

"To stop them," Dol says. "To ruin the hatcheries. To end your species."

What? Sax doesn't understand. Can't understand. Here Sax is, willing to work with those who want to subvert the galaxy's established order, and they're saying the first step is to destroy the future of his own species?

"The rest will never change," Fraykt warbles from the wall, and Sax takes the reminder to drop a miner and pull the table away, letting the Vyphen drop to the floor. "The other Oratus, they're too loyal. They will fight to stop us."

"And the Chorus will make more of you once they feel the threat," Dol adds. "They'll overwhelm us. Use you to massacre every other species in the galaxy if they have to. The Amigga think they can build a new universe for themselves—they won't mind destroying this one first."

"Bas agreed to this?" Sax says for want of other words.

"She's already gone," Dol replies. "On a light craft that left the Spire hours ago. You're supposed to go to Evva, help keep her alive."

And Sax will, eventually. His pair, though, comes first.

The *Mobius* is besieged. Sax leaves the lift alone—Fraykt's followers pulled the Vyphen to the Spire's only hospital and Dol ditched away as soon as Sax made it clear what he was going to do.

Now he only has to convince Plake to take her ship and crew to a place crawling with angry Oratus who'll want nothing more than to eviscerate all of them.

Except finding Plake in the stacks of nutrient goop crates and the small army of loader robots shoving them around is hard. It gets even harder when a face Sax never expects to see again pops out of the *Mobius'* boarding ramp and scuttles down to meet him.

A single glance explains everything; Nobaa's wearing the vest Engee crafted for Sax, the one built to control the *Mobius* so that Sax wouldn't need to be in the cockpit the entire time. Nobaa's managed to tangle the thing around himself on hooks and hangers pounded into the sides of his carapace. It looks terrible, but then, Nobaa doesn't seem like the Teven to care about such things.

"Didn't think you'd be making it back!" Nobaa exclaims as the reedy creature meets Sax. "Thanks for the vest, by the way. Made it much easier to stake out my spot on the ship!"

"I never gave that to you."

"You threw it away right outside my apartment! What else was I supposed to think?" the Teven leans towards Sax. "I'm taking the cabin right next to Engee's."

"That's mine. Ours." Sax's claws twitch.

"Oh, Plake's moving you now," Nobaa says. "You're getting the cargo bay to yourself. It's the only space big enough, and, she says, you deserve it."

Sax takes a heavy breath. Thinks about Bas. Calm thoughts. Nobaa's not worth his time.

Sax convinces the blabbering Teven to take him to Plake, and Nobaa goes away from the *Mobius* towards another, larger, freight carrier. The kind that's designed to shuttle goods from the surface to a massive spaceship. This one's loading on slats of refined ore into what amounts to a rounded-edge nearly as tall as the docking bay's level.

These loaders don't have struts—just a reinforced hull with embedded jets that rest on the floor. The entire right side of the loader opens up and lays flat, allowing for quick moving of goods into the ship. Plake, for some reason, appears to be arguing with a burly brown Flaum near the small bubble serving as the loader's cockpit.

"She dashed away as soon as she saw the pilot," Nobaa's whispering as they close. "No idea why! But it's not a fight I want to get into, and Engee might need my help with a project, so, bye!"

The Teven pivots back towards the *Mobius* and, thankfully, blessedly, disappears. One more crew member for Sax to avoid.

Plake and the Flaum notice Sax coming well before he reaches them so they've stopped whatever they were talking about and turn to greet the Oratus with defensive stares. Sax feels like he's walked into a personal argument, but doesn't care.

"We need to leave," Sax says to Plake. "We're going after Bas."

"Shut up," Plake says, nodding towards the Flaum. "Innes doesn't need to know this."

"I really don't," Innes says, crossing his furry, and huge for a Flaum, arms. "Fact, I'd be thrilled if you took this crazy Vyphen away from me right now."

Sax catches the way Plake clenches her feathered hands, tenses her arms, and the Oratus steps between the two of them before Plake decides to start a fight. Not that Sax wouldn't mind getting another brawl going, but he's got bigger priorities here.

"Plake, what do you need from the Flaum?" Sax hisses. "I will get it. Then we will leave."

"Whoa there, big guy. You're not getting anything from me," Innes says.

"What he owes me," Plake warbles at the same time, then points at the loader. "How much are you making off this run, Innes? How much?"

"You're an idealist," Innes huffs. "Shouldn't matter to you what I do."

Sax reaches out with his right foreclaw. Fast. Innes sees it, tries to react, but no matter how strong a Flaum gets, he's not competing with an Oratus for reaction time. Sax gets the claw up tight against Innes' throat, a single press away from ending the creature, and Innes freezes.

"Sax, let him go," Plake says, but not before waiting a long second. "I don't want him dead."

"Then he should pay you what he owes," Sax says.

Even though the Oratus hasn't ever had to deal with currency—the Vincere's limitless expenses have handled everything for Sax since he became a conscious being—Sax gets the idea of debt, of what's owed and what's not being paid.

And the idea of getting something back, rather than nothing, even if that something is just the satisfaction of knowing your enemy suffered for their choice.

"I don't owe her anything!" Innes tries protesting and the voice is tighter than usual as the Flaum tries to keep his throat from catching on Sax's claw. "It was a fair deal."

"I was desperate. You cut me out." Plake shakes her head. "Let's go, Sax. I thought once this Flaum had honor, but he's like all the other skimmers out here. Burning anyone to make a profit."

Plake turns and heads back to the *Mobius*. Sax gets his face real close to Innes, opens his mouth a slight bit, then pulls the claw away and follows.

Innes makes the smart call and says nothing to their backs.

. . .

Sax doesn't manage to get Plake alone—following her to the cockpit brings Agra-Red and the Whelk's omnipresent miner into the picture. Sax, though, suppresses the itchy instincts that come with a weapon pointed at his back . There's a conversation that needs having, answers that needs getting, and Sax isn't going to take off with Plake again until he has them.

"This wasn't a random choice," Sax says when Plake settles into the netting that supports her piloting. "You came to Rathfall and Astre's Spire so we could meet Fraykt and Dol."

Plake doesn't bother hiding it. "I could've chosen a few places. There's a lot of people that don't like the Amigga, Sax. That don't have any love for the Vincere. Fraykt and Dol, though, don't tend to trust newcomers. I figured they'd learn if you two were for real."

"After what we did on *Scrapper Station*? That didn't convince you?"

"You talk about being loyal to this commander," Plake says. "What happens if she dies? Are you and Bas going to run back to the Vincere? We need your help, Sax. You and your pair. But we had to know you'd work with us, even if Evva's not around."

"And the thinking was to separate us, capture me and throw me out?" Sax hisses. "That's idiocy. Stupid."

"It worked, didn't it?"

Sax pauses. Breathes. Thinks for a second how he would have handled it if, moments after landing on Rathfall, they'd been asked to take part in a revolution against the Amigga. Against their own species.

"We would've joined anyway," Sax says. "Where else are we going to go? The Vincere would kill us if we tried to return."

"Then we were wrong," Plake shrugs it off, her feathers remaining unruffled. "We make mistakes, Sax. At least this wound up where we needed it to be."

"Not quite," Sax shifts into a harder stance, makes sure his claws are visible. "We're not going to Evva. We're going after Bas."

For the first time, Plake actually looks surprised. "That's not what Fraykt said."

"He changed his mind after I crushed him with a table."

Plake's confusion gives Sax the excuse he needs to relay the rest of the meeting, and its results, in a steady drip of slow menace that, by the end, has Plake shaking her head and giving in to what Sax wants.

"Oratus are so much trouble," Plake mutters at the end of it. "Don't know why the Amigga ever created you."

"Because we're effective. How soon can we launch? I don't want Bas to get there long before we do."

The *Mobius* gets ready fast when Plake wants it to. Silver and Black report back not long after the call to depart goes out, returning flush with the profits of Sax's broken nest of pollen-chasers. Engee and Nobaa are already on, tweaking gadgets in the crannies of the ship. The last one back, oddly, is Coorvin, who takes up a spot beside Sax in the cargo hold as the *Mobius* warms up its jets.

"Is this what you expected when you left *Cobalt*?" Coorvin, his fur looking a much healthier white than the patchy gray it'd been under the Amigga's control. "Joining a fight against your own makers?"

"I stopped expecting anything a long time ago," Sax replies. "The Vincere sent us often enough into places where we had no idea how many we'd have to carve up, or how far the Sevora infection had spread. You learn to rely on instinct, and on those few you can really trust."

"Like Bas?"

"Only Bas."

Coorvin nods. Stays silent as the *Mobius* rumbles and rises. The quiet churn takes Sax's own loneliness at being apart from his pair and has him looking at the Flaum. Coorvin had survived on *Cobalt* for who knows how long, virtually alone and in thrall to a domineering creature that never cared one bit for the Flaum's own survival.

"You're alone." Sax says the words without a question.

"I have been for a very long time." Coorvin glances up towards the ceiling, where the cargo netting—useful here to keep them stable during the leap in a mostly-empty bay—hangs.

"The Oratus that lose their pairs?" Sax says. "Most die soon after. They throw themselves into impossible fights. Accept suicidal missions."

"Like Evva?"

"Could you call going against the Chorus anything else?"

"Meaning," Coorvin says. "That's the hardest part, Sax. With Dalachite, on *Cobalt*, I had constant goals. A drive to keep it alive, to help its experiments succeed. Without Dalachite, I have nothing."

"And now you have this?"

"Yes. Now I have this," Coorvin says. "If you lose Bas, or she loses you, this cause might help you as it's helped me."

Sax, though, doesn't find the idea comforting. Anyway, he's not going to lose Bas. Not now. Not ever.

Vee stares at the torch in his hand like Diego stares at him—an alien thing that's changing his worldview by its very presence.

"You use fire for light?" Vee hisses. "I have never seen this before."

"Now I know he's an alien," I say, watching the Oratus with a slight smile.

We'd had our nutrient goop breakfast—supplemented by a bit of cave mushroom soup for a side of 'real' food, and now Diego has us gearing up to go. The other members of Diego's watchband stand somewhere between at-the-ready and drowsy, their hands near their pistols and their eyes half-closed.

I feel the early hour even though it's impossible to tell in the cave's separate reality. Diego rustled us up before dawn, declared that we ought to get started because the further we get before the creatures start to roam, the better.

When I ask Diego what creatures he means, the Lunare just laughs. Says if I find out, it'll probably be too late.

"He's exaggerating," Viera brushes him off.

The night sleeping on the rocks seems to have helped her most of all. Viera springs up, helps me pack, and even manages some of the cooking, which I've never seen her do before. Her lips curl up often and laughs came easier for her down here.

The mark of home, I think, and I hope the jungle would bring about the same for me. If I ever see it again.

"Kaishi," T'Oli says, slurping its way over to me. "May I travel next to you?"

"Sure," I reply. "Why?"

"Because I want to be able to protect you," T'Oli replies, and while it's sometimes hard to distinguish tone in the slapping voice of the Ooblot, I get that it's being sincere.

"Protect me?" I don't mean to question T'Oli, but I kind of do. What's the slime species going to do if an attack comes?

In answer, T'Oli surges over my feet, up my legs and across my body until its eye stalks are level with my head. T'Oli's heavier than I would've thought, like wearing bulky ceremonial robes, if they were cool and wet. Then the Ooblot hardens and I'm suddenly wearing armor.

"I get it," I say. T'Oli stops its reach just beneath my neck. "Thanks."

It's a little disconcerting to have a large pair of eyes blink at me directly in front of my own, but T'Oli liquidates and drops away quick.

"You've seen masks?" T'Oli says as Diego calls for us to get moving.

"I've worn them."

"Sapphrite told me the Amigga developed them from Ooblots," T'Oli replies. "They never could perfect the hardening, though."

"Do they steal from every species?"

"They steal from everything."

What I don't ask, what I don't need to ask, is what they do with the things they steal. I know, because I'm increasingly certain that's what I am.

I'm in the middle of the pack, with Vee picking up the rear and

Diego and Viera leading. From the very first step, I can hear Viera start to pick at our guide's thoughts.

"So why're you trusting us?" Viera says as we get going. "Just you, with a group of strangers, at least two of which are very dangerous."

"Two dangerous ones?" Diego's gruff growl carries back through the rocks. "I get the creature with all the claws. Who's the second?"

"You're looking at her."

Diego starts to laugh as his boots crunch along the rock, when Viera flashes a shard of stone I'd not seen her pick up. It's small, and it gleams in the torchlight, pressed up against Diego's throat.

"Don't get any ideas," Viera says.

"Same to you." Diego rubs his throat after Viera pulls the stone away. "What do you think happens, you show up at a Lunare waystation without me? They'll shoot you. And that's assuming you even find your way through this maze."

"We'd figure it out," I say up to them.

"Or, you could be thankful I'm taking my damn time to guide you, and be nice about it." Diego actually sounds miffed.

"If you get us to the rest of your people safely, I will be," I say.

Once we leave the outpost, the cave narrows until we're going single-file, black and beige rock pressing in around us. Unlike smoother caverns that I'd found by following streams as a child, these are rougher, with jagged edges and sharp turns avoiding large stones. Man-made.

Periodically, our torchlight is joined by fungal growths adding hazy colors to the scene; blues and pinks, mostly, in bulbous splotches spreading like diseases along the walls. The mood brightens every time we come across these markers of biological progress, a neon countdown to our goal.

"A week," Diego says when I ask how long this is going to take. "And that's just to the nearest village, the outer arm of Lunare territory."

"You carved a tunnel this far for nothing?"

"Not for nothing," Diego replies. "Plenty of mines and other things between here and there, and Lunare like to explore. We're not content to sit in the shade and watch the seasons pass us by."

"That's not—"

"Diego," Viera interrupts. "Answer her questions without the comebacks."

"Are humans always like this?" Vee asks T'Oli, behind me.

"Haven't been around them long, but they do seem prone to arguments," T'Oli replies. "I think they can be violent when the situation calls for it, and sometimes when it doesn't."

"We're not perfect," I say to them, almost laughing when I see how much Vee needs to scrunch himself together to fit in the tight quarters. "But we're not evil."

"Evil," Vee hisses his way around the word. "I would never use that to describe a species as a whole."

"Not even the Sevora?"

"The Sevora are prey, Kaishi. Prey that fulfill their imperative. As I exist to destroy them, so the Sevora exist to take control of others." Vee's rasping out a deeper argument, but it's hard to take him seriously when his claws are all tight together, his shoulders are hunched, and his legs and half-tail are scraping against the ground.

"You don't think taking control of others is inherently evil?"

"I don't think they have a choice, so if it is their only possible course of action, then I cannot consider that an evil act."

We have to catch up to Diego and Viera, whose fires are flickering further, so I turn away from Vee, but don't stop thinking about what the Oratus is saying. I had a Sevora in my mind once. It had lived there, spoke with me and read my thoughts, and never took control. Ignos, the Sevora, claimed it had no choice. That it couldn't direct me as it could, say, a Flaum.

Which means Vee is wrong, which means the Sevora very much could live without controlling others.

Which, to me, makes them plenty evil.

As we walk, I notice occasional spikes driven into the rock ceiling. They're cylindrical, with a mesh lining of tight-woven metal.

Even when I raise the torch to one, I can't make out what's sitting inside.

"What're these?" I ask Diego when we've gone past a third one.

"Being underground doesn't mean we don't have problems," Diego replies. "You ever see one of those glowing red, you go the other way. Means there's dangerous gas, and the plant inside it can't keep up."

"Keep up?"

"No different than your jungles, Empress," Diego spits the title. "Everything either eats or gets eaten down here, even the air."

It's difficult to tell how much time passes before Diego calls us to a halt for the day. Without a sky, without even the changing temperature of the air, and only the smell of wet rock, I can't gauge where I am, when I am.

But my muscles let me know they're tired. My ankles are sore from having to keep their footing on smooth and rough stones all day. My arms ache from holding the torch, and my back's letting me know that it's not thrilled at having to carry the pack for so long. So I'm not upset when Diego slings his own pack off and sets it on the ground.

The chamber's about as large as the shuttle's living space. Enough for us all to have our own bedrolls, but not much more. There's a patch of pink-glowing fungus in the center ceiling that provides enough light for us to douse our torches. The glow also illuminates several exits.

Diego points to one, "That's the latrine. Like the other ones, you go back there if you need to take care of yourself. There's a hole, use it." Then he angles towards the middle one. "There's a spring back there, ought to be warm. Good for baths. The last one's where we're going tomorrow."

"You managed to make these every day's length away?" T'Oli asks. "That's remarkable."

"It's not precise," Diego huffs. "We use what nature gives us."

Not long after, feeling the dirt sticking to me with my sweat and more, I decide to take up the offer of the spring. Head that way with a torch and T'Oli for company. Make it about five steps into the spring's cave, before both the Ooblot and I notice something different.

This tunnel's not hard-edged like the others. The rocks are broken, yes, but these stones look like they've been whittled away, as if something's gnawed at them as opposed to using the picks and drills Diego says are the core of the Lunare digging operations.

"What do you think made this?" I ask the Ooblot.

"I can think of many things," T'Oli replies. "The most likely, though, is some sort of creature. Which, given my current assessment of human capabilities, would provide a better reason for this tunnel to be here."

"What do you mean, capabilities?" the way T'Oli said that has me raising an eyebrow.

"Compared to other species, like Vee and the Oratus, your senses seem average, at best." T'Oli doesn't put any judgment in the tone, only simple fact. "That one of your kind could smell and taste spring water through the rock from any distance away seems unlikely. Rather, my guess is that this tunnel already existed."

"Yeah, well, at least we're smart enough to use it." I counter, and keep walking towards the spring.

"That's only smart if the creature that made it is no longer here."

"I'm sure Diego would warn us otherwise."

"Yes, because, as we've discussed, humans are excellent judges of their environments."

Now I stop, glare down at T'Oli. "You don't have to keep insulting us."

"Kaishi, Ooblots are literally puddles of amorphous genetic material. Before you would feel attacked by a word of mine, consider the source." T'Oli waves its twin eye stalks back and forth and, I have to agree, the Ooblot does look pretty pathetic there on the ground.

The pool is lit in mirrored green, the plants hiding beneath the surface and shimmering their light up through the bubbling water. Steam rises from the surface, coasting towards invisible escape in the ceiling. I can feel the heat from the edge, and I jam my torch between a few rocks, slip off the dirty clothes, and dip a toe in.

T'Oli races by me, slurping into the spring, where its body expands and ripples until the Ooblot looks like a lily pad.

"You like this?" I ask T'Oli, giving my feet time to acclimate to the heat.

"What, you don't think Ooblots need to clean ourselves the same as you?"

Guess I didn't. I shake my head, then lower myself inside the pool. After the lip, it drops off fast and I have to tread water, at least until I find the right spot where I can rest my shoulder on a stone lip.

To say that the pool's relaxing would be to rob it of its due; I simply haven't felt anything this good since Damantum's own bath houses. My soreness vanishes, I breathe the moisture into my lungs and feel the warmth excise the day's dust. Whatever dirt I have sloughs off and disappears into the depths.

T'Oli floats further, eventually disappearing towards the far end of the pool, beyond the edge of the fungus light. There's no sound save the bubbling, nothing to see except the mist and the soft green.

"You never seemed this happy in Damantum," Malo says, and I see him standing there, on the edge of the pool. Through the mist, he's indistinct, but I think he's smiling.

"Because I was always being threatened, or had Ignos telling me what to do." I take a hand, swish the water in front of me and watch the waves. "I wanted to explore the city. Try new things. Learn why you called it the greatest place on Earth."

"I would have shown you, if you'd asked."

"I know." I look at Malo again, and he's sitting by the edge of the pool. "I was scared."

"Why?"

"Because that would mean doing something for myself. I thought it would be selfish, with Ignos and so many people depending on me."

"I depended on you too, Kaishi. You depend on you."

"Wish you'd told me that sooner." I look back at the green light. It's easier than staring at that face.

"I'm telling you now."

"When it's too late to do anything about it."

"Is it?" Malo's using that same joking tone, like when he gave me the pepper-covered fish. "You might have more time than you think. Humanity's not gone yet."

"Yet." I glance towards Malo, and he's even more shrouded than before. "What should I do, Malo? You're gone, Ignos is gone. I'm just guessing."

"What do you think the rest of us are doing?"

I laugh, shake my head and shut my eyes for a second. Take a scoop of the warm water and run it through my hair, over my face.

"Kaishi?" Malo's voice is different now, more alarmed.

"Yes?" I brush the water away with my arm, clear my eyes.

"I don't think we're alone," T'Oli says, the Ooblot rushing back towards me.

I look past the Ooblot, in the darkness at the far end, and see nothing. There's no rushing water— like when some of the jungle's river predators swim towards their prey. But T'Oli's skimming towards the edge with speed, so I move too. Get out, slip on my clothes, and then yelp when T'Oli slithers onto me and hardens.

"What are you doing?" I manage to ask, glancing at the twin stalks.

"The pool vanishes into another cave at the far end," T'Oli says, its voice vibrating against me as it slaps himself to make the sounds. "Curious, I went further. There's a den."

"A den for what?"

"Have you heard of Fassoths, Kaishi?"

"No?"

T'Oli's eyestalks twitch the way they often do when it's about to launch into a long explanation of something or other. I keep my attention, though, on the water, which is now lapping against the near side of the pool. Splashing up on the same rocks that were, a moment ago, serving as my arm rests.

"I did not expect to find one here—" T'Oli starts, and then I see the shadow.

Or rather, the pool becomes the shadow. The green light goes away as a massive dark blob covers it. I grab the torch and hold it out, which lets me see, in glorious orange clarity, the sopping wet, white-haired, huge head that rises up from the water.

I immediately question if it is a head, because there's no eyes, no ears, no mouth that I can see. Only a furred oval. It's weird enough that I step back, my booted feet scraping against the rock.

Turns out that's a mistake. The oval swivels towards me. Starts moving towards the pool's edge.

"Unless humans have a strong defense mechanism I have not yet witnessed, in which case you should immediately deploy it, I suggest fleeing," T'Oli says.

"Yeah, we've got none of those," I reply and keep backpedaling.

My running starts as soon as the rest of the creature climbs out of the pool. Two thick legs come first, planting clawed feet on the ground. That's when I recognize what I'm looking at.

T'Oli called them Fassoths, but I've seen them before. The Lunare used beasts like these when they fought us in the desert, when they killed the former Charre emperor. Then, we had better versions of the pistols Diego and his cohorts have. Then I had an army.

Now it's only me, cloaked in an Ooblot, sprinting and stumbling through a dark cave as death comes scrambling after.

Fassoths don't make any noise of their own. I hear the claws scrape on against the rocks, the thud as the beast's big body bounces off walls. Or maybe I'm drowning out the Fassoth with my own shouts, because my voice is going full tilt between breaths.

Which is why, when I barge into our makeshift camp, I'm expecting a host of traps set. Weapons drawn and dead-set stares trailing after me, waiting for a chance to lay into the beast.

What I get is nothing. Nobody. Even Vee, the brave Oratus, is gone. Most of our things are still on the ground, though a half-second glance confirms someone snagged the food packs.

"Keep running, Kaishi!" Viera's voice, from the tunnel Diego said leads onward. "We can't fight that thing in here!"

Great. I manage to get across the camp before the Fassoth bursts out behind me, a movement made known by the sudden flying of our bed rolls through the air as I duck and run.

"Your odds of outlasting the Fassoth are slim," T'Oli says as I career down the tunnel. "Find a place to hide and stay still."

"Great advice. Let me know when you see a spot."

The tunnel's one slim pathway, carved walls giving precisely zero room to slip away. I think, though, that I'm holding my lead until I feel a push on my back that sends me flying. The torch in my right hand goes for a trip, bouncing off a looming boulder and rolling on ahead as I crash into the ground.

A dozen cuts and scrapes open in an instant. T'Oli somehow draws its eyestalks in, hardens them as I roll over, and in the process I get two Ooblot-eye-shaped jabs to my chest as its solid form clogs the space between me and the ground.

All of that pales a second later, though, when the Fassoth pins and pushes me into the floor. I feel snaps in my chest, and spiderwebs of sharp pain ripple out. I scream in there, but I'm pretty sure I black out for a hot moment too.

Survival instinct, though, doesn't let me go that fast. Neither does Viera—I assume it's her, because I can't picture Diego coming back— whose miner unleashes a different kind of crack. The Fassoth must like her as much as I do right then, because it goes charging after the Lunare. Though not before trampling me with its other legs on the way.

Then there's only me and rock-T'Oli, on the ground in the dark, my torch long gone, as ever-more-distant sounds of miner shots ring through the cave.

I can't move. I mean, I can, but doing so hurts so much that I don't want to. That I'd rather sit there on the floor and wait for death to find me. Maybe the Fassoth will come back and take me out of my misery.

"Kaishi?" T'Oli says. "Are you still alive?"

"Yes," I manage, though speaking feels like dredging my voice across hot coals.

"Then we should be moving. The Fassoth, if Viera and the others fail to kill it, will eventually come back for you."

"Good."

T'Oli hesitates. I can feel the Ooblot slowly liquidate itself, slide off of me and run through my hair en route to the ground in front of my face.

"Forgive me, Kaishi, but unless I am missing something, I believe the Fassoth's return would be very not good for you."

"You're missing how much everything hurts."

"Ah. Then that snap I felt was not an idle sound?"

"That was me breaking in half." I wiggle my toes after saying this and feel a momentary relief that I still can. The Fassoth didn't actually snap me in two.

"More sarcasm. I'm beginning to think this is how humans deal with difficulty."

"Now's not the time, T'Oli." I close my eyes. Start to take a deep breath and stop immediately. Only shallow gasps from now on.

I can't just lie here, right?

No.

I test my hands, both hurting from rock-scrapes, and press them against the ground. Push, slide my knees beneath me and rise up, slowly, until I'm standing, then leaning against the side. Spots burst in front of my eyes in time with the spears of pain coming from my right side.

"Standing is a good start, Kaishi," T'Oli says. "It will be easier to escape the Fassoth if you can walk."

"Yeah," I say. "Can you see anything? Cause I sure can't."

"Ooblots, sadly, are not equipped with night vision," T'Oli says. "I can, however, guide you."

"Then let's go."

I keep my right hand on the cave wall as we walk. Every step sends spiking aftershocks up my system, and now that it's out of immediate danger, my body's wasting no time reading off a litany of minor wounds covering every part of me that T'Oli didn't protect. Wrists, knees, elbows, they're all beat up. I brush off a drop of what I assume is blood from my nose, but I can't see it on my hand.

There's plenty of noise in the distance beyond the standard drip-echoes of the cave. Every time I hear a miner blast apart a rock, or the crack of Diego's pistol, I get a little hopeful. Means one of them is still alive. Though I guess it also means they're still on the run.

"Kaishi, we have a problem," T'Oli says.

"Think we might have a few, T'Oli."

"There are three options here that I can feel. Which way should we go?"

"Towards the sounds?"

"The echoes make it difficult to discern where they're coming from. Can you tell?"

Hah. Can I tell. That I'm standing ought to be enough of an achievement right now. Every sense I've got is playing at half-speed as my mind slogs through an ever-present swamp of pain.

"T'Oli, pick a direction, and let's go. Worst thing that happens, we find another one of those things and get ourselves eaten."

"I don't think Fassoths would be able to eat me," T'Oli says. "You, however, they would likely find a delightful snack." I hear T'Oli oozing across the floor. "This way, I think."

And on we go.

After far too long stepping through the deep dark, I see light. Not white, artificial light like on the Sevora ships, nor the yellow heat like Ignos. But a blue halo coming out of somewhere ahead.

"Know what that is?" I say, dimly aware that I've been saying nonsense things to T'Oli for a while now as we've trudged through these endless black holes.

The Ooblot responds for a while, answering my pithy complaints with its usual straightforward commentary. It's refreshing, in a way. T'Oli doesn't indulge me, just states what's necessary to say and nothing more.

T'Oli doesn't change now.

"It's one of the fungal growths," the Ooblot says. "Nothing dangerous."

I stumble on. The pain's more or less numbed now, owing partly, I think, to my realization that I'm not going to die from my wounds. And if I'm not going to die, I might as well try to live.

We round the corner and the fungus blossoms into full bloom. It's not a small room but a vast chamber with at least a dozen natural pillars I can see stretching back, all of them coated in the plants. For a moment I forget everything as the dazzling azure sucks away my breath, draws me into the vast maps of sparkling stones coating the walls.

It's beautiful, stunning, incredible.

So much so that I don't notice the bones covering the floor until I step on one.

Solis. Sax hasn't seen the small world since his birth, or, really, since he first came into consciousness. A gray rock ball with a single, jagged green scar slashing through the barren waste. A creche carved from nothing to grow a species not safe to raise anywhere else. There's a white dwarf star spinning nearby, close enough to baste Solis with enough heat to allow the Amiggas' experiment to work. The planet serves as both nursery and teacher, often a fatal one.

The *Mobius* exits its leap far enough away to see the array of Vincere ships hanging in space around the planet. Enough to make an easy landing impossible.

"This is why we weren't supposed to come here," Plake says as the opposing forces become clear. "We're not getting the *Mobius* through that force."

"Then how did Bas expect to land?"

"A single small shuttle. All I know is that the Flaum piloting it's on our side. Had some way of sneaking Bas through that."

"What about the far side?"

Solis isn't developed. Only a quarter of the planet, so far as Sax knows, is used for the Oratus project, with the rest of it left alone.

Probably so the Amigga could add on further creations if they wanted to.

"Even if they don't chase us down, you're saying we land and, what, walk all the way over?"

"Not doing that for you, Oratus," Agra-Red says from behind. "I already think this is a stupid idea."

"Nobody asked you, Whelk," Sax fires back.

"Stop," Plake closes her eyes for a second, then looks again at the terminal. "Looks like they have a pair of smaller frigates, meant for craft like this, and then a big cruiser. Way too big for something like Solis."

"It's not meant for fighting," Sax says. "That's where they train us, if we survive that long."

"So it's a boat packed with Oratus?" Agra-Red says. "Let's not go there. Ever."

"Scared?" Sax hisses, giving the Whelk a wicked grin.

"I don't want to waste the power turning them all to slag," the Whelk replies, patting the assault miner that never seems to leave its side.

"Wait," Plake says a moment later. "You're saying that big ship is packed with Oratus? New ones?"

"A hundred or more," Sax says. "It can hold thousands, but unless they've made it easy for Oratus to earn their letters, it'll never be near full."

"Can they be turned?"

Can a weapon be twisted against its wielder? Sax himself is proof that it can, but there's a difference in the experiences he's had compared to what the Oratus on that ship, most only just removed from a harsh introduction to life on Solis' surface, have gone through. Would they turn their backs on the Vincere just after joining it?

"Unlikely," Sax says finally. "Why would they trust us?"

"Not us," Plake replies. "You."

At this, Sax laughs. "Look at me, Plake. I'm a traitor. My scales are bent and burned. I'm sitting on a ship with a ragtag group of outcasts. Why would they care about me?"

Plake looks at her own feathers, and Sax realizes she's glancing at the part of a Vyphen where medals would hang. Where rank would be established if she wore a Vincere uniform.

"I thought, when they removed us, that I was done," Plake says. "I was, I am angry. But there's something you get when the Vincere stop controlling your life. Freedom. Independence. I could choose where to go. My failures were my fault, not because I'd been thrust into an impossible situation without support. Not because the equipment I had wasn't up to the task."

"Or you weren't good enough," Sax says. The Vyphen weren't removed only because they were less pliable than the Oratus, but also because they were less effective.

Plake acknowledges this with a slight nod. "Now, though, I get to make my own choices. I don't do the bidding of anyone but myself unless I want to. Sax, your species hasn't been given a choice. They never have, and as long as the Chorus exists, they never will."

"That's the message you want me to send? That we should fight against the Chorus because otherwise they'll control us?"

"I think that's the only message we have. If we can't turn these Oratus, then as soon as the Sevora are gone, the Chorus will use them to kill every last one of us."

If the plan is to get the Oratus to fight back against their creators, they first have to find a way to get Sax onto that large ship. A plan pushed to the forefront when the Vincere frigates take notice of the *Mobius* hanging out on Solis' fringes and send a few fighters to investigate.

"Use the escape mod," Coorvin says after Plake explains the dilemma, over intercom, to the entire crew. "Send Sax. He can say that he managed to escape."

"They'll never believe that," Plake says. "And Sax is wanted. He's a known traitor."

A traitor. Sax hasn't thought of himself like that, but Plake's words aren't wrong. He's actively working against the creatures that made him, working against the society that's given him life and, at first, a purpose.

The term, though, is freeing. Sax *is* a traitor. He's cast off his chains. He has no obligations anymore.

Except to Bas, of course.

"I'll do it," Sax hisses. "Only I'll need a hostage. Like Coorvin says, they won't trust that I made it away without one."

"They'll still imprison you immediately," Plake replies.

"But if there's a bit of doubt," Coorvin offers. "Even a little, that might give Sax another chance."

A beeping noise sounds from the cockpit—Vincere craft are getting closer.

"I'll do it!" the squeaky voice coming from the intercoms has Sax wincing. "I owe Sax that much. Wouldn't even be here if he hadn't found me!"

Nobaa. Why?

Sax doesn't have the time, unfortunately, to argue and none of the other crew volunteer, so it's a swift scramble to get Sax a miner and squeeze him into the escape mod with Nobaa.

"After we kick you, we're leaping away," Plake says. "Send a message to Astre's Spire when you're ready for pick-up and we'll come back."

"We're going back there?" Agra-Red grumbles. "It's the most boring—"

"Quiet." Plake jerks a feathered hand towards the Whelk, though Sax can't see Agra-Red's response from inside the cramped mod. "Can't believe I'm saying this, Oratus, but good luck."

Sax gives the Vyphen a flash of his teeth, then presses the panel to seal the mod. The door slams shut, the vacuum seals activate, and Sax feels the slight judder as the mod kicks away from the *Mobius*.

"Do you think Engee will think I'm brave?" Nobaa says. "This is pretty courageous, right? Giving myself up for your grand mission?"

Sax sighs and closes his eyes, waits for the pick-up.

It's strange being stuck in a capsule with little view of the outside. All Sax can see, in fact, is dark space. There's too much ambient light from Solis' nearby star to get a glimpse of a nebula or other twinkling dots, but even a blank black is better than staring at Nobaa and his endlessly blathering mouth.

Rescue comes partway through Nobaa's seemingly endless iterations on how the Teven's going to undermine the Vincere ship's control systems and use them to confuse, frustrate, and drive the ship's crew insane with blaring alarms, randomly locking doors, and food dispensers set to continuously spray nutrients onto the floor.

"Evac mod, we're tracking you. Who's inside?" the intercom buzzes with the stern, light voice of a Flaum pilot.

Sax feels the Oratus should be given the chance to fly fighters too, but they're too big. Creating a craft that could hold an Oratus in comfortable position yet still be able to twist and turn in heavy atmosphere isn't a problem the Amigga think they need to solve. So instead the Vincere trust their space acrobatics to the most prevalent and, until he'd met Nobaa, what Sax thought was the most annoying of species.

"This is Sax," the Oratus says, right foreclaw pushing in the panel for a response. Now that he's said his name, though, Sax isn't sure where to go. So he falls back on instinct. "I broke free of the Vyphen traitors holding me, and I'm ready to come home."

It sounds weak, but then, that might be what they're expecting; an Oratus who played with rebellion, found it wanting and forced to fight his way free without his pair? Yes, that could mean a tired voice. A sad soul.

The Flaum pilot takes her time in responding, and then only gives an acknowledgment that Sax is going to be taken in.

"That worked!" Nobaa exclaims when the intercom cuts. "They believed you!"

"I'm too valuable to kill outright," Sax hisses. "At the least, they think I have information to give. Either I'm being honest, which means they'll interrogate me and, probably, waste me for being disloyal, or I'm lying, in which case they'll waste me for being a traitor."

"Neither of those sounds like the outcome we want."

"Neither of those is the outcome they'll get," Sax says. "Just remember your role; get out, get access, and clear a path for the *Mobius*. If we can't get a full on fight started, then we need to get down to Solis and find Bas."

"Of course! It'll be easy. I can hack . . ." Sax stops listening to Nobaa's drivel and lets his eyes drift back to the window.

There's a shiver as something latches on to the escape mod and redirects its path. After a moment, the big Oratus ship swings into view, a monstrous oval spiked with antennas, and coated in glowing docking bays. They're heading towards it.

At least, that's what Sax gets to think, for a moment, until one of the two frigates swings in front of the viewport, its docking bay looming large and close. Too close to miss now.

They're going on the wrong ship.

Through the viewport, Sax watches as the escape mod settles into the frigate's empty bay. Clear bluish-black floors meld with yellow-aged walls and white lights to make for a sterile Vincere appearance.

"Why's it so empty?" Nobaa says. "Are they that scared of us?"

"They think this might be a bomb," Sax replies. "Suicide or otherwise."

"Do Oratus do that? I thought you were too valuable?"

It's weird to think of himself as some sort of commodity, but Sax supposes that, yes, there's a price for him and every other Oratus. Sending one of a limited species on a bombing run against a low-value target wouldn't be smart. Wouldn't be profitable.

Then again, the Chorus doesn't deal in profits. The galaxy they've built serves as a mechanism to support their experiments, their ambitions. They wouldn't care how many Oratus have to destroy themselves so long as the Chorus comes out ahead.

Sax and Nobaa are separated the moment the mod arrives on the frigate. Stiff Flaum and Whelk shuttle Sax through the docking bay and towards the bridge—Sax has been on plenty of these sterile frigates before, and knows where he's heading. What he doesn't understand until he's stalking through the halls—flanked by miners on either side, in front and behind, is just how bland these ships are. *Scrapper Station*, Astre's Spire, and, most of all, the *Mobius* teem with the evidence of life; stained walls, nicked surfaces, littered junk and half-finished projects. Stories told in the ambiance.

Here, though, the Vincere keep things clear and clean of the past. Sax can't tell what lives have been shared in these hallways, and the silver sheen on the walls tells no tales. Even his vents pick up only the most mild scents from the creatures around him—tasteless goop to eat and plenty of showers mean his captors are blanks.

Before, Sax would have thought these things meant perfection and order, essential traits for a military force. Now it reminds him of the Chorus' ultimate objective; a universe they control.

The distaste must show in his stance, because when Sax is brought into the small bridge and face-to-face with the ship's Oratus commander, a brilliant gold-scaled one who introduces herself as Rav. The second thing she says is:

"You don't look like you belong here."

"I lived in these ships for a very long time." They're no longer his home, though.

Rav doesn't bear the scars of long-time war—her scales are too perfect, her claws unbent and sharp. Sax suspects she's never been on the front lines, relegated to back-water command posts like this one. The question is, why?

"I'm not supposed to interrogate you," Rav hisses, throwing a glance towards the Flaum manning the bridge's Q-Net communications array. "They're sending a transport to pick you up. Apparently you're going to be torn apart, mentally and physically, so they can find what's wrong with you."

"They?" Sax asks the question knowing the answer.

"The Chorus."

"What do you see in front of you, Rav?" Sax says, trying to think like Bas. "A damaged, broken thing, or another Oratus?"

Rav tilts her head, bares her teeth slightly. "I see a traitor."

"To what? The Chorus? Because I choose to do something other than their will?"

"Because you choose to be yourself," Rav gestures with her fore-claw around the bridge, to the pair of Whelk standing—as much as a Whelk can stand without legs—behind him with their miners ready. "The Vincere needs loyal soldiers, or else how can we keep the galaxy safe? What happens if every Oratus takes your path, if the Sevora are given free control to spread themselves throughout every inhabited planet?"

"So choosing to think for myself means I'm letting the Sevora win?"

Rav locks eyes with Sax. "Yes." Then she looks past him. "Take the traitor to his room. Keep him there until the transport arrives."

The frigate isn't equipped for much in the way of prisoner transport, much less one the size of Sax. So instead they stick the Oratus in an empty, square cabin without much inside except a long bench on the right. One that could have been covered with a cushion but, for Sax, is left hard and bare.

There's a screen occupying a wall opposite the bench, one that could be used to show calming landscapes, watch entertainment, or a dozen other things but that, for Sax, remains black and dead.

Yet, when the door shuts behind him, Sax relaxes. He didn't realize how tense it would be, confronting his own side, dealing with the accusing stares of lowly soldiers and staff that, before, would've been legitimately concerned with becoming his next meal. Now, Sax isn't something to be feared, he's something to be scorned.

The cabin's door sits flush with the wall behind him, and the panel controlling it's been overridden from elsewhere. Sax taps a couple of the buttons just to see what might happen and each one greets his attempt with an indignant buzzing. The screen does the same when Sax experiments a second later.

So they expect him to sit and wait. Stew, perhaps, in his own decisions.

Instead, Sax hunts for the cameras. Finds one hastily latched onto a wall above the door, peering down at him from its black nub.

What would they do if Sax attacks it? Would they open the door, miners in hand, and try to stun him enough to repair the thing? Or would they let him sit, hope that Sax doesn't do anything rash as they're unable to see him?

Sax opens his mouth at the camera, crouches and jumps, swiping with a foreclaw and shredding the camera off the wall. As soon as Sax lands, he rakes the door's panel with his claws, knocking it off its perch and sending it sparking to the ground. A couple hard swings with his tail and the wall screen is coated in cracks, which has to make any camera looking through the glass a distorted affair.

"Why?" Rav's voice snarls through an overhead intercom a second later. "What's the point, Sax?"

Sax takes a bit of smug satisfaction from knowing they're using the frigate's alert system to talk to him—the cabin's private intercom was on the door panel. Sax can't exactly talk back to Rav here, but at least he knows she's frustrated.

"You're not getting out of that room," Rav continues. "I'm ordering the outside guard doubled. The Chrous transport's already leapt into the system, so your pointless destruction will get you nothing."

But it's satisfying.

And now he knows they're blind.

The dull pearl bones carpet the floor, and at first I want to panic, push away the pain and run. The bones aren't human. Not all of them anyway. Even the one I just stepped on is longer than my own leg. Thick, with a knob on either end.

"T'Oli, do you know whose bones these are?" I manage to ask.

"Given the size, it seems plausible that these belong to other Fassoth," T'Oli says. "Unless your planet has other large predators with a predilection for dark, damp environs?"

The Ooblot surges ahead of me, rolling over the bones and deeper into the cavern, around those blue-coated pillars. I don't really try to keep up, instead focusing on my awkward shamble, trying not to fall into what would be a nightmare.

"If the bones are here, though, doesn't that mean it comes back to eat?" I ask.

To the right, as I pass by the first pillar, I see the grand sphere of a Fassoth skull, almost perfectly unbroken save for a crack in the upper right temple. I only guess it's a Fassoth because there aren't any holes for eyes or ears, or a mouth.

"I don't know much about how Fassoths live, Kaishi," T'Oli replies from up ahead. "But your thought seems likely."

"Which means we shouldn't be here."

Two choices, then. Either we turn around, hope that Viera and the others took a different path and that they've killed the Fassoth chasing us, or we keep plunging ahead this way. Hope that the Fassoth or whatever lives here doesn't decide to come back. Or isn't waiting behind the next pillar.

The bones thin as we go deeper, where a small stream makes its burbling self known. It cascades along the left wall, filling a small pool before vanishing through some unseen crack in the rocks. I can picture this as a Damantum house—the boneyard being the dining area, the stream marking the kitchen.

Which means we're coming to the bedroom.

Beyond the stream, the fungal growths dwindle as the cavern closes together into a dead-end. A smooth, rounded closure whose ground is coated in soft-white hairs. T'Oli's waiting for me there, its eye stalks scanning the area.

"I can't find another way forward," the Ooblot says as I wander up, right hand on the wall.

"So we chose the wrong way."

"Depends on what you consider wrong," T'Oli replies. "We didn't find the Fassoth, so, in some ways, we chose the right one."

"What I don't understand, is you said you found the Fassoth's den on the other side of the pool. And I can't imagine Diego and the others taking up this close to two of these things." I glance back towards the blue pillars. "It's too dangerous."

"A full day's walk away is distance enough, and Fassoth would be wary of attacking a large party," T'Oli says. "They simply may have hid while Diego and the others moved through."

"Still doesn't explain the two dens."

"Do human families stay close together?" T'Oli asks.

"Generally," I reply. "Why?"

As I finished the answer, there's a clear rustling from back up the cavern. The sound of many thick feet pounding on the rock, and heading this way.

"Fassoth," T'Oli says. "Are the same."

I press against the den's back wall. T'Oli starts to sluice up me, to form its armor again. Not that the Ooblot's protection saved me the last time.

Of all the ways I thought I might die, trapped in a cave with a monstrous beast wasn't on the list until this moment. I'd pictured growing old in my village, possibly going out through disease or a hunter's spear. Maybe getting sacrificed to Ignos.

But this? No.

So when the Fassoth shows up, as it picks through the bones, kicking some aside and, using one of its eight legs, handling others, I try to think. Try to ponder some way out.

The Fassoth doesn't seem in a rush to get to me, so I watch it move. It looks larger than the one that emerged from the pool, and there are gaps in its white fur where scars make themselves apparent. Some of the bones it puts down are snapped, or have grooves cut in their smooth surface, as though the Fassoth is somehow sucking out the marrow through its feet.

What I don't see, though, is a weakness. A way around the creature and out of the cavern. Especially when moving faster than, oh, a slow walk would make me pass out from the pain.

So when the Fassoth finally finishes with its inventory of the bone hoard and ambles towards me, I feel around my feet for a loose rock. Figure that, if nothing else, I'm going to go out with a short, pitiful fight. T'Oli twitches against me, but says nothing.

Not like the Ooblot has to worry—it'll live through this. T'Oli can go all stone and it'll be fine. Maybe T'Oli can take my bones when the Fassoth is done with me, bring them to Viera and the others so they know.

The Fassoth, so close now, dips a foot in the creek's pool. I can smell its sweaty stink, hear its thick breath. It's made no motions towards me, though. No aggressive gestures as I keep myself pinned to the wall.

No eyes. The thought hits me hard. No eyes, and no visible ears. The Fassoth might not know I'm here. I haven't made a sound, haven't moved.

Only now the creature's moving away from the pool, towards me and its bed of white fur. If it gets so close, it might be able to hear my breathing, or the rapid-fire beat of my heart.

So I throw the rock. Launch it hard across the cavern to the left side, where it strikes a pillar and rattles into a pile of bones. The Fassoth jerks immediately, tracks the rock as it flies and then shifts towards where it lands.

Then it bursts.

I've seen juar—large, predatory cats—do the same, but the Fassoth is larger. Has more legs. The Fassoth I'd first seen used by the Lunare were tame, controlled. This one leaps through the air, legs flailing out, and it crashes into the bones, scattering them everywhere.

"Go," T'Oli pats quietly.

And I do. Push off from the wall and run. Towards the right.

I make it all of two steps before the side of my chest breaks me with stabbing pain. It's like I can't feel my legs anymore, can't focus, can't land the next step and I wind up falling. Splashing into the end of the creek, and the icy cave water soaks my clothes, and me.

At least it numbs the pain.

The Fassoth isn't fooled. I see the creature wheel around towards me, and as the rock I threw fails to keep moving, the Fassoth begins creeping my way. I crawl, dragging myself forward, trying to get my legs beneath me, but they're half-frozen from the water and I'm half-stunned anyway.

I can't outrun this thing.

Which means I have to fight it.

"T'Oli," I say, causing the Fassoth to start, to lift its eyeless head and point it towards me. "Can you form a point? On my left hand?"

T'Oli, to its credit, doesn't ask questions. The Ooblot just goes.

Slimes away from me, disintegrating my armor and going, instead, along my left arm and over my wrist, then, building off of itself, T'Oli extends my hand until it ends in a hard-rock spear.

The Ooblot's two eye stalks fold back along my arm, turning to look at me.

"Yeah, like that," I say to the stare.

The Fassoth rumbles over, standing over me. It raises its front right leg and there, between the claws, I see how it eats. How it survives. In between those deadly points, there's a mouth. A slit filled with jagged, broken teeth.

"Stay away from me," I growl, and punch up with my left arm, right into that mouth.

The pressure, the strength of the hit ripples along T'Oli's form, to my arm and along my body as the Fassoth rears back from the strike. There's no roar, no angry call as I'd expect from anything else getting such a wound. Only the shuffling of dirt and bones, only the *drip drip* of the creek.

Life or death determined in silence.

"Having never been a weapon before, I'm not sure I like it," T'Oli says by thawing a small portion of itself near my elbow. "Awfully brutal."

"Welcome to life for the rest of us." I use the seconds bought with the strike, while the Fassoth changes its calculus on its prey, to get to my feet.

I back against the wall, the creek running just in front of me, and watch as the Fassoth heads around the pillar, careful to hold its wounded leg off of the ground. I, though, keep my Ooblot spear raised in front of me, ready.

"You know any way to scare these things?" I ask T'Oli.

"They're trainable," T'Oli says. "If you have the right tools, and catch them young."

"Thanks." I edge along the creek, towards the boneyard and the cavern entrance.

Not that I think I have any chance of outrunning the monster, but if I can knock it away, make it hesitate, that might be enough to flee.

The Fassoth, for its part, seems to be content waiting. It paces me, following along the middle of the cavern. At first I wonder what it's doing, but then I recall the fight with the juar, in Damantum's Pits. The Fassoth is a predator, I'm its prey, and it wants to figure me out.

Well, it's not the only one learning.

When my boot brushes the first bone, I reach down, press away the pain in my side and pick it up with my right hand. I throw it back across the cave, towards the wall near the fur. It clacks off, hits the ground, and sure enough the Fassoth jerks its head back that way.

I stay perfectly still. Don't even breathe. And in a second, the Fassoth takes a couple of steps towards the thrown bone.

I toss another bone. Then a third, without taking another step. When the last one bounces with a hollow clack, the Fassoth can't resist anymore and it launches towards my trick.

And now I have it.

It's a lumpy, lurching run but it's the only one I have. T'Oli waves through the air—attached to my left arm—as I scatter bones with every step. With my right, I scoop up and throw one after another, flinging them at random around the cavern.

Clattering noise from everywhere, and I'm hoping it confuses the beast.

For a moment I think it's working. I hear the Fassoth jump after the last bone I throw, hear the beast bounce off of a pillar and see the light change as blue fungus goes flying. But apparently the Fassoth isn't as easy to fool as I thought—the very next second brings clattering claws racing up behind me.

"Now!" T'Oli says, its eyestalks peering over my shoulder, behind me.

I turn, swinging my left arm in a wide slash. T'Oli manages to harden itself into a razor's edge, and the cut goes right across the front of the Fassoth's head. The slash leaves a bright red line in the fur, and the Fassoth rears back.

What it doesn't do, though, is run.

Instead it plows forward, even as I get T'Oli oriented so the charge costs the Fassoth another gash. The beast plows into me, pushing me back and knocking me to the ground. The world blurs as my nerves overload at the impact, and I'm thankful, because now I can't really see as the Fassoth's toothy foot descends towards my face.

I feel a cold flash from my left arm. As the Fassoth's foot crashes in, T'Oli slides in front of it. The Ooblot catches the strike, wrapping itself around the Fassoth's foot. The creature stops its attack and stumbles back, probably wondering why its front right leg is covered in hard rock.

My head sits back against the stone floor—I can't keep it up anymore—as the Fassoth commences to panicked battering, hitting its front leg on the ground, whacking it into the pillars and the walls to try and get T'Oli off.

I want to help. Want to find some way of rescuing T'Oli. Only I can't move, and my head's blowing up with pain.

So I do the only thing I can.

I scream.

The sound surprises everyone; the Fassoth, who pauses its crazed whacking of the Ooblot to turn towards me, T'Oli, whose rock eyestalks flip my way, and even me, as I didn't think I had that much air left in my bruised lungs.

I guess fear can do amazing things.

T'Oli's the first to recover, climbing up the Fassoth's leg. I sit up as the Ooblot makes its way towards the Fassoth's monstrous neck. The beast, though, isn't fooled and rolls. Bones fly everywhere as the Fassoth wriggles on its back before continuing upright. When the white-furred creature stands again, T'Oli's nowhere to be seen.

Stand up, Kaishi. You're not going to die lying down.

I don't really succeed. The best I get is a stumble against the wall, near the cavern's exit. I try to throw another rock, and this time actually hit the Fassoth, which ignores my efforts completely.

The beast grumbles towards me—still favoring that right foot I cut—and I start to pray. There's nothing else to do. Nowhere I can run. So I call to Ignos, and ask, if not for his help, then for his courage.

I don't hear an answer.

The Fassoth raises its left foot, and I try to duck, but it catches me with its claws and throws me to the ground. The foot lands on my back, cutting into me, and I fall into the pain.

I'm coming to you, Malo.

"Not her." A crack—impossibly loud—shatters the cavern after the words.

The Fassoth's foot jumps off me as a second crack breaks out. Then a third and a fourth in quick succession. I brush my face against the floor to look up, to see the Fassoth back-pedaling as shot after shot pours into the thing.

Viera comes into view, a pistol in each hand, unleashing one crack after another until both weapons click empty. She holsters the left one, then reaches into her pocket and pulls out a handful of bullets. Starts reloading the pistol in her right. The Fassoth, for its part, is moving around, trying to keep the pillars between it and the Lunare.

"You still alive, Empress?" Viera says without looking back at me.

"For the moment."

"Try to keep it that way." Viera snaps the chamber back. "Vee, you're on her."

"As ordered." The hiss comes from above me, and I twist further to see the Oratus, bleeding from plenty of his own cuts, missing a pair of claws from his right foreclaw, and holding two torches, standing over me.

Viera begins a dance with the Fassoth, keeping her distance while slowly reloading her second pistol, bringing both weapons back to ready. She makes enough noise, kicking at rocks and bones to keep the Fassoth on her, but the creature's not quite so reckless anymore. Its fur is blossomed with red, and it's moving slow.

At least, that's what I think until the Fassoth bursts forward, scrambling on its back four legs while raising its front limbs to bat towards Viera.

I shout. Vee hisses.

Viera pulls the triggers. Both pistols work again. One after another. Four cracks, five cracks, their fiery flashes sparking over the blue glow. I see her face, her set, grim, look beneath her white, tangled hair.

And then she's gone, buried beneath an unmoving Fassoth as it collapses onto her.

"Go! Help her!" I manage to croak, though Vee's already moving.

The Oratus goes to work, pressing with his legs, with his claws, and then Viera's there, crawling out from beneath the beast and coated in the results of her handiwork. She's as beaten and battered as all of us, but Viera's able to stand. Able to walk to me and, after putting her pistols back, help me up.

I point, then, towards the spot where the Fassoth ran T'Oli into the ground, and Vee goes to check. Retrieves the stone slab of the Ooblot. Still in one piece, T'Oli's eyestalks are flattened into the surface of its body. None of us knows if T'Oli's alive, so Vee settles the stone Ooblot into his midclaws.

"I'll carry T'Oli until it's ready," Vee hisses.

"And Diego?" I ask.

"First one took him," Viera replies, pats the pistols. "That's where these came from."

"How?"

"He didn't run fast enough." Viera throws a look at Vee. "Then he held its attention long enough for me to take it out. Thankfully, Diego was a bit paranoid, so he brought a ton of ammunition."

Losing Diego is a hard blow. Not because I have any fondness for the man—he was, generally, a jerk to all of us—but because we're now lost down here. We've got no guide, and no way to convince any Lunare we come across that we're friendly.

"How about you?" Viera asks. "How bad are you hurt?"

Rather than list off my injuries, I break into a half-hearted laugh. "I'll survive. May need new ribs, though."

Viera nods. "Then we should head back. They'll have medical supplies at the gateway."

"No." I almost fall over, but Viera catches me. "We keep going. We've lost too much time already."

But we do go back a little, to our ditched campsite, where the rest of the gear and other supplies sit. I'm tempted to return to the pool, but instead hold still while Viera wraps cut up clothing around my ribs. Tries to keep them in place. It doesn't help much, but I appreciate the sentiment. The effort.

"You didn't give up," I say to Viera as she finishes the wrapping.

Vee looks like he's asleep already, T'Oli still cradled in his claws.

"We fought through space, through other worlds, Kaishi," Viera says, using her torch to set the fire pit, full of dried fungus and other random growth, alight. "Dying to a Fassoth now would be a stupid way to go."

"We were close."

"But we're alive." Viera steps back from the small fire. "That scream, you know. That's what let us find you."

"I was trying to scare it. For T'Oli." I tell my version of the fight.

"You used T'Oli as a spear?" Viera asks when I'm done. "Clever."

"Don't know if T'Oli liked it, but we didn't have much choice."

"You could have chosen to die," Viera says. "But you didn't give up."

I catch the sentiment. Offer up a smile. "No. Though I think I might pass out now."

"Do it. I'll keep watch."

Part of me wants to offer to do the same. Or tell Viera to wake me in a bit to take her place, but the truth is that I can't bring myself to say the words. My body's demanding sleep, and as soon as my head hits the mat, I'm gone.

. . .

Our progress is achingly slow, but the nutrient goop is filling and we have a lot of it. T'Oli wakes up by the second night, more or less the same as always, though the Ooblot mentions no desire to become my spear in the future.

At first I'm afraid we'll be stuck lost in the tunnels forever, but it seems Diego exaggerated the difficulty; the Lunare didn't carve a dozen routes through the Earth. There's only one main path and a number of tiny diversions, most leading to pools or small storage caches with emergency supplies.

We avoid any smooth tunnels, anything that doesn't bear the tell-tale marks of Lunare picks and their crude hacking. No further Fassoths come to hunt us down, though we're also quiet, keeping to soft murmurs as we move so that the cave's natural rumblings tend to be louder than we are.

My damaged ribs never fade, but familiarity turns the pain manageable and I gradually pick up my pace. We're all hurt, though, so speed is never a serious concern. We won't be much help to humanity if we die en route, anyway.

Viera, more than myself, Vee, or T'Oli, takes over the lead as we go. She holds a pistol in one hand, a torch in the other, and strides with confidence I haven't seen before. Maybe because Viera feels this is, more than any of us, her home. Maybe because she knows nobody else is willing to take up the leader's burden right now.

I'm certainly content to let her have it.

Especially when, late in the third day, we stumble upon a small village, built around a lake that would have been considered tiny if we were in the jungle. Our tunnel spits us out over the lake, where a man-made path leads us across the water and towards a dozen houses and a few accompanying buildings.

I've never seen Lunare homes before, and these are built from the ground up to the ceiling, the structures blending into the rock at both ends.

"They're support and shelter," Viera says when I ask why. "We have to hollow most of these areas out, so the buildings help keep the ceiling from falling in."

There are other pillars cast around too, including a few lunging out of the lake, rising to smash into the top of the cavern. They remind me of trees, in a way, only deep gray rock instead of wood.

The first Lunare to notice us are a pair of fisherman, casting their nets into the lake. I can't imagine what fish make it down here, and how they manage to reproduce if they do, but there's a woven basket between the two men, so I assume they must catch something.

When they see us, though, their net comes in fast and the closer one reaches for a pistol holstered around his belt, keeps his hand on it as we draw near. I'm expecting panic when he notices Vee, but the man's eyes only widen a little. His partner takes the gear and makes a speedy walk away, leaving his friend behind.

"You came from the other side," the man says once we're in conversational range.

"We did," Viera says, then nods back at us. "We're tired and hurt. Is there a place to stay here?"

"You think you're just going to walk in with that thing?" the man nods to Vee.

"Yes. We are."

"Viera," I interject. I'm too tired for another fight. "Please, I don't know your name, or your home, but we've come a long way and only need a place to rest. We mean you no harm."

"That's what they said too," the man replies. "The ones we're fighting back to the west. They said they came with nothing to hide, no reason to hurt. Didn't last long. How do I know you're not with them?"

Viera sighs next to me, brushes away a dangling bang with the back of her wrist. "What lies beneath?"

I'm about to ask what she's talking about when the man squints at her. "Our truest self."

"Why do we go?" Viera continues.

"To find what we must."

"And who do we carry?"

"All who carry us." The man relaxes his pistol grip, shakes his head. "Been a long time since I've heard that one."

I'm looking back and forth between the two, and notice Viera's wearing a small smile.

"It's been a long time since I've said it," Viera replies. "Good to know the old verses haven't been forgotten."

"Not yet. Not by all of us." The man seems to see us for the first time, only now, instead of suspicion, he gives a steady look of trust. "Head to the common house. They'll have room for you. Refugees haven't made it this far yet. Tell them you talked to Anjo."

Leaving Sax alone in a room designed for rest and not, say, keeping a dangerous weapon captive, leads to poor results; Sax takes a running leap, bounces up the door and makes it to the ceiling, his claws catching in the slats of the air vent. With a kick, Sax digs his talons into the silver tiles on the ceiling—punching his sharp feet through the thin metal.

With his foreclaws, Sax tears the vent away and sends it rattling to the floor. The duct behind it isn't nearly large enough for Sax, at first, but when the Oratus peers through his new-made hole, it's clear the small duct intersects with the much larger, main one feeding this portion of the ship with sweet, sweet air. What's life-sustaining for the crew is going to bring them a very fatal surprise.

Sax rends the small duct sides to widen the path, pushing away streams of wires. He tucks in his midclaws close to his chest vents as he starts climbing up, stretching his talons and tail out behind him to create as thin a form as possible.

If Bas saw him now, half-stuck in this mess of metal, she'd laugh so hard. Sax can't quite suppress a hiss of his own at the situation—he'd never have thought he'd be scrambling through the innards of a Vincere ship.

But he squirms anyway, because knowing the circumstances are ridiculous doesn't help Sax get out of them. It's a centimeter by centimeter crawl, with Sax's foreclaws clearing the way. He has to test every pipe, every section of wire for give so he doesn't damage or break something that might burst hot liquid or fiery electric sparks all over him.

"Sax? What are you doing in there?" it's a Flaum voice this time —Rav probably has better things to do than babysit a prisoner. "We're hearing a lot of noise."

Sax doesn't try to respond. If they burst in now, they'll know where he is in a moment, and have stunning bolts blasting his tail in the next. And if Sax gets on that Chorus ship, he'll never see Bas again.

So Sax picks up the pace. Scrabbles forward towards the wide duct. He leaves plenty of claw marks on the ship around him, and the frigate leaves a bunch of small cuts on Sax's scales as his body bends and warps.

There's no warning when the door to his cabin opens. Just a beep and a shunt—guess destroying the door's panel didn't help—and there's a half-dozen footfalls as the Vincere guards run beneath Sax into the room.

"Sax!" One of them shouts, as if calling his name is going to get Sax popping out from behind a curtain, laughing and declaring the whole thing a joke.

What Sax does instead is finish tearing his way into the breezy main duct, where warm air rushes by and an infinite silvery corridor goes both to his left and right. He has to make a choice now, as the Flaum have performed the minimal detective work to figure out where Sax has gone and are attempting to climb up into the vents.

Problem is, Flaum are small creatures and Sax doubts they've brought a ladder with them.

Which way?

There's only one thing on this ship that really matters, only one way Sax can come close to completing his original mission: Rav. Sax bets she's still on the bridge, so that's where he goes.

Sax doesn't have a map, has no easy way of telling the layout of the frigate, but he knows Vincere ships and knows, too, that the heat keeping the ship warm comes from the bank of batteries back by its main engines. The bridge, kept far away from those same engines—a means of keeping the commander at the farthest spot from the area most likely to blossom into a fiery death at a malfunction or well-placed shot—is at the opposite end.

The Oratus follows that warm breeze and clambers through the ductwork. Here it's plenty wide for Sax, though it's short enough he has to keep crawling. Small and medium offshoots dot his path as Sax moves, and he manages to ignore almost all of them until, bouncing off the walls, comes a voice that makes Sax wince.

"You're running old systems! I could do better, if you give me just a few minutes!" Nobaa's speaking to someone. "The Oratus used me as a hostage. I love the Vincere. Love you guys!"

It's coming from Sax's right; a cramped offshoot that's still larger than the one he tore up to get here. Navigable. But is Nobaa worth risking his mission for?

No.

Sax turns back to his path, is about to go on, when the tiniest flicker of a flash makes its way up into the vent. Followed by a panicked yelp.

"You can't kill me! That's not fair!" Nobaa's shouting.

"Why not? This isn't a prisoner ship, and you don't have anything to trade," a Flaum voice says. "If word gets out that more Oratus are turning traitor, that wouldn't be good for us. Others might get the same idea. Rav told us you're not going to leave here, and I've got other things to do. Make peace with yourself, Teven."

Sax tears his way through the duct before he really thinks about what he's doing. As soon as he hits the vent staring down into the larger room—apparently made for medical evaluations—where Nobaa's backed against the wall, Sax uses his head to smash the vent down. The metal grate crashes into the Flaum aiming his miner at Nobaa and, with his fore-claws tearing a wider hole, Sax squeezes through and lands on the captor.

Sax rips away the miner, lifts and throws the Flaum against the room's walls. The red-furred guard hits the wall hard and collapses to the ground.

"You rescued me!"

Sax takes a deep breath. Looks back towards the duct, then at Nobaa. Maybe . . .

"Let's go," Sax starts, moving towards Nobaa. He figures he can throw the Teven up there and Nobaa can pull himself the rest of the way.

"No, wait!" Nobaa's carapace looks strange now, covered in empty hooks and belts. "I need my things."

"Your things don't matter."

"You want to survive this?" Nobaa counters. "Then I need my gear so we can take this ship over the right way."

Nobaa's idea of the right way is a lot more complicated than Sax's —for one, as Sax understands it, there's not even a need to slash and tear through any Flaum at all.

"If you really want to murder some things, I'm sure you'll have the chance," Nobaa says as Sax opens the door out of the medical room where they'd been holding the Teven. "This ship is full of people."

The frigate doesn't have an expansive med bay, only a dozen rooms, most of those smaller than the one Nobaa was in. They're clustered around a single monitoring station currently occupied by a robot that, after a flash scan from across the room declares Nobaa and Sax to be in good health, ignores them.

"Kind of small, isn't it?" Nobaa says. "For a ship this size?"

"Not a lot of space combat that leaves you alive," Sax replies. "Better to give the rooms to more weapons, more energy, than beds that won't do you any good."

Nobaa doesn't have a response to that other than a twitch of his arms as he turns his carapace to get a good look at the place.

"Where's your gear?" Sax hisses after a moment. "They'll find us soon."

"I don't know," Nobaa says. "I thought it would be out here. They took everything after bringing me onboard."

This frigate doesn't have cells, so it probably doesn't have a designated spot for a captive's gear either. Which means they'd toss Nobaa's electronics in the same spot as the rest of the general junk the frigate's maintenance people might need. Or it's near the docking bay, waiting for the Chorus' transport to take it back with them.

Sax tosses these options at Nobaa, who doesn't have a suggestion.

"You're no help," Sax hisses at the Teven.

Before Nobaa can properly describe how hurt he is by the insult, there's a shout from outside the med bay. Alarms bang suddenly, the harsher tone indicating everyone should find immediate shelter. The robot acts on it—whirling into activity and calmly calling for everyone in the med bay to seal their doors.

Sax takes a couple long lunges and gets to the med bay's entrance, a double-wide sliding door leading out to another corridor in which Sax can see plenty of armed Flaum and Whelk heading their way. Sax hits the panel to close off the med bay, which, so far as he can tell, is going to buy them a second of time.

"We need a way out!" Sax hisses back to Nobaa.

"You're talking to me like I know this place! Wasn't this one of your ships?"

It was, but med bays weren't a space Sax frequented. That's what the masks—and his raw talent—kept him out of. The Oratus runs his eyes around the space, and falls on the only thing that might make a difference.

"Take the miner, buy me time," Sax hisses to Nobaa, passing off the Flaum guard's miner to the Teven, who, at least, holds the weapon like he knows how to use it.

"Shouldn't you be the one doing the fighting?"

"I wish I was." Sax blows by the Teven, heading for the terminals left vacant by the robot.

There's several of them, showing bars and numbers that, Sax guesses, have to do with the occupants in some of the rooms. What he's looking for, though, is a channel to the bridge, and he finds it on the right terminal. Taps the icon with his right midclaw.

"Rav," Sax says as soon as the terminal beeps that a connection's been made. "Call off your force."

There's hissing laughter on the other end. "You're better than I thought, Sax, but the Chorus's transport is docking now. Give yourself up. Don't hurt the Vincere more than you already have."

Rav didn't go for it the first time Sax made his pitch. She refused to play the part of traitor with him, refused to turn on her own troops or try to convince them to join Sax's cause.

"They're going to kill you," Sax hisses. "All of you. All of us. I've seen it, Rav."

Behind him, around the wall, the med bay door judders open. Nobaa, standing near Sax and using the corner, immediately lets loose a pair of bright-blue stunning bolts. Smart—stuns use less power than deadly shots, and everyone they don't kill will be one less reason for Rav to despise them.

"The Amigga are making better versions of us, just like we were to the Vyphen. Then we'll be replaced. But Rav, we can't reproduce. We're not a natural species. When they decide we're done, we're done."

"And you think that by fighting the Chorus we can live somehow?"

"If we take Solis, yes! That's where the hatcheries are. Where the Oratus can survive!"

There's a heavy hiss on the other end of the line. Nobaa unleashes a few more bolts, and Sax sees a couple return shots burn blue into the far wall past them.

"Rav?" Sax asks.

"Even if I believed you," Rav says. "Even if there's a chance you might be right, then what? The Chorus would destroy us all before they let your plan succeed."

"They've been trying to destroy me for a while now, Rav, and I'm still here."

There's another blue blast and Nobaa falls back from the corner, his little limbs slinking limp to the ground, the miner beside them.

Sax is out of time.

He can't wait for Rav. Sax reaches down, grabs Nobaa's fallen miner in one midclaw and the Teven in the other. The med bay goes in a ring around this terminal bank, with the single open door directly behind Sax, through the back wall of a supply room.

"Oratus! Give up!" It's the skittering, stern voice of a Flaum soldier. "No reason you have to die here!"

Sax glances left, right. Only patient rooms. And above is a flat ceiling—no time to crawl up into a vent even if he wanted to.

"We're coming around to get you in ten seconds!"

That means Sax really has five. He spies his answer in one: the medical robot, moving from one room to the next and now passing by them on the right. Sax raises the miner and uses his left foreclaw to adjust the miner's power, pushing it to maximum. Turns, and aims at the robot's power supply, housed within its base, between the metal balls allowing the machine to get around.

Fires.

The bright red bolt strikes a robot never meant for combat duty. The heat burns through the robot's shell, strikes the big power supply, and overcharges it. Because Sax is ready, because he's gouged his talons into the floor and has his tail bracing against the same, the explosion doesn't send Sax flying.

It does, though, splash his eyes with heat, burn his claws and set all the lights in the med bay to a deep yellow warning glow. Alarms—true alarms—start off like wailing monsters as smoke pumps out from a dozen small fires, smoke that's as quickly shunted towards the vents as the frigate's systems take charge of preserving itself.

As Sax acts now to keep him and Nobaa alive. He twists around the corner to the right, talons pounding. The squad coming to capture him is in disarray, blown about the entry. Some are trying to help others, plenty more are lying still.

Sax hopes he didn't kill any, or at least too many. Every death hurts his cause here.

Back in the main corridor, Sax turns away from the bridge and runs. There's plenty of people there, mechanics and medics dashing towards the explosion and plenty more pushing to get away from it.

Nobody bothers to engage Sax, who towers over most of them and uses his foreclaws and tail to clear away anyone who doesn't notice the Oratus trampling through.

Lit signs show up at intersections, signaling what lies which way. Sax goes by a cafeteria, a fitness center, and a simulator section before hitting what he's looking for—cargo. The frigate's not going to be hauling freight, but there's a good chance that Nobaa's gear would find its way there.

The Teven's still not conscious and Sax has no idea how long it's going to take a small creature like Nobaa to wake up from a heavy stun, which means even if Sax finds the Teven's things, it's going to require hiding out on the frigate for a long time.

Time Sax doesn't have.

Sax hisses away some of his anger, drawing plenty of frightened looks and a couple of squeaks from the crowd, who add distance from Sax as the priority to their paths through the ship. It's a problem, as Sax is getting away from the aftermath of the explosion, and the panic isn't following as far.

As Sax nears the frigate's aft and its massive engines, he hunts for a place to drop the dead weight in his midclaws; Nobaa isn't helping Sax unconscious and there's a good chance the Teven's going to get shot hanging limp in the middle of a big target.

And Nobaa's body is far too small to make a good shield.

In this, the constant overhead announcements tracking Sax's progress and ordering all non-combat personnel to stay out of the Oratus's way serve as an advantage. Hallways are clear, rooms are empty, and nobody accosts Sax as he barges into a storage room and stuffs the Teven in a food locker. Nobaa doesn't exactly blend in with the crates, but he's not likely to get blown apart in there either.

Back in the main corridor running from bridge to stern, Sax catches some more shots from another cadre of Flaum and Whelk guards. The fire doesn't come all that close to hitting Sax, and the bolts are a dim blue—low power. The reason's clear—there's plenty of valuable equipment in the frigate, and Sax is running out of places to go. Why risk damage when they'll have the Oratus trapped soon anyway?

Soon, though, isn't now.

Sax takes the opportunity to jump and dart along the corridor towards the engines, past all sorts of glowing lights and locking doors showing ways to cafeterias, crew quarters, and maintenance bays. As the Oratus moves, the crystal white lights shift to red spectrums, adding to the constant warning drone to hide.

The corridor ends in a wide, locked and sealed entry to the engines. These are thick silver shields, meant to cushion and even block any explosion if the frigate's big thrusters decide to end themselves in a fiery death. It means Sax has run out of room.

There's a single panel near the doors, one that Sax uses to call the only place he can. To act on the idea that's made its way into his mind as his talons have scraped and scratched their way this far.

Sax taps to call the bridge and there's a blip as the Oratus on the other end clicks into the line.

"Rav," Sax hisses. "You don't have to trust me."

"I don't have to trust you? That makes it easy."

"Trust Evva instead. She's a four-letter Oratus. A Vincere commander. She's abandoned her post. Why?"

"Because she's insane? A traitor?"

"Because she learned the truth, Rav."

The Flaum and Whelk soldiers have caught up with him. They're arrayed across the corridor, miners raised. Sax keeps talking, because as soon as he stops, he's not getting another chance.

"That the Amigga are all evil, and we're all being played for fools?"

"Exactly."

There's a heavy silence on the other end of the line. Sax keeps his eyes on Rav's guards. Why haven't they shot yet? Sax hasn't heard Rav give an order for them not to.

"Sax, even if I wanted to believe you, even if I wanted the Oratus to rise up and take their destiny into their own hands," Rav says. "There's a problem."

"What problem?"

"The Chorus has already won. I'm sorry, Sax."

The line clicks off. Sax looks back at the guards, raising his claws. They'll fire in a second, but if they don't, Sax isn't going to wait. He tenses his talons, looks to the right, where a set of lower pipes would provide grip for a bounding jump into the side of the Flaum line. Strike there and limit their field of view and maybe, maybe in the chaos there'd be a chance of survival.

But Sax doesn't get his chance to act, because there's a sharp hiss from behind the line, an order that causes the guards to split apart—Flaum stepping rapidly, Whelk sludging along the floor—to show something Sax didn't think was real. Something he's never seen before.

The Amigga created the Oratus to be weapons. Grew and designed the species to take the reins of war. That, though, was a narrow view of what Oratus could be capable of. There'd been plenty of rumors, gaps in new Oratus joining the Vincere, that suggested the hatcheries on Solis were being used for purposes less clear, less about keeping order in the galaxy and more about cleaning out what the Amigga didn't like.

Its scales aren't a single color. Instead, they shiver and shift as the Oratus moves, their surfaces reflecting the red and black lights, the glow of the dozen miners primed to fire, so that their owner appears less as a physical object and more as a wavering line, a reality-blending blur.

"They sent you?" Sax manages to say, which is all he can think to speak to a legend brought to life in front of his eyes.

The mirrored Oratus aren't supposed to exist. Everyone assumed they were a tale told in the shadows, the price paid if one considered disobeying the Chorus' orders. If one ever turned on the Vincere.

Yet, Sax and Bas hadn't ever seen one. Hadn't heard of one. How could they be afraid of what didn't seem real?

"Your charges are clear," the Oratus speaks, and even its voice is a reflection of itself, distorted and chilling. "You are a traitor to the Vincere, to the Amigga, and to your own species."

Sax moves to the left, watching the blur go opposite him. Sax has to keep a little distance, give himself a half-second to adapt when the mirror Oratus decides to strike.

"You'd trust the Amigga over one of your own?" Sax replies. "Who's really betraying their species?"

The mirrored Oratus doesn't reply. At least, not with words. It leaps up, high enough to catch the ceiling and hook onto a vent with its foreclaws. The Oratus swings forward, red lines playing over its scales between darker reflections of the watching Flaum and Whelk, and lunges at Sax with its talons.

Sax dives forward, tucking in his tail as he rolls and feeling the shift in the air above him. Sax twists as he comes out of the somersault, winding up on all six claws and talons, crouched and ready if the mirrored Oratus makes a quick attack.

"What is your plan?" the mirrored Oratus asks instead, keeping on its talons.

Sax realizes its eyes are mirrored too—probably covered by a mask helping with the imaging.

"My plan?" Sax hisses back a reply. "You're asking that now?"

"It will save me time," the Oratus says. "Tell me, and I can deliver you a clean death now, rather than a slow one later."

If there's one thing Sax can't stand, it's mockery. He rises up, matching the mirrored Oratus on his talons.

"Our plan is to end the tyranny the Amigga have over this galaxy," Sax hisses. "Starting with the Chorus."

"Then they were right," the mirrored Oratus hisses a laugh. "I've received more briefings than you can imagine, Sax. Removed all manner of traitors to the Chorus. Incompetent officials to high level Vincere officers. Even other Amigga deemed a risk. But never, never have I encountered any with such lofty ambitions."

That isn't what Sax expects to hear. He's thinking the mirrored Oratus has a mask that's recording everything, and as soon as it gets the information it needs, the Oratus will just signal to the guards who'll burn Sax down in a blaze of miner fire. This is all just a show.

So why is the mirrored Oratus bothering to have a real conversation?

"I've risked my life many times for much less." Sax picks a path. "About time I took a chance for something greater."

The common center that Anjo directs us to is about the only bustling part of town that I can see. It's set against what must be the town square; a circle of packed earth with a large stalagmite rising up from the middle. Like our Tiers in the jungle, the stalagmite is covered in drawings and various dyes.

One stands out—a black and white version of a Fassoth, its many legs chasing after what looks like a pack of Lunare. Even the simple drawing sends a chill and I look away, over towards the warm fires glowing in the common house windows.

"Been a long time since we've seen human civilization," Viera says to me.

"I thought you said it's only been a season?"

"Feels a lot longer than that."

I nod. Even though these cavern towns are far different than the Solare and Charre villages, there's a lot about them that's familiar; the low hum of human voices rather than the hissing and clattering of the other species I've been around, the simple smells of cooking food rather than the stale purity of nutrient goop, and the ramshackle dirtiness, the imperfections of everything around us.

Humanity, I realize, is not rote perfection. It's not refined and coated with the sheen of eternal tweaking. We're rough, but strong. Stupid at times, but we try.

"It's good to be back," I finally say as we head towards the common house's doors.

Rather than the wooden portals of Damantum or the hanging cloth shields of Solare villages, these doors look like sheets of light stone, set on hinges along the sides. The opening itself is square, and on the borders, Lunare script reads that any looking for food, for company, will find it here.

"Will we be welcome inside?" T'Oli asks us.

"No idea," Viera replies. "Stay quiet and I think you'll be fine."

"I have little experience in human combat." T'Oli squirms up and onto Vee's shoulders. "What should I do?"

"Let me handle it." Viera turns back to the stone door, pushes it open, and we head into a wash of warmth and laughter.

The common house floor is dominated by a set of six stone tables, each big enough to seat ten or more, laid out across the main room. In the center, a large black-rock hearth burns coal bright, with the chimney heading up and disappearing into the ceiling. Behind it sits a long counter lined with crude-sculpted stone stools, on which sit a variety of Lunare laborers.

Beverages and food—cooked meats and roasted root vegetables, from the smell—spin by us as a pair of wait staff keep the small crowd fed and drunk. The place is, at best, half full. But it feels like far more than that when everyone turns to look at us. When even the sole musician, a man playing a simple drum near the fire, stops his beat and stares.

Even Viera seems frozen by the response, as if she's never been the target of so many different inquisitive and suspicious looks before.

I have.

"Hello," I start. "We're not your enemies." Figure that's a safe way to begin. "We came from the far side, and we're looking to get back home. A man named Anjo guided us here, and said we would be welcome for the evening."

"You, maybe," shouts someone from behind the counter. "But not them!"

I find the man, and he's a grease-coated cook staring dead at Vee and T'Oli . I notice too that there aren't many surprises sitting on the faces of the guests. They're not stunned at the presence of a tall, beaten-but-scaled and clawed creature standing in their doorway. Interesting.

"They're here to help fight against the other ones." I'm not sure if the word 'Sevora' holds any meaning here, but I have to try it anyway. "They want to fight the Sevora as much as you do. As much as I do."

"And who are you?" this time it's the musician asking, the cook in back resigning to a huffy glower. "Why should we listen to what you have to say?"

"Because I lost everything to be here," I reply. "Because I have everything to gain from helping you. Because I used to be the Empress of the Charre, and now I'm nothing more than a wounded woman who knows what we have to do to survive."

Now faces are turning to each other, questions are being muttered, and I feel the spotlight turn bright on me. So I think back to when I first stood on the Vaos with Jakkan, to where the high priest taught me how to sell myself to a populace.

Especially one in fear of an advancing, hostile force.

"You have questions. You have fears." I take a deep breath. Father said cadence was everything. "You have every right not to listen, not to trust us. But if you hear what we have to say, then maybe you'll understand. Maybe you will see that we mean to help, not hurt."

The words pour on from there. I stand past the entrance and tell stories, talk about *Cobalt*, the Oratus and the Sevora. Every time I see the audience starting to drift away as unfamiliar terms and strange ideas roll over them, I slide back to direct appeals. To the idea that humanity must stand together against massive threats. Against things that don't care if we, as a species, live or die.

When my throat is parched and I feel I can't speak anymore, it's the musician that brings me an earthen mug full of bitter stuff. I nearly spit it out after the first sip, but force it down. Beer, I think, and recall Malo's warning about the Charre peppers; you must be able to eat and drink what they do, if you want their help. If you want to be seen as one of them.

At the end of it, I don't know if I've convinced anyone, but the looks are more curious than cautionary now. One of the waiters, a young boy who seems enthralled with Vee, directs us to an empty table, and that's where we sit, at last. If not entirely accepted, at least we're not being attacked.

"Nice work," Viera says as we sit down. "I thought I'd have to shoot at least three of them before they'd leave us alone."

"This place doesn't seem so strange," T'Oli remarks as we sit down. "Though it has been a long time since I've enjoyed this sort of beverage."

"What sort of beverage?" I ask the Ooblot, who coils up on a stool and hardens its lower half so that its eyestalks and a small puddle spill onto the table itself.

"The one you're holding. If I might have a sip?"

I glance at the mug. Look at T'Oli's puddle. "How?"

"Like anything else," T'Oli patters. "Pour it on me."

I lift the mug, tilt it a little bit so that the beer runs up to the lip, and then let some pour over. I'm expecting it to hit the Ooblot and scatter all over the place, but instead the beer simply dissolves into T'Oli's skin, leaving a faint amber spot against the white.

"Not so bad," T'Oli says. "Though it could use cleaner water. More pure ingredients."

"You're drinking beer in a cave," Viera says. "What more do you want?"

The way T'Oli's eye stalks turn to regard Viera with earnest clarity, I know the Ooblot's about to answer the Lunare's question literally. I try to stop that disaster before it starts.

"Vee, what do you think?" I ask.

The Oratus hasn't stopped moving his head since we came in here. He's watching for something, and I'm curious about what.

"There's fear here," Vee hisses. "It's a strong smell." Vee turns back to me, sets his four claws on the table. "We should not stay."

"What, why?" Viera asks. "After Kaishi gave that speech? They're not going to hurt us."

"Look at them," Vee hisses back. "They are desperate. I do not know the density of your human settlements, but this seems like a large concentration for one this small?"

"Is it?" I ask, taking another stock. Sure, there are about twenty people in here, and maybe a dozen houses in the entire village. That number doesn't seem too ordinary.

"He's right," Viera says, and her voice has a different edge to it now. "Look at them. They're not locals."

I can't tell. Most are wearing the same sorts of loose clothes, boots. Some have bandannas on, others have pistols holstered around their hips. All of them are dirty—and so are we. There's not an obvious look I can pick out.

"I don't see it?" I finally say.

Viera's about to speak when the boy comes by again, asks if we would like anything to drink. Viera orders a round, and when I'm about to ask how we're going to pay for that, she pulls a small pouch of stones from her pocket.

"Diego didn't need this anymore," Viera says at my look, and now that the boy's gone, she nods towards the cook. "See how he's acting? How the rest of his staff are keeping eyes on everyone?"

I shrug. "Yes? So?"

"It means they don't know these people well," Vee hisses. "A small place like this, every person should be known. This should be comfortable. Instead, everyone is on edge."

"Why would they be?" T'Oli says after the boy deposits a set of four mugs in front of us. "They have food, shelter, and drinks?"

I'm thinking here. What would make a Charre town this worried? What would disrupt a normal village of Solare?

The answer comes walking over after we get our drinks, a gruff woman flanked by seven men.

"Name's Celice," the woman says and I'm struck by how gravelly, how deep her voice goes. "You're from the wrong side of the mountains?"

I feel Viera move her right hand to her pistol, and I tighten my grip on the beer mug. It's full, but the mug itself is hard. If I had to throw it, the mug could probably do some damage. But for now, I try not to start a fight.

Especially as I'm still in a world of hurt, and none of us are feeling ready to swap fists with this crew.

"Further than that," I reply. "We came over there from space, from beyond the sky."

Celice doesn't look fazed by that at all. "That's what they said too. You know what's happening back the other way?"

"We've guessed."

Vee, for his part, hasn't moved except to help T'Oli pour more beer on itself. The Oratus seems unconcerned by Celice and her crew. Which, if I was a scaly death-beast, I probably wouldn't be too worried either.

"It's worse than whatever you're thinking." Celice leans over, plants her hands palm down on the table. "Wouldn't be surprised if Avril's lost the first tunnels by now, even with all your Charre and Solare friends fighting on their side."

"We're trying to get there. What we know could help them."

"If you had thousands more with you, like that one, maybe," Celice nods at Vee. "Otherwise, all you're doing is marching to suicide."

"What's your point?" Viera interjects. "You didn't come over here to warn us away."

"No," Celice replies. "I didn't. We left the front on orders. Keep an open chain of Lunare control through the mountains, so that we could retreat all the way out if we have to. Which is where you all come in."

"What do you mean?"

"We want to go back," Celice says. "The fighting's there. The enemy's there. We're tired of sitting around this place, waiting. You're going to be our reason. Our way home."

I blink. That's it? They want to escort us?

"Sure?" I say. "That's fine."

Celice flicks her eyes to Viera, who shrugs. "Whatever Kaishi says."

Celice nods, stands up from the table. "Then we're going tomorrow. Better see the town's doctor, too. You're all looking a little beat."

She's not wrong. After T'Oli and Viera finish their drinks—I let mine languish—the four of us arrange for a room at the common house and head towards the only sort-of clinic this town has, which amounts to a house with an older couple inside.

What they have, though, are supplies. Wraps and poultices for our cuts, which they wash out and bandage. Ointments for our blistered feet and soaps for our dirty hair. Sandy paste for our teeth to keep them from falling out. Afterwards, we head to the bath house and its spring, thankfully Fassoth-free.

When I finally fall asleep that night, on a hay bed next to Viera, with T'Oli puddled on the floor and Vee curled up on our mats in the corner, it's the first real rest I've had in a very, very long time.

Celice and three of her guards meet us in the morning. She leaves the rest of her force behind as a garrison, and we spend the next few days venturing through tunnels far better lit, signed and marked than before. They're wide enough for cart trains, for all of us to walk abreast, and even, occasionally, have carved art and paintings on the sides.

I do find myself wishing for the sky, for Ignos to shine, but the closest we get to that are the periodic ventilation shafts, through which, if I listen carefully, I can hear the whistling wind far above.

Celice gives a dire account of the war as we move. The Sevora appeared not long ago in the skies overhead, seeming first like black smudges high above. Then came shuttles packed with creatures nobody had ever seen before.

Here, Celice stops for a second to thank me.

"Why?" I ask. "I wasn't even here."

"Because you showed us what was coming," Celice replies. "You brought the first ones, like him, here."

I'd forgotten that Sax and Bas visited the Lunare hunting for me. They'd exposed Earth to the new threats from space.

"We weren't entirely unprepared," Celice continues. "Avril had contingencies. We were already overtaking the jungle, about to assault the Charre themselves—"

"Wait," I say as we walk beneath a glittering, magenta-glowing ceiling. "You were attacking the Charre?"

"Of course," Celice says, as if such a move is obvious. "You were gone. Their leading general, gone. They were in disarray. What better time?"

I want to fire off some insults, spit a bit of fire at the cruelty of taking advantage of people, but then I remember the Sevora in my own head. Ignos, constantly telling me when to push others, to use them and twist their goals to suit my own ends. I'd done that, which is why I became Empress in the first place.

"So the Sevora come and you what, run?" I finally say.

"We offered them shelter," Celice says. "Damantum's too wide open, especially for an attack from above. The Charre aren't stupid—they listen to their priests and come rushing in, along with the Solare tribes we've taken."

"So charitable," Viera says. "That's not like Avril."

"When you're facing annihilation," Celice replies, "every body counts. Those that could wield weapons got them, others we sent deep into the tunnels to secure routes like this one. You might not like Avril, Viera, but she wants humanity to survive as much as you do.

"And it's a good thing she did, because we didn't hold long on the outside. Nothing we can do about their . . . fliers. The ones that come out of the sky and send burning death into us. We've been in the mountains ever since, waiting and holding and hoping for a miracle."

Celice's expression as she says this shows she doesn't think we're it.

I can't disagree with her. A wounded Oratus, an Ooblot, and a couple of battered humans aren't going to swing the tide of this fight. At least, not without some help.

Sax charges as he finishes the words. His talons slash the metal floor and he dives at the mirrored Oratus, who doesn't see it coming.

At least, that's what Sax thinks for the fraction of a second before the mirrored Oratus shifts ever so slightly, his blurry, flashing scales throwing Sax off his line, making Sax's claws slide off scales rather than cut deep. The mirrored Oratus takes advantage as Sax flies by, gouging Sax with his foreclaws.

The Oratus body is all weapon, though, and Sax whips his tail as he falls, gets it underneath the enemy's talons and sweeps the creature from his feet. Sax's momentum carries him into the far wall, and the gray Oratus grips, spins, and turns with his midclaws before leaping back at his downed target. Sax lands on the mirrored Oratus, claws raking, mouth biting, and receiving equal treatment in turn. Slashing, stinging pain cuts through Sax, he feels the muscles in his arms and vents tear but Sax doesn't care—he's in the bloodlust now. Everything is red and raw energy. Sax is going to die, so he's going to give everything he has for this.

Which is what?

For the first time in his life, a thought stops Sax, and the mirrored

Oratus takes advantage, pushes his talons beneath Sax and kicks him off. Sax flies from the floor and rolls into the left wall. He feels his energy draining away, his blood pooling on the floor and all he can think of is that he's given himself for nothing. If he dies here, his mission ends. Losing it all in a fight with a creature that, even if he wins, would cause the Flaum to burn Sax down where he stands.

Sax can't die for nothing anymore. He has a cause.

"Surprising, but stupid," the mirrored Oratus hisses, and there's a slurping sound in his voice now. Sax must have clawed the Oratus deep in the creature's vocal cords. "You didn't need to hurt yourself that way. Now I'll have to fix you up for them to kill you all over again."

Sax stares at the mirrored Oratus, feels the cold metal floor against his head. He wants to talk back, but the act of opening his mouth feels like lifting a ship off the ground. Instead, Sax thinks about Bas. What she's doing, where she is. If she's even still alive.

The mirrored Oratus blurs over to Sax, glares down at him. "For the last time, tell me your plan. Why are you here?"

"I told you," Sax manages to croak. "The Chorus must be stopped."

The mirrored Oratus takes his right talon, presses Sax's throat, and he can feel the claws pushing in. "That's not enough."

"That's all you're going to get."

The mirrored Oratus pushes further with his talon, but Sax doesn't care. What's more pain to what he's already endured?

"I thought you were taking him prisoner," this hiss comes from someone strong and new. Rav. "What do you think murdering an Oratus on my ship will do for morale? They need to listen to me, not think I might be a traitor."

"I don't care about your sensitivities," the mirrored Oratus hisses back. "This creature *is* a traitor. You should be proud that you facilitated his capture."

"Then take him away," Rav replies. "I won't have him killed on my ship."

The mirrored Oratus hesitates, then lifts his talon off of Sax's neck. "Fine. Help me drag him to mine."

Sax can't see her, but he feels Rav look at him. "I don't think your prisoner's going to live long enough for a leap. We'll patch him up, first."

The mirrored Oratus snorts, but doesn't refuse.

Rav orders a pair of Flaum to help Sax to his feet. Three more keep their miners trained on him, even though Sax isn't going anywhere, and they all know it. Sax knows it too; he's focusing on breathing, and standing and on not giving the mirrored Oratus any more satisfaction. They take Sax along through the hallways, away from the engines and Sax's last idea. The medical bay's ruined, so instead they sling Sax into an empty crew cabin, where a Flaum patches Sax's wounds with bandages and injects him with just enough Stim to keep Sax alive.

All the while, the mirrored Oratus watches over Sax. All the while, the mirrored Oratus talks. Tells Sax all about the various horrible treatments he'll be receiving at the hands of the Chorus. At the end of it, when he's concluded any number of options for how Sax may meet his gruesome end, and when Sax has had himself pieced back together, the mirrored Oratus leans in real close.

"I'm not telling you this to scare you," the mirrored Oratus hisses. "I'm telling you this because you deserve to know the ways in which you will end."

From there, with Sax barely awake, they take him to the docking bay, floating on the transport. A pair of Chorus pilots, red-furred Flaum wearing special armor and patches bearing a single white spire jutting through black space, start launch procedures. Sax is locked into a couch at the back end. The mirrored Oratus sits across from him, giving Sax an endless dead-eyed look.

At least until the transport fails to start. At least until its microjets don't fire.

Sax manages a weak, toothy grin.

The mirrored Oratus drips contempt at Sax and his smile.

Because of the refracting scales, Sax only gets the outline of the sneer, which deepens into a dead-lipped frown as the transport doesn't lift.

"What's going on?" the mirrored Oratus throws his voice towards the two Flaum in the cockpit, who are busy squeaking at one another.

"The power's cut," the right Flaum replies. "All readings are negative. I'm not getting anything from the jets."

"Looks like you'll be staying here a while longer," Sax says. "Good thing you made friends with everyone on this frigate."

"They're not my friends. They're servants, like me. All of us, even you, must bend to the will of the Chorus."

"Is that what you say to yourself?" Sax says. "All of this is the will of a bunch of blobs in a tower? You could tear any of them apart in a minute. Why take their orders?"

The mirrored Oratus exhales a heavy sigh from his vents and stands, scales shifting to match the yellow light in the shuttle's interior. "Because I believe in something called loyalty. In paying back my creators for giving me life."

"That was their choice," Sax says. "You should make your own."

The mirrored Oratus doesn't reply, instead stepping around to the panel controlling the boarding ramp. With a claw, the mirrored Oratus opens the transport's door and, after giving the ramp a moment's head start, descends, leaving Sax onboard and captive.

But only for a moment.

The two Flaum continue their rapid-fire chittering, with one on the left eventually jumping up from the pilot's chair and heading back towards Sax. The Flaum makes it near him, keeping well back from Sax's claws as it heads to the door, when there's a bright flash and the red-furred creature drops to the floor.

Sax hisses in surprise, seeing the other Flaum holding a pocket miner that it's pulled from somewhere. That Flaum dashes through the shuttle quick and slaps the boarding door's panel, sucking up the ramp and slamming the door. A moment later, after unlatching Sax from the net, the red-furred Flaum steps back behind its former colleague, miner aiming Sax's way, though the twitching hands show cautious fear more than malice.

"What?" Sax manages to ask.

"The Chorus has fewer friends than you think," the Flaum says. "The Resistance has more allies than you know."

"And the jets?"

"He'll find them working." The Flaum glances towards the door. "We should leave."

"No," Sax says. "I have a friend on the ship. I'm not leaving him. And I have an idea; open a channel to Rav."

Sax felt a shift in the last conversation he had with the frigate's commander, and he's going to bet everything that another push could sway her over to his side. With the frigate, Rav would be able to force a way for Sax to get down to Solis, to find Bas.

The Flaum gives Sax a wide-eyed side-glance, a look Sax recognizes well from his own experience. It's wondering if he's crazy, if it made a terrible mistake in choosing to help him over just following orders. But Sax is still an Oratus, and his damaged body is plenty able to handle the furball, so quick enough the Flaum decides a chance of life is better than a swift, certain death. They retreat to the cockpit and the Flaum opens up a channel.

"Why haven't you left?" Rav's voice scratches through. "You're clear. The bay is open."

"There's been a change in plan," Sax says.

Dead silence on the other side. Silence that's eventually broken by the hard thump of something crashing against the outside of the transport. The scrabble of claws digging into the hull.

"He's figured it out," the Flaum says, his voice dulling into the tone of the doomed. "This ship's not meant for combat—he'll tear his way in before long."

"What are you doing?" Rav's voice comes back. "What happened to the Oratus?"

"He's clawing his way into his own ship," Sax replies. "I'd be grateful if you stopped him." Then, to the Flaum pilot. "Start the engines."

"Why?"

"Do it," Sax orders. "Rav?"

Rav cuts a dire, lost laugh. "You want me to stop him? How?"

"Tell your Flaum he's the true traitor. That their race as well as ours depends on stopping this Oratus."

There's a ripping shriek from outside, and Sax turns to see bright light from the docking bay filtering in through a long gash. In a second, the mirrored Oratus will rend a hole big enough for itself and Sax is in no condition to fight. A quick scan of the shuttle shows no miners here either, save the small one clutched tight in the Flaum pilot's hands. Such a small weapon, unless perfectly shot, wouldn't do anything more than annoy the mirrored Oratus.

Sax teeth and claws will have to do.

"Last chance, Rav. Last chance to choose your own species." Sax is kind of proud of that, thinks Bas would be proud of him too. Here he is, talking like someone who knows something outside of the ways of war.

Or maybe Bas has rubbed off on him over all this time.

Sax sees a pair of claws, their edges visible as black lines against the silver gray skin of the shuttle's inside. They close across the gash and tear, peeling the hull back like it's simple paper. Its entrance created, the mirrored Oratus pulls itself inside.

"Seems like we've lost power?" The Oratus growls at the Flaum pilot, sparing barely a look at its downed companion on the shuttle floor. "It seems like Sax is not the only traitor the Chorus is dealing with."

Sax spreads his patched and bandaged claws out wide. "Maybe I am a traitor to the Chorus, but at least I'm fighting for something."

"But you'll die for nothing," the mirrored Oratus says, stomping towards Sax.

Sax doesn't feel like dying quite yet though, so as the mirrored Oratus stalks closer, Sax, using his tail, smacks the flight stick behind him, sending the transport lurching forward, its microjets very much alive.

The mirrored Oratus realizes what's about to happen, realizes it has no time to get to cover, and neither does Sax, nor the Flaum. The transport rams into the back of the docking bay, the impact throwing Sax backwards, into the crumpling windshield of the transport's front as glass bursts around him. The mirrored Oratus completes the crash a split second later, barging into and over Sax as they fall, with the ship, to the bay floor.

The impact sends Sax's head for a loop, the universe splitting and blacking out even as the shrieks of rending metal and sparking clicks from snapping wires fill every available audio space Sax has. He lands on wreckage, the shuttle's ceiling crunching close but not collapsing, with the smell of leaking energy ozoning the air. Smoke pours from batteries rent apart too close to food stores and the flammable fabrics coating the couches in the transport's back half.

Consciousness doesn't flee Sax entirely, though. Instinct survives, and pushes Sax up. He's hurting, his left foreclaw and his tail, so recently burned is again bearing the hallmarks of too hot, too close flame.

Sax staggers away from the wreck through the same hole his enemy's claws created, but doesn't make it more than a few steps before the haggard hiss he's waiting for emerges.

The mirrored Oratus pushes his way free, tilting over and crashing through the right wall shielding the shuttle's cockpit. The slab cracks down on rubble, casting up a shower of smoke and dust as it hits, which frames the Oratus in the evidence of his own escape. The creature's mirrored scales no longer glisten, their reflective array now a battered black, coated in dirt and oil and grease. Chemicals drip off of its tail, while long scars across its chest show it landed hard on the exposed batteries powering the transport's microjets.

It's a dark, broken thing now. It stumbles towards Sax, its roiling green eyes the only bright thing it has left.

There was a moment, a time when the mirrored Oratus would

have taken Sax back to the Chorus. Delivered Sax to its Amigga over-lords: Sax would be readied for trial, for sentencing and eventual damnation. But this one is past the point of reason now. There's only vengeance, eyes full of anger and rage. Things Sax knows. Things he understands.

The mirrored Oratus is beyond conversation and it leaps towards Sax, flying through the air with too much strength. There's no way the creature could be that hurt and able to fly that high, until Sax realizes the Oratus must have been wearing a mask. One no doubt damaged by Sax's claws, one that gave its last protection in the crash. Doing enough to keep its wearer alive and deadly.

Sax can't fight that, so he doesn't.

Instead, he goes the other way. Dashes beneath the mirrored Oratus' charge and blitzes back towards the wrecked transport. Claws-on-metal tells Sax the Oratus has landed, but he's focusing on one thing sticking out of that inferno; a long burnt-metal shard that, moments ago, stood as the top bar holding the cockpit's windshield. The crash sheared it off, but half of the bar juts out of the fire like a spear.

Sax gets the first burn on his foreclaws as he scrambles to the wreck when he feels a hard yank on his tail. A light stab as claws break through his scales, and then Sax is getting whipped around, flung through the air. He's too heavy to fly far, and Sax hits the floor hard and rolls on wounded shoulders. He manages to stop himself and looks back towards the approaching mirrored Oratus, that scarred black form looking even more horrible in the bright bay lights.

"You'll never win," Sax hisses as the Oratus comes closer. "You'll kill me, it's the Amigga who get the victory. You're hurting your own kind."

"You think I care." The Oratus goes for a kick at Sax's face, but gives it away with a rippling tense of its strong legs.

Sax snakes out his foreclaws, catches the talon—at the cost of another gash on his left foreclaw, but at this point there's too many to count—and Sax yanks the Oratus forward. Here the sharp grip of claws embedded into metal winds up hurting the mirrored Oratus, because his back talon doesn't give and let Sax trip the creature. Instead, he holds steady while Sax yanks the Oratus' leg forward. The bone pops above the constant crackle of the burning freighter, and the mirrored Oratus roars as Sax uses the pulled leg as leverage to swing himself around and tail-whip the mirrored Oratus across the face.

The impact and the sharp jerk that follows lets the mirrored Oratus free itself, and Sax is plenty gratified to see the enemy fall into a deep limp. An emotion that quickly dies when the Oratus twists and sends its own tail crashing into Sax's head. The impact kaleidoscopes the bay and sends Sax skidding across the floor until he comes to rest against a set of empty fuel containers. They're bulky cylinders, old and probably permanent fixtures of this frigate until Rav manages to get an assignment on somewhere inhabited.

Right now, though, they're what Sax needs to pull himself to his talons. To give the mirrored Oratus one last level stare. If he's going out here, in this ruin of a bay, bleeding out from a dozen deep cuts, he's going to do it standing up.

"You do our race proud," the mirrored Oratus hisses as it limps towards him.

"And you betray yours." Sax keeps his tail wrapped around the spent fuel container—his legs are mostly numb and Sax is sure he'd collapse without it.

"We all choose our masters," the mirrored Oratus replies.

He gets close to Sax, and Sax can't help but try, with his fore- and midclaws to get in a rake, but the mirrored Oratus catches all of them. Twists and snaps each of Sax's wrists in turn, leaving his claws broken and limp. The pain's immense, but Sax lets it all flow into the giant black hole that's formed in his mind; a calm, endless void that grows as Sax's hold on life gets more and more tenuous.

"I deny yours," Sax manages to hiss.

The mirrored Oratus nears. Then, with a sudden jerk, all four claws knife deep into Sax's vents. The mirrored Oratus leers close as it strikes, the hot air from its own vents blowing against Sax. Who responds in the only way he can.

He bites.

A quick, darting snap that gets Sax's teeth around the throat of the mirrored Oratus. Sax rends the scales, stabs beneath and tastes every part of the burnt grease and the warmer, softer stuff beneath. Every ounce of strength Sax has goes into his jaws then, digging harder and further.

Sax doesn't think he'll live, but neither will this thing.

The mirrored Oratus breaks into a frenzy, tearing and stabbing with its claws. Each cut takes away more of Sax. His vision goes spotty and dark, he loses the feeling in his legs, his tail. Keeps his whole energy in his jaws.

Tighter, harder.

For as long as he can.

Celice doesn't mince time or words. She moves with an angry purpose that fuels the rest of us. Up till now, I saw the Sevora and their invasion as an abstract, a menace we were going to confront eventually, but Celice embodies its effects; she wants to fight, to win, to save her home.

I do too.

After the first day's journey, which ends in another village, bigger than the last, we see the wrong signs. This one's common house is more crowded, and not only with soldiers. Carts litter the streets, and Lunare with them, curled up in makeshift tents and blankets. Others set off back the way we came, muttering talk of getting away, saving themselves.

"This isn't going well," Viera says to me as we continue the next morning.

"I thought we might stand a chance," I reply. "I hoped that if the Sevora couldn't take us as hosts, that they would leave us alone."

"You weren't empress long enough to learn empires kill what they're afraid of."

"I am still the Empress, Viera. I've just lost my empire."

"You think we can take it back?" Viera throws the question out with zero hint of sarcasm, and with plenty of exhaustion.

"You don't believe we'll win, do you?" I reply. "You think this is it for humanity?"

Viera pats the pistols on her belt. "I've got a pair of these. That's it, Kaishi. Avril might have a few tricks too, but nothing much better. The Sevora have ships that come from the sky and burn us away before we even see them. How do you win that fight?"

It's a problem I've been pondering as we've stalked through the caves. One I've been talking to T'Oli, to Vee about too. There's one solution we all keep coming to. One answer.

"We need help." I nod at Celice and her men, parting another refugee train to let us through. "They're going to fight to the end, and they don't deserve to do it alone."

"Kaishi, we're not the help they need."

"No. Remember Sax? Bas? They hate the Sevora. They said there's a whole army of them. Vee says the same thing."

"So you want to call in different monsters to fight the ones already here?"

"It's either that, or we die," I say.

She doesn't have a reply to that, and we keep on moving. The tunnels blend together, and my heart aches at not seeing the sky for so long. The stream of fleeing people thickens until it's a torrent. They squirm back from Vee and T'Oli, and a few bother throwing insults their way, though a sliver of teeth from the Oratus shuts them up quick.

At night, the four of us toss strategies around. Ways we could get in contact with the Vincere, the force Vee says might be able to help us. T'Oli says sending the message is simple, provided we get a shuttle. Which, of course, is the hard part.

Until we get to the Lunare capitol, Marilo, in its vastness, and everything changes.

. . .

You can read a lot in a person's expression, but I get more from the way the refugees are running now, the way they're pulling along their children with little else strapped to their backs. The carts are mostly gone—the ones that do rumble through, pulled by tamed Fassoth, are full of dead-eyed people—and rather than the low murmurs of the lost, the caverns ring with the shouts of the panicked, the afraid.

Celice starts cursing to herself as we get closer to the opening into Marilo's huge underground lake.

The view from the tunnel lip provides all the reason Celice needs for her epithets. All of the dark-forged glory of the Lunare is laid bare before us, and half of it, or more, is engulfed in bright-burning flames. Streaks of hot red laser pour out of several craft, hovering above the city near the cavern ceiling, but even that doesn't hold my attention for long.

Because I can see the sky. And it's clear blue.

Somehow, in some terrible way, a giant hole has been carved in the mountain under which the Lunare settled. It's uneven, with slicing cuts in the rock, and some of the edges still glow a molten orange.

Down through this opening pour shuttles, disgorging what look, from this far distance, like Flaum. The troops disappear down into the city, vanishing into the smoke or behind buildings.

"How do they land?" Celice manages to say as we watch another dozen dive into her home.

"Oh, they have magnetic boots," T'Oli says. "They'll drop a landing pad or two, and then it's like jumping into a soft bed. They'll bounce off and be ready to go. Quite efficient, really."

"Quiet, T'Oli," I say. "Celice, where's the army? I thought you said Avril had assembled a massive force?"

"They came behind," Viera points at the hole. "I bet they didn't want to deal with pushing through Avril's force, so they created their own back door."

I'm about to ask another question—namely, what now—when Vee

flashes past us. The Oratus makes his own path through the fleeing populace simply by showing up; nobody wants to stay in his way.

"What are you doing?" I call after him.

"Hunting!" is the hiss I get in reply, and then he's gone.

"Can't keep an Oratus from his purpose," T'Oli says. "Literally, you can't. It's programmed into their DNA."

"I don't know what that means, but we have to help him," Celice says, then looks at me. "You said you're the Charre Empress? Plenty of these people are yours too. I hope you find a way to save them."

Then Celice and her men, pulling at their pistols, push forward after Vee.

"Going into that's only going to get us killed," Viera says.

"So will staying here, just more slowly." I look at the hole again.

The shuttles seem to be coming in, going low enough to drop their complement of Flaum, and then zooming back up and out of the hole.

"If we get on top of that building there," I say, pointing at what looks like a bricked tower looming over the lake. "We might be able to get on one of those shuttles."

"On? How?" Viera asks. "You want to jump on them?"

"I have an idea," I glance down at T'Oli. "You ready?"

"Always, Kaishi. An Ooblot never lacks for energy."

We run towards the city too, then. Or rather, walk fast. My ribs still hurt plenty if I try anything faster than a jog, but the crush of people heading against us means it's slow going anyway.

I just hope we make it in time.

A red flash bursts the ground in front of me as I skid to a stop, my heels sliding on the cobblestoned street leading into the city. That bolt is followed by others, tracing a line across the path and stitching up the side of the building to my right. At first the shots only melt stone, but then one strikes something more and the inside breaks open in fire and black smoke.

"C'mon, Kaishi, out of the open," Viera says, pulling me to the side, underneath the awning of what looks to be a bakery.

"We have to get there." I point out ahead, not quite to the center of the city, but to the tall, arched building that's high enough. "That's not going to happen by hiding."

"There's a middle ground between getting yourself vaporized and getting where you need to go," Viera replies.

We edge forward to the last bit of the faded green awning. There are three more buildings—the middle one mostly a melted ruin—before we hit the next cross street. Smoke burns up and out, clouding the area and making my lungs itch, but I take a deep breath anyway and make a break for it.

"Go!" I say, as if I have a clue when the Flaum are going to shoot next. "Use the smoke as cover!"

Viera and I hug the walls, moving behind the belching fountains of black smoke. T'Oli's wrapped himself around me, providing armor and some small support to my ribs. Every time I pass beneath a burning window, heat washes over my hair and ash blows into my face, but I keep going. Stopping means death.

In front of us, a man dives out of another building, holding what looks like books in his arms. He takes a wild look at us, starts to move in our direction, and then vanishes in another flash of red. Nothing's left of him save a few burning pages floating to the ground.

I can't stop though. Have to keep moving. Horror at one death means I'll fail at stopping thousands more.

We hit the cross street as a pair of Flaum round the corner in front of us, one covering down the street, one turning our way. Wearing Nasiya's Sevora badge on their armor, their brown-black fur puffs out. They're moving with miners raised, but with an easy pace. It's a slaughter, and they know it.

So Viera gets the first shot off. Takes the lead Flaum between the eyes, sending its partner swiveling towards us.

Too slow.

I'm already running, and I push off with my right foot to the left, then rebound off the building wall as the Flaum tries to track me. I tackle the smaller creature and drive it to the ground as T'Oli flows up my right hand, shifts into a sharp point that lets me finish the job.

By the time I stand up, Viera's already holding the first Flaum's miner, playing with its triggers. She nods to the other one.

"Let's make the fight a little more fair," she says.

I can only agree.

We slip through more broken alleys, past burning markets and crumbling buildings. There aren't, thankfully, many bodies—Avril must have started evacuating the city before the raid began. The Sevora, though, don't seem to care; the Flaum expend plenty of energy zapping anything and everything.

The Sevora want to destroy us. Not conquer, not take over, but obliterate.

So when we reach the tall building, I'm coated in soot, my lungs burn from breathing in so much smoke, but I've still got the Flaum miner in my hands, and it's still ready to fire. Viera's right at my back, and I wonder if my breathing sounds as bad as hers. Or maybe that's just the continuing ripple of explosions, scattered cries, and the whine of shuttle engines.

Our target rises up in front of us, and I think it must be some sort of government building, or a temple like the Vaos, only tall and square until sharpening to a flat spire at the top. The front of it—the parts not blackened by laser-fire, anyway—is a mesh of intercut designs. Gemstones are interspersed in the pattern, coming together at the nexus of various grooves.

"I'd call it beautiful if this was any other time," I say to Viera as we crouch in the shadow of a half-shattered wall.

"The Siamante," Viera says. "Where Lunare commerce begins and ends."

"You confine your trade to one building?"

"The major deals." Viera nods at the Siamante. "Any party wanting to get themselves established here has to make their case here, in front of the government and other big Lunare players."

"They used to, anyway," I reply.

"I was in there once," Viera whispers. "For a Solare tribe that wanted to supply jade."

We shouldn't be talking about this now. We should be rushing across the road, into the Siamante and finding our way up, a way to take one of these shuttles and stop this madness. And yet, right here in this ruined city, I want to hear more.

"Did they?" I ask. "Did we help the Lunare?"

"Yes," Viera says. "We approved the deal. Gave that tribe plenty of black-glass for their weapons and their ceremonies. Not that it helped them—the Charre wiped them out not too long after."

"We're always the targets." I stand. "Come on. Let's go."

I glance up, look for a shuttle and see none. There's no Flaum on this street—they're pushing out from the city center now, establishing their front. Then, I have no doubt, all of these buildings will burn.

But the Sevora push means we can run over the cobblestones to the wide stone doors, pull on the rings bolted to the tall gray portal and open our way in. Once Viera slips through I pull the door shut behind us, sealing us into the Siamante.

The sounds rumble through the wide room, a space with rows of padded benches on either side of a central rectangle dominated by a pair of desks. At the far end, set against the back wall, is a single throne-like chair with a thick shelf in front of it. I can picture a hundred squabbling Lunare in here, shouting at each other over the price of sapphires or who has the right to mine a particular mountain.

What I don't have to picture are the three Flaum above, wandering through one of the overlooks. They're hunting, at least going by their searching eyes, by the occasional human shouts shortly followed by a bright red blast.

At the sound of the shutting door, those Flaum turn and see their new prey.

"Split!" Viera yells and I jump towards the right side.

A pair of walls on either side of the door hold stairwells leading up, and Viera goes to the one opposite me. The steps are short, marbled stone scuffed with long years of boots to which mine add their prints. Above me, the grooved patterns—absent any gems—continue their meanders on the ceiling.

"Did you mean to leave Viera with the Flaum?" T'Oli asks me as I jump up the stairs.

"Leave her?" I huff. "This is strategy."

"A rather convenient one."

I get to the second floor and ignore the continuing steps, choosing to crouch and move into the long rows of hard benches. Across the way, I see dust and rock flying as Viera engages in some drawing fire with the Flaum. Their whole trio is set up around the stairwell, taking potshots at my friend.

None look towards me.

I rest my arms on a bench, line up my aim, and pull the trigger. There's no kick, no sound other than the slight hiss of the miner's gas ionizing and launching forth in blazing power. Power that streaks across the chamber and hammers the wall above the Flaum. My surprise attack only showers them in pebbles.

"Good shot," T'Oli says as I dive away from a few fast returning shots.

"I've never fired one this large before!"

"I suggest you try again."

"Thanks," I try to think like I'm in the jungle, avoiding enemy hunters.

The key is never being where they think you are, which means either moving, or making them think you're moving.

"T'Oli, go three benches over. Make some noise." I nod to my left, my back against the bench.

The Ooblot flows off of me, careens its liquid body and a pair of stalks across the floor until it hits the distance I asked for, and then T'Oli proceeds to bang its body back and forth. The Ooblot sounds like something's slamming the stone benches with a giant mallet.

But it draws fire. Which lets me turn, put up the miner, and see that there's still a single Flaum pinning down Viera while the other two, who've spaced themselves out, take their shots at my Ooblot friend.

It feels vaguely wrong to blast someone in the back, but I shoot the Flaum anyway, and this time my shot hits the Sevora-controlled creature in its shoulder, causing it to drop its weapon and howl a high-pitched curse. One that's cut off a half-second later by my second shot, adjusted and lethal.

I duck back behind the bench, which is getting smaller as the other Flaum blows off one chunk after another. When I feel the piece covering my back burn away, I throw myself towards T'Oli as the Ooblot heads towards me, expanding itself to act, again, as my only defense.

Then I poke my head up, swing the miner around, and see Viera top the stairwell as the two Flaum center their weapons on me. T'Oli sweeps over my face as I duck back down, as intense heat follows the close-cutting lasers.

"T'Oli?" I say as the Ooblot flops off of me, curdles up on the ground.

"I've felt better." T'Oli's body, even hardened, is blackened in ways I haven't seen before. As if the rock-like skin has been melted together. "This, this is going to take a while."

"Stay down," I say, crawl a meter away to the next bench and try another pop-up.

Turns out I don't need to. Turns out Viera's reduced the Flaum to smoking ruin. Turns out we have a clear path to the top.

After confirming the Flaum are down, we keep climbing and pass a few huddling packs of Lunare who take one look at our miners and shrink away.

I want to tell them to run, but seeing as the Siamante still stands, it's probably better if they stay hidden here. So that's what I say; hunker down, hide, and hope for a rescue. Viera tells them to take the miners from the fallen Flaum below and, with a few flicks of her fingers, shows the humans how to fire them.

"That's how a resistance starts," Viera says to me when we're done, when we're climbing the steps alone.

"A dozen scared traders?"

"A dozen desperate ones."

"How would you know that?" I ask. "You've always been with the Lunare. Part of the strongest nation on Earth."

"We crush these insurrections all the time." Viera doesn't seem the least bit troubled by this. "A town decides they want to govern themselves instead of taking the latest decree. Some mine owner doesn't want to pay taxes. It's easy to start a rebellion, hard to make it last."

"Clarity's Dawn survived by hiding," T'Oli interjects. "Staying in the shadows, waiting for the right moment."

"Patience helps." Viera makes it to the top landing, where the left and right stairwells meet far above the Siamante's front door, and nods towards the roof. "That's our way out. Won't be much cover out there, so now's the time to make a plan."

"There's not much to plan." I look at T'Oli. "You can fly one of those shuttles, right?"

"Not in this condition." T'Oli swivels its eyestalks to look at the hard-charred part of itself. "I need to be flexible enough to get all the levers, the toggles. Can't do it like this."

"Which means it's you," Viera says to me. "Think you can do it?"

"We don't have a choice," I reply. "If we don't send that message, then we're all dead anyway."

The rest of the moves are simple; go out, wait for a shuttle to dip low to drop off the next set of Flaum, and dive on it. Burn our way in and commandeer the craft.

Viera leads the way up onto the roof, and the first thing I notice as she flings open the thin slate door is how much darker, how much thicker the smoke is up here. It's as if I'm standing in the middle of a fire—Viera and I start coughing right away, and I notice T'Oli press its large eyes shut.

Even in that ashy black, it's not hard to track the shuttles. Their engines give off a light-blue glow, and the whining sound carries above the scattered screams and crackle-burst of crumbling buildings. Red flashes blink in the distance, muted bursts carrying through the dark like far off lightning. I try not to think about what each flash means, another life snuffed by the Sevora.

"There, beneath the spire." I wave and realize it's pointless—I can barely make out my own hand, and the spire's only visible because it rises over most of the smoke.

We gather at the edge, feet balancing on the stone ledge, and wait.

The Sevora shuttles look like, well, the Sevora themselves. Long ovals, with what looks like a wrap-around windshield over the front. A series of bays open alone the bottom of the shuttle, from which ladder-like tentacles extend, and the Flaum drop from those, magnetic boots flashing as they land.

We watch a pair let off a new squad of twelve and start their journey back up before we decide the next one is the target. So far, the tops of every shuttle look like sealed armor, impassible. Which means the tentacles and their open bays are the only option.

"They pull back slow enough," Viera says as the last shuttle soars by the Siamante and up into the sky. "If we time it right . . ."

"If we time it wrong, though, we end up smashing into the ground," I say. "There's no recovery."

"Failure means death? Seems like we've been here before."

"T'Oli?" I glance at the Ooblot, a blob on the floor next to me. "Any advice?"

"Don't miss."

"Always inspiring, T'Oli. Always."

Another shuttle's approaching whine draws away my sarcasm. Time to track our ride up and out of here. T'Oli hears the cue too, and it slithers up my back, perching near my shoulders. I notice T'Oli's not playing the armor dance anymore—apparently getting shot's robbed T'Oli of its guardian drive.

Guess I'll have to dodge this time.

The shuttle coasts by us, Flaum standing on their perches, and after they drop off onto the street, the shuttle does a slow rotation.

"Easier than that sewer tunnel on Vimelia," I say to Viera. "Easier than the trees back home."

"Just jump, Kaishi!" Viera echoes her own words, pushing off of the ledge as the shuttle picks up towards us.

I'm surprised at how little I hesitate, how quick I press off and fly into the air. How fast I fall towards that rising shuttle and its array of retracting tentacles. Barely a second passes before I hit the smooth metal bar and its cross-section pieces. My knees bang off of one, my hands reach out and snatch.

My left hand slips—the momentum's too much—and my right wrist flares as my whole weight pulls on it, as my legs dangle off, towards the diminishing city beneath us. Then I feel something cool form around my right hand. T'Oli—swirling around my arm and sealing me to the rung. The Ooblot gives me a chance to pull up my feet, get myself situated even as the tentacle pulls back into the bay.

The small door slams shut behind me, and I'm inside.

Lemon-yellow globes flash to life as all the doors shut, and I see Viera, miner already slung from its strap over her back and in her hands. She raises it towards me as I look at her.

"Viera—" I start when she fires.

The red bolt flashes over my shoulder and I hear a chittering scream, then a thump.

"Nice shot!" T'Oli warbles from my shoulder, where it's currently reforming itself. "I thought that one would definitely get you both."

I shake my left shoulder to bring my miner around as I press my back to the shuttle's outside wall. The only thing behind Viera is the sparse end of the crew bay, which consists of nothing more than hanging handholds. The Flaum don't get to ride to their assaults in comfort.

Back towards the cockpit, though, there's more than the smoking ruin of the pilot. Viera and I step over the downed Sevora into a spectacular view over the mountain range as the shuttle clears the cavern and heads for the skies.

Browns and grays spread out beneath us, merging eventually into greens and blues as the mountains meet the jungles I know so well. Somewhere across that horizon is Damantum, or, at least, what's left of it.

There's a bank of terminals set across from the netting the Flaum occupied, with a single flight stick locked into its autopilot position.

"Where do you think it's going?" I venture to ask, moving around to get a better look at the screens.

"Nowhere we want to be," Viera replies.

T'Oli launches itself off of me as we continue our flight. The Ooblot swarms over the terminal, hunting and searching until T'Oli finds something it likes. Flapping its cream-colored skin, T'Oli flags us over to what looks like a dusty, small-screened terminal with a wide set of lettered keys.

"This is what we're looking for," T'Oli says. "It's an emergency broadcaster. It'll send out a signal that can be caught by the Amigga's Q-Net. Then they'll come find us."

"None of that makes any sense to me," I say, and confirm that Viera's equally confused.

"Light and sound can only travel so fast," T'Oli's going all teacher-voice on us now, and both Viera and I take looks out the windshield to see how close we are to a Sevora ship. None visible, yet. "If we sent a message from here towards, say, an inhabited planet, we might be long dead before they even received it. The Amigga knew there might be a need to talk across vast distances quickly, so they developed the Q-Net."

"Ok, T'Oli," Viera interrupts. "This is fascinating and all, but we're going to need to shift plans here. There's a big Sevora boat up there now, and we're heading right towards it."

"Grab the flight stick and get away," T'Oli replies, as if this is the most obvious solution. "It's going to take them some time to realize we're actually running."

"On it." I settle into the netting, put my hands on the flight stick and judder it out from the autopilot position.

Immediately the shuttle swings as I angle it down and away from the Sevora ship and black space. Back towards the mountains, towards the jungle far below.

"The Q-Net is made up of small satellites scattered all throughout the galaxy." T'Oli drones on as I try to figure out where all the buttons are.

Some are similar to the Amigga shuttle we flew over here, but the Sevora change other things around, and it takes a few random guesses, which result in a few sudden lurches and one half-roll before I feel like I've got a good idea on how this thing flies.

"And that's how quantum computers work." T'Oli's voice fades back into my concentration as my concerns about crashing our ship die down. "Essentially, if we can get a message to the Q-Net, they'll learn about it almost instantly at the Chorus, and since leaping folds a ship across space-time, the Amigga could get a Vincere force here fast."

"Sounds great," Viera says. "Kaishi, any guns on this ship?"

"My miner's right there." I point to my weapon, lying on the ground next to me. "Why?"

"Because I think they've noticed we're not friendly anymore."

A couple of the terminals have started flashing red, but it's not till a couple of blue-lit beams shoot by overhead that I realize Viera's serious. I immediately twist the shuttle into another roll, leveling it out over the mountains, and the craft shudders and groans as I make the move. Almost as loudly as Viera, who's cursing up a storm as I send her bouncing around the inside.

"Watch that wind resistance," T'Oli says. "You're not in space. Too sharp a turn and this shuttle will snap apart like a tree in a tornado."

"Just get that message sent, will you?"

"Oh. I have to find a Q-Net satellite first. It might take a while."

"We don't have that. Go faster." I risk a look back—Viera's

cursing is getting farther away—and I notice she's back by the bays again.

"Open up the doors, Kaishi!" Viera calls. "If this boat doesn't have any weapons, we'll have to improvise!"

As if I know how to do that. Thankfully, though, the Sevora aren't completely obtuse when it comes to the icons on their shuttles. I tap at the terminal that has six glowing squares, each one with a small line descending from it, and Viera's happy shout comes back my way.

"Now you just need to get us near one of them!" Viera says.

Near one? The shuttle rattles suddenly, and the terminal to my right, showing what I think was the battery's power, bursts out in a spray of sparks. I juke hard, sending our oval ship to the right and down, closer to those mountains. I keep looking up through the windshield, but I can't see anything, only blue sky and a few clouds.

"They're following you!" Viera yells. "Can you flip us?"

"I wouldn't try that, Kaishi," T'Oli says, but it's too late.

I pull back on the flight stick as T'Oli delivers the warning, and the Sevora shuttle veers back, replacing mountains and ground with horizon, sky, and then mountains again, only on the other side of the windshield.

For the first time, I see what's chasing us: a pair of three-pronged, rock-like craft whose ends glow bright red against the soft blue of home. Fighters, Ignos called them.

Well, I'll give them one.

20 / A LONG WALK

Solis hangs against the stars. Sax watches through his own eyes, through the screen hanging against the ceiling. Thick green-purple fluid laps around him, over and across his scales. Some his natural gray, others a decidedly more metallic color. The patches cover his body, mar it like an infection. Each one a product of haphazard surgery, of the frigate's limited resources.

Then again, the Oratus are an unnatural creation. A product of engineering. This, perhaps, is the only course that makes sense.

Sax wouldn't mind so much if the patches didn't itch. Supposedly the fluid, in addition to helping his nerves, his muscles repair, is also suppressing his body's reaction to its new additions. He's to stay in the bath until the Flaum doctor—the frigate's sole medical officer—and its robots determine Sax's cells won't commit genocide against their new brothers.

He's alive.

The thought keeps coming back like his heartbeats. Sax marvels at it.

"The Chorus have asked if their transport arrived," Rav says as the door to Sax's cell shifts open.

Behind the red-gold Oratus, Sax can see tufts of Flaum fur and the points of miners on either side of the door. Rav may have kept him alive, but she's not exactly trusting him.

"What did you tell them?"

"That it never showed," Rav says, standing over Sax.

There's plenty packed into that statement—for one, it makes Rav, and her crew, traitors. They'll be attacked and eliminated by the Vincere, and with another frigate and the massive Oratus-housing ship in orbit around Solis, saying that a ship any of them could have seen didn't arrive is a huge risk.

Sax's eyes must say what he's thinking, because Rav nods towards the door and the Flaum guarding it, "I already spoke with my crew and they agreed. I've asked to meet with the captains of the other two ships here, and they're coming over before communicating with the Chorus."

"How did you manage that?" Sax is stunned, though perhaps he shouldn't be—loyalty to the Chorus doesn't seem to be all that strong anymore.

"By showing them the recordings," Rav replies. "Your fight, the words you said. We all have crews, Sax. Hundreds that depend on us to make the right decisions. If we plunge blindly ahead and let the Chorus decide whether our species survive, then we deserve to die. It's time the Amigga share their control of the galaxy."

Oratus are trained to work in pairs, at most in sets of four to accomplish missions. They're not expected to share a common bond with their species, or with anyone outside their immediate chain of command. Sax has only ever cared about himself, Bas, and defeating the next enemy.

And yet, now he has a larger focus. There's a bigger goal out there, larger than destroying the next ship or even saving Bas from her mission on Solis.

Her mission.

"I need to get down to the planet," Sax says.

"Why?"

"My pair is on a mission that shouldn't succeed. Not if there's a chance the Oratus can turn against the Chorus."

"You're not well enough," Rav hisses. "Not yet. Tell me what she's doing, and I'll have her stopped."

Does Sax trust her here? Does he have a choice?

"You won't hurt her?" Sax says.

"Why would we?" Rav reaches in with her left midclaw, into the healing broth, and grips Sax's right. "I swear, Sax, we're in this together. Every Oratus we have is valuable. Tell me where to find her, and I'll bring her back."

Sax weighs the options and decides to trust this Oratus. Rav's repaired his body, and she isn't shipping him back to the Chorus. She must be on his side. So he speaks, tells Rav what he knows, and the frigate commander declares she'll go back through the logs of ships recently come to Solis, find the little craft Bas came in on, and track it down.

"Now, heal," Rav says. "I'll need you when the other captains come by so you can convince them to join our cause."

Rav, though, isn't quite done. "There's someone else who wants to talk to you. Someone we found wandering a corridor, that you stashed away."

Sax doesn't have to see the little Teven making his way into the room to know it's Nobaa. Rav shifts to the side to let the Teven up to the bath's edge, and Nobaa immediately starts throwing his spindly arms from his carapace towards Sax's metal patches.

"You both know, too," Rav says. "That you owe me quite a lot for destroying most of my med bay."

"Guess you'll have to help us, then," Sax says. "Because we have no money, and no power."

Rav doesn't laugh. "You have your claws. This little one has his mind. I'll take those."

With a swish of her tail, Rav leaves the room, though the door stays open. No doubt those Flaum standing guard will tell her everything said in the room, but at this point Sax doesn't care. He's too tired, too changed to worry about keeping secrets.

"Do you like them?" Nobaa asks after he's looked at each of the metal patches on Sax's chest and legs. "They were my idea."

"Your idea?"

"They thought you were dead. With the med bay gone, they didn't have enough supplies to heal you up and repair the muscle," Nobaa sticks a small hand from a hole near the top of his carapace and waves it around the room. "Plenty of metal, though! We grabbed some scrap, sterilized it, and used the engineering equipment to put it together."

"Will it work?"

"If I'm right, you'll be even stronger than you were before!" Nobaa giggles. "We reinforced the patches, so you can take more hits. They should even stop a miner's bolt, at least the first one. You want to know the best part, though?"

Sax closes his eyes briefly. Nobaa is so exhausting.

"Your claws, Sax! They were all broken and burnt, so we replaced them."

His claws? Sax didn't notice this. Now he looks and, instead of the dull-and-dirty white they'd used to be, Sax's most prized possessions are now the glinting silver of shined, unnatural stuff. Sax can't help it, he tries to lunge for Nobaa, a snapping bite that can't get there because, well, Sax can barely move.

The Teven jerks back anyway, his eyes cowering in the carapace holes and his hands waving high in the air. "I know! I know! It's not easy to take but you have to believe me, they're stronger this way."

"Those were mine," Sax manages to hiss. "From birth."

"Yes, but these are better. They'll never break, Sax. I mean, not unless you try with a combination of—"

"Nobaa. Stop." Futility and growing resignation drain away Sax's anger to a simmer. "Leave. Now. Or I'll figure out a way to leave this bath and devour you."

"Sure, sure!" Nobaa waddles back. "Just, trust me Sax!"

All the Oratus can do is glare until the Teven is out of the room and the door is shut behind him. Sax, alone with his fabricated claws and patches of metal skin, tells himself that these are the wages of war. That these are the sacrifices required for his species to survive.

What settles in his mind most of all, though, is who took his body away from him.

The Chorus.

The next time Sax wakes up, he feels weighed down by a thousand bricks. Healing without the right creams, the right baths with true molecular repairing liquids rather than stabilizing ones is a mistake Sax refuses to make again.

Now, though, time is passing and Bas is either in danger or about to make a move that could end future Oratus forever. Sax doesn't have the luxury of waiting anymore. Rav hasn't said whether she found Bas or not.

The door to his room is shut, and while Sax could probably call for help, he's not going to. Not now. He starts first with his talons and his tail, pressing them through the thick fluid towards the tub's floor. The move comes with aches, pains, so Sax buries them beneath an avalanche of frustration and determination.

An Oratus is meant to move, not to sit.

When he strikes the bottom of the tub, Sax pushes himself back. His head hits the wall first, hard enough to jolt, but not enough to hurt. Sax keeps pushing, pressing with his talons and swimming with his tail until, with his neck and back using the wall for support, he's standing.

The gooey stuff drips from his arms and away from his vents. His new metal claws gleam in the room's white light. Sax keeps himself from looking at his own body, at the strips of scales sliced away and replaced with bands of knitted metal.

Instead, he focuses on his right leg. The lift is slow, as though Sax is shoving up a body ten times his own size, and his muscles quickly burn like neon fire. There's a point, a singular moment where the pain intensifies and it feels like his leg might tear apart when Sax could give in, when the cool relief of failure is right there.

He falls. Presses with his tail and left leg and throws himself over the edge and out of the tub, landing on the hard floor. The impact rattles Sax's teeth, shudders up and down his arms, and Sax feels the metal plates, his skin wrapping and roiling as it moves them. None of them, however, pop. Nobaa's work holds.

The door opens a moment later, two Flaum standing there, miners at the ready. They take a long stare at Sax, before the lead one, a patchwork project of gold and brown, speaks, "We heard a roar?"

"A roar?" Sax manages to hiss, and at their look, the Oratus realizes he just might have bellowed out when he hit the ground. "An accident."

"Do you need help?" the Flaum asks. "To get back in the tub?"

"No," Sax says. "To both."

With his foreclaws, Sax rolls onto his chest and pulls himself the rest of the way out of the tub, which eventually requires all of his limbs working together to get to a standing position, as the room's too thin for Sax to lie across on the floor.

The two Flaum stay right where they are, miners still ready.

"What are you trying to do?" the gold one asks.

"I'm going to the bridge," Sax says.

"No you're not," the Flaum replies. "Orders are to keep you here till you're healed and, uh, you're not looking good."

Sax takes a step towards the Flaum, keeping his right claws against the wall for support. His muscles are weak, his vents tired, and a faint itching pain has started up around the metal plates in his body. All of these are inconsequential. All of these are pushed away.

"I will do as I wish," Sax hisses, his mouth hanging open a fraction too long as the energy to close it doesn't come quick enough. A big splash of spit leaks from his mouth and hits the floor, the Flaum paying it rapt attention. "You can choose to die, or get out of the way."

The Flaum opt for a combo package instead, backing out of the room and placing a call to Rav.

"You're a stubborn one," Rav's voice comes over the intercom moments later, as Sax is about to reach the room's doorway.

"You already knew that." Sax keeps moving, keeps his eyes on the next step.

The corridor here isn't a main artery; it's thin, and the outer walls shift translucent as various species walk by. Black space and the stars speckling it cover the view, with the edge of Solis visible off to the right, its reflected light shedding misty rays. The two Flaum guards establish a perimeter, waving by any passing crew member and making sure they keep out of the range of Sax's claws.

Not that Sax cares. It's one step at a time, and now he shifts to his left claws and leans on the inside wall.

"What are you trying to prove?" Rav asks over the next intercom. "You'll just hurt yourself."

"I'm done resting, Rav." Sax is about to reach the next door when one of the guards darts in front of him, swipes a badge at the panel and locks it, which lets Sax use the door as a crutch a moment later. "You've brought me back, and now I'm going to find my pair."

"Even if it kills you?"

"What better thing to live for?"

Sax keeps moving, and he realizes he's attracting onlookers. Crew members and soldiers, Flaum, Whelk, Teven and more who cluster to watch this wounded, mismatched Oratus struggle step after step towards the bridge.

For Sax, every move brings with it pain, but it's as nothing to what he earns, what keeps him moving forward. Bas is on Solis, and when he gets to the bridge, he'll make Rav get her meeting, get her support, and then go planetside.

When the big bridge doors slide open, Sax nearly falls in. Only through the sheer weight of his tail is Sax able to keep himself up. He doesn't want to, hisses at himself to keep standing, but Rav moves forward to help him anyway. If before, during their conversations, Rav looked at him with mistrust, or calculated concern, here there's only open respect.

"You made it." Rav says slow.

"I had to."

"You had to?" Rav asks, her tail flicking behind Sax, and he notices most of his following horde scatter back into the ship. "You took most of my crew away from their posts. Caused all kinds of disruption, including to yourself."

"I'm ready, Rav," Sax hisses. "By the time you get your commanders here, I'll be ready. Call them."

Sax, though, isn't looking at Rav while he speaks. He's staring out over the bridge, through the giant screens at the world glowing in front of them.

"I want to go home."

As the fighters get close, I can see they have no windshield. Like flying rocks, all mottled stone and sharp angles.

"More protection that way," the Ooblot says when I ask why.

That's the end of the conversation, though, as I yank the shuttle into a flip-turn, giving Viera a chance to play tag with her miner. She spews red fire at a fighter as it rockets past, and a couple of the bolts bite into the ship's side without any apparent effect.

"Nice shooting," I offer anyway.

"For all the good it did," Viera shouts back. "Don't know if this is going to work, Kaishi."

We're bigger, they're faster. Two of them, one of us, and I'm not sure how long the shuttle's going to keep taking punches without plummeting to the ground in pieces. We have to change the game.

So I dive at that big hole in the ground, back towards Marilo in all its ruin. The fighters are already looping around to follow me, but their turn takes time and I manage to scream past a couple more descending Flaum shuttles before my pursuit gets oriented.

Then we're plunging into smoke, between the rocks and into the massive cavern.

"I'd slow down," T'Oli says. "At this speed, you're likely going to turn us all into mush."

"Working on it." I'm pulling back on the flight stick, sliding down the speed on the control terminal.

"You know I can't send the message to the Q-Net from within here?"

"Some things have to wait, T'Oli," I reply. "You won't be able to send the message if we're blown apart, either."

With the slowing speed, I guide the shuttle out from over the city, passing above the lake, where, once the smoke clears away, I can see squads of Sevora Flaum pursuing the refugees along the road we ran not long ago. They're gunning down the fleeing humans, and the sight of it lights a fire in me.

"Viera, we're going strafing," I yell back to her. "Be ready off the right side."

I bring the shuttle around low, trying not to wince as humans dive and cower when we swing near. If I could yell to them to keep running, I would. More frustration to add to my fire.

Ahead, walking along the wide rock path split on either side by the large lake, ranks of Sevora move forward with miners raised, spraying red fire at the humans. None, yet, seem to think we're anything other than support.

"Get ready," I shout a warning, though I doubt Viera needs it.

I pull the shuttle to the right, then twist it as we go over the water, flipping Viera's side towards the Flaum. I slow the engines, so that we're hovering as we pass over the bridge. Viera, with our moment's surprise, goes to work. A steady stream of red flashes out from her miner, laying into the packed Flaum troops who, until this point, probably hadn't faced any counter attack.

They take it exactly the way the Lunare took Malo's surprise assault on them so long ago—with stunned immobility. Viera's miner goes through its energy quick, and she drops it to pick up mine, and only in that brief pause do the first Sevora start to counter, start to send a few hasty bolts our way while others realize they're in a tight space without cover.

The panic that takes hold is not an asset.

When the second miner runs out of juice, most of the Sevora forces on the bridge are ruined, and those that aren't flee back towards the city.

Right in time for those fighters to find us again, as we're hovering dead in the air.

The two fighters home in on us, emerging from the smoke. They're flying cautious in the tight quarters. I do a quick consideration; we're too slow, too big to get away from them, and Viera has no firepower left. If I move forward and we crash into the lake, we do nothing. But if we stay here? The shuttle's going to smash onto the rock bridge and maybe destroy it or, if not, serve as an obstacle for the pursuing Flaum.

One more refugee might live another day.

"T'Oli, it's been an honor," I say as the two fighters settle in close to us. "Glad I got to know an Ooblot."

"And I'm happy to know a human," T'Oli replies, shifting itself to hard stone.

The fighters unleash their first salvo, a trio of crimson bolts that crash into the shuttle and send lightning racing across the terminals. I squint and block sparks with my hand, feeling their heat in my palm. Any moment now.

I'm expecting the crackling roar of an explosion, but what I get instead is a loud boom. No, a cascade of deep cracks banging in the air, and something strikes the left fighter hard. The Sevora ship lurches forward as its rear caves in, and the craft plunges down into the lake. The second fighter doesn't fare much better as the booms continue and a pair of large, rounded metal balls bang into its sides, sending the fighter spinning into the cavern's wall, where it crumples and slides into the water.

"Where did those come from?" I'm ecstatic, confused, all together.

"Avril's come home," Viera shouts from the back. "And she brought help!"

I remember that I control the shuttle, so I use the flight stick to turn us, pick us up from the ground, so we can see. Pouring into the cavern from the far side, barely visible through the smoke, are Lunare and Charre soldiers. Trundling with them, some already breaking into the back side of the bridge, are those land boats, pulled by chained Fassoth, with their cannons roaring.

The Lunare have made modifications since we last fought them; the cannons aren't just fixed to the sides anymore, but sit on raised platforms, giving the Lunare manning them the option to swing those cannons around, even to aim them up, where they're now firing at the Flaum shuttles. Pistol and long-gun cracks mix with red flashes of Sevora laser.

"Why haven't they shot us?" T'Oli asks. "Not that I'm disappointed, but we look like the enemy, right?"

I'm wondering the same thing, until I hear cheering coming from behind us, through Viera's open bay.

"The refugees," I say. "If they miss, they might break the bridge, or hit their own people. Avril's making a safe choice."

"Then you'd better stay right here," T'Oli replies.

"Viera, go!" I yell to my friend. "Tell them we're friendly. Then T'Oli and I will take off and deliver the message."

Viera doesn't hesitate, and I'm glad, for even if the Lunare manage to win a small victory here, it's only going to last until the Sevora get tired of fighting, until they decide to simply immolate everything. These caverns, the jungle and all of the Charre lands could wind up like the blowing ashes on the other side, and I will not let that happen. The faster we get that message out, the faster we get help here, the more of my world we'll save.

"How high do we need to go for this message?" I ask the Ooblot. "All the way up to space?"

"I nearly had a link established before we abandoned the sky,"

T'Oli replies. "Just outside of the hole should do. Which is good, because I don't believe this shuttle will fly much longer."

"What do you mean?"

T'Oli points out the broken terminals, shorted by the fighter's laser fire. On the screens still working, plenty of graphs and meters blink in reds with bars near their bottom lines. I learn which ones mean power, which mean shielding, and which mean life support, and how all of them are close to failure.

"So you don't think the Sevora will take this back when we're done with it?"

"As scrap, maybe," T'Oli says.

I settle back into the netting, watching the burning, broken city. The Sevora aren't sending any more shuttles in through the hole—after losing three, they abandoned that tactic—which means the Lunare should eventually triumph. With the space that'll give us, I'm thinking we might actually get this message off.

"Which means what, Kaishi?" Malo's voice whispers in my head. "What do you think the Vincere are going to do when they come? You think the Amigga's army will save you?"

I blink. Glance at my wrist. The Cache.

"T'Oli, give me a moment." I stare into the bracelet, see that green flash and vanish into its endless library.

What I'm looking for are species, ones left by the Amigga, ones destroyed and saved. What I find is complicated; this is a Sevora Cache, and the parasites don't know everything, so I get half-formed entries about strange creatures, ones the Sevora might have hosted for a time before they're eliminated and never encountered again.

A couple stand out. Ones the Sevora infected and spread through quickly, until, according to the Cache, most of the population had been turned into hosts. These, once the Amigga found them, were eliminated. Turned to ash.

So the Amigga aren't afraid to torch a species that's lost. It's not great, but I see the point. If something's useful to your enemy, you take it away. What's worse, though, is that the Amigga don't even try to save them. The Sevora records show an orbital attack, burning the planet to oblivion, including those small factions that weren't yet enslaved.

Is that what they'd do to us?

The go-ahead doesn't come from Viera making her return to the shuttle, but rather from Vee bounding onto the bridge and up through our bay doors. I've pulled myself out of the Cache, and the Oratus' return gives me a welcome reprieve from the repercussions of our plan's potential success.

Vee himself isn't looking all that bad for his hunting expedition; a few new burn scars on his scales, some bits of fur sticking from his teeth and a face full of satisfaction.

"I bring you assent from your people," Vee announces as he stalks to the cockpit. "They will not fire at you if you fly."

"You bring assent?" I look past him, glance out the windshield. "Where's Viera?"

"Telling your story," Vee hisses. "She did not think I would add anything, and said the amount of blood on my scales was distracting." When he notices me looking, Vee laughs. "I took a dip in the lake to spare your soft heart the trouble."

"Glad to have you back, Vee," T'Oli says from the Q-Net machine. "I must say, it's been dicey without your natural killing abilities around."

"Yes? You must tell me."

T'Oli launches into a recounting of our venture up the Siamante as I lift the shuttle up and towards the ceiling of the cavern. As we rise, it's clear that some of the fires are being put out. The red flashes have disappeared, and the large boats are taking up positions around the city, with all of their cannons aiming towards the very hole I'm flying to. It's an impressive, if useless display.

Nothing the Cache told me suggests the Sevora, or the Amigga, will bother with another land invasion. Unless something changes, they'll cut their losses and blow everything apart from space.

We lift out of the hole, into the bright light of Ignos. It's nearing evening, and traces of orange and purple slant into the sky. It's lovely, and for a moment it lets me ignore the dark Sevora ships hovering far overhead.

I don't get near them, instead following T'Oli's suggestion to park the shuttle on a crumbled, frost-bitten plateau not far from the hole.

"Will this work?" I ask T'Oli.

"Perfectly," the Ooblot replies. "Already on it."

"Great. I'm going to step outside for a moment. Get me when you're ready to head back."

The ground is hard and frozen, a few sparse weeds fighting for survival up here as wind whips my hair around. It's cold and cutting, and I love every second of it. Mountains spill out around me, wild and ferocious. The jungles of my home are behind me, hidden by the peak. Ignos hits my face, and his slight warmth is everything.

Home. This is what we're trying to save.

I hope we don't destroy it at the same time.

Read on for an excerpt from Humanity Rising - The Skyward Saga Book Five, or find more adventures at Black Key Books:

The Sevora normally send a few shuttles through the atmosphere, buzzing down and hitting our cliffside position with plenty of laser fire. We duck and cover, using the rocks for protection, then burst out and engage in a sloppy melee that lasts until the Sevora decide they've had enough and retreat.

This time, though, instead of four shuttles, there are dozens. Behind them, too, greater shapes are descending through the clouds; larger spike-like things, coming towards us with their round bottoms shimmering as reflected light bounces away.

"Looks like they're done playing with us," I say, then turn towards one of the warriors. "Send the signal—we need everyone ready to hold here, and the city needs to empty."

Avril's going to wake up to a thrill, but better that than not waking up at all.

"Cover positions!" Viera shouts as the first shuttles scream closer.

Everyone, myself and Viera included, dive into carved out niches in the rock. Some hang over the hole's edge back towards Marilo, resting their feet on notches made for the purpose. A hundred fighters disappear in a moment, and good thing too, because the Sevora start shooting in the next.

Lasers don't make noise when they scream down. There's no crackling, no whistling from an arrow's feather. There's only a flash and a spray as rock fractures and bursts. The hiss as snow vaporizes. Explosions, like when the Lunare use their cannons, don't erupt—rather, small fires start as the ground literally melts.

I see several fighters on the unlucky end of a near strike—the laser superheats the air around where they are enough that their fur-lined armor bursts into flame, prompting a frantic roll-around. My own shelter, beneath a thick slate slab, keeps Viera and I safe, and I try to ignore the screams of others less lucky than us.

"Think this is the end?" Viera asks as the flashes continue.

"I don't think we've come all this way to die here," I reply.

"Hope you're right." Viera glances at her pistols. "There are so many cool weapons out there I haven't used."

I can't stop the laugh.

The fire dies away as the shuttles get close. Once the flashes stop, it's a sign to burst out of our hideaways, and I go, black-glass spear in my right hand and a kukri looped at my waist. Viera has her pistols ready, a more conventional Lunare sword hung over her back.

"For Malo?" Viera says as we leave cover.

"Always!" I call back.

The spirit of my friend, who fell getting us off of the Sevora's home planet what feels like years ago, guides my spear as I rush towards the first quartet of Flaum dropping from the shuttles over-head. Their boots flare and catch each of the furry creatures, about my height, though of slighter build, as they land.

My first target sports clotted amber fur, which blows across its face as it's exposed to the mountain wind. Those distracting strands offer me the opening I need to slip the point past its guard, which amounts to a thrown up arm with a small hand wrapped around a miner's trigger. The stab connects and I start to pull back for a second jab when the Flaum pinches the spear into its side, pressing the point in further.

It's a move that has to be incredibly painful, but when you're being controlled by something else, something that can ignore your suffering for its own ends, such maneuvers become viable. I'm not expecting it, so when the Flaum twists away from me, the spear's torn from my grasp.

I draw the kukri, a knife that bends along the blade, ending with a heavier, flat point ideal for the more mundane tasks of life like chopping fruit or clearing leaves. I use it to perform a slashing cut, one that doesn't so much hurt the Flaum as force it back, giving me a meter's space to adjust.

On either side of me other warriors engage with the rest of the Flaum, using our numbers to drive them back towards the cliff's edge. Viera works her pistols, along with other Lunare marksmen, to keep other Sevora shooters from picking us off from the shuttle doors. This is the instant stalemate I've come to expect, and one that gets thrown awry as more Sevora shuttles blow in above and behind us.

The amber-furred Flaum makes its move, ignoring its wound and the spear sticking out of it to aim the miner towards me. In that instant, though, I jump forward, kukri swiping at the Flaum's weapon-wielding arm while the rest of me barrels into the lightweight creature.

I'm not a large person either—most of the warriors on this cliff face have me beat handily in height and weight—but Flaum are more fur than anything. The kukri's swing gets the Flaum backpedaling, and my left-shoulder charge hits its chest, knocking the Flaum into a falling stumble. With my left hand, I grab the handle of my spear as the Flaum chitters out a panicked screech, and draw back my weapon.

The Flaum, and the Sevora inside it, tumble over the cliff. There's a chance those boots it has can find enough metal in the mountainside to stabilize its fall, but I'm willing to live with that risk; there's more pressing targets.

"This isn't working, Kaishi!" Viera's yell cuts above the madness, and I see her wielding her sword in her left hand, a pistol in her right.

Viera ducks under a Flaum firing as it descends to land near her, then sweeps with her blade, taking the creature's legs out from under it. A quick finishing shot at the tripped Flaum buys my friend a breath, which she uses to tell me to run.

"There's too many!" Viera calls.

I rush back to the line, which now is more of a circle around the long hole back to Marilo, getting pressed in on all sides by the Sevora forces. Miners flash their bolts and our warriors fall, the Sevora forming a defensive line and allowing the ranks behind to lay down covering fire.

I'm passed back, Viera pulling me along. I try to turn, to stand with my own forces, but my friend won't let me, until I shake her off, twist away and look in the faces of the creatures gunning us down.

"Kaishi," Viera protests over the screams, the shouts and rings of metal-on-metal. "We run now, or we die!"

I've run before. Left my people to fend for themselves against a hostile galaxy, and I'm not doing it again.

"Then I die with them."

Continue the adventure with Humanity Rising, *available now.*

ACKNOWLEDGMENTS

This novel is the product of my family and friends refusing to let a dream die. My wife Nicole, for letting me write in the early mornings and making sure I didn't starve. My brothers and parents for their continual comments, support, and enthusiasm.

And, of course, you, the reader, for giving me a reason to write.

ABOUT THE AUTHOR

A.R. Knight spins stories in a frosty house in Madison, WI, primarily owned by a pair of cats. After getting sucked into the working grind in the economic crash of the 2008, he found himself spending boring meetings soaring through space and going on grand adventures.

Eventually, spending time with podcasting, screenplays, short stories and other novels, he found a story he could fall into and a cast of characters both entertaining and full of heart.

A.R. Knight plans on jumping through to other worlds and finding new stories to tell in the limitless borders of our imagination.

Thanks, as always, for reading!

For more information:
www.adamrknight.com

To Elmer and Evelyn